"It looks as ~~if you~~ *another conqu~~est, Elizabeth?~~*

Elizabeth whirled to face the man who ~~had just~~ spoken to her. Her smile was frozen on her face, and she raised a hand slightly, as if she were reaching out for help. She would have recognized his voice anywhere, even though it had been fifteen years since she had heard it.

"Blake," she whispered. His name came out as an aching caress. She couldn't help it. She had been caught unprepared, and her feelings burst forth before she could do anything about them. "Blake..."

He was standing in front of her, looking much the same as he had, although perhaps a little more filled out, a little more mature. He was still unbelievably handsome. He was smiling slightly, but there was a hardness in his eyes that seemed at war with the smile on his lips....

Dear Reader,

When two people fall in love, the world is suddenly new and exciting, and it's that same excitement we bring to you in Silhouette Intimate Moments. These are stories with scope and grandeur. The characters lead lives we all dream of, and everything they do reflects the wonder of being in love.

Longer and more sensuous than most romances, Silhouette Intimate Moments novels take you away from everyday life and let you share the magic of love. Adventure, glamour, drama, even suspense— these are the passwords that let you into a world where love has a power beyond the ordinary, where the best authors in the field today create stories of love and commitment that will stay with you always.

In coming months look for novels by your favorite authors: Nora Roberts, Heather Graham Pozzessere, Emilie Richards and Kathleen Eagle, to name just a few. And whenever you buy books, look for all the Silhouette Intimate Moments, love stories *for* today's woman *by* today's woman.

Leslie J. Wainger
Senior Editor and Editorial Coordinator

LEE MAGNER

Stolen Dreams

SILHOUETTE·INTIMATE·MOMENTS®

Published by Silhouette Books New York

America's Publisher of Contemporary Romance

SILHOUETTE BOOKS
300 East 42nd St., New York, N.Y. 10017

STOLEN DREAMS

ISBN: 0-373-07382-8

First Silhouette Books printing May 1991

Books by Lee Magner

Silhouette Intimate Moments

Mustang Man #246
Master of the Hunt #274
Mistress of Foxgrove #312
Sutter's Wife #326
The Dragon's Lair #356
Stolen Dreams #382

LEE MAGNER

is a versatile woman whose talents include speaking several foreign languages, raising a family—and writing. After stints as a social worker, an English teacher and a regional planner in the human services area, she found herself at home with a small child and decided to start working on a romance novel. She has always been an avid reader of all kinds of novels, but especially love stories. Since beginning her career, she has become an award-winning author and has published numerous contemporary romances.

For my late great-uncle, bookman Jack Stephens,
who would have been amused to see me writing
"sweet and lovelies"

Chapter 1

The bride and groom were still kissing, and it was beginning to look as if they might never stop. Their nattily dressed friend, Blake Malone, grinned. It had been a whirlwind courtship, but he could already see a happy future in store for his longtime associates.

The stone walls of the gothic chapel began to echo softly with sighs and happy sniffles. Then a cough or two blended in, followed rather swiftly by an undercurrent of tittering.

"Save some for the honeymoon!" Blake whispered in amusement. Since he had given away the bride, his friend Shelby Marlowe, he was standing close enough to the newly married couple for them to hear his soft, teasing advice.

The groom, Blake's business partner Grant Macklin, reluctantly broke off the kiss and retorted with a lopsided smile, "We don't need to save. We're not going to run out."

Blake laughed. "No," he conceded. "I don't suppose you will."

As he thought about Grant's words, Blake's amusement began to fade. There was a familiar ring to that sentiment... *not saving*... *never running out*... He frowned slightly, trying to recall. Then a bitter memory long buried deep inside his mind worked its way to the surface, and Blake grimly recalled the sweetness of it—and the incredible pain.

Blake had once felt the way Grant did. There had been a woman... No, Blake thought. She'd been barely eighteen, more girl than woman. His eyes narrowed. Physically she'd been little more than a girl, but she had turned out to be as cool and calculating as a much older woman when it came to deciding whom to marry. She had been much more sophisticated than he'd given her credit for at the time, to his very anguished amazement. His jaw tightened as he recalled kissing her and never wanting to let her go, being oblivious to the world, to anything but her. How he had loved her. How he had thought she loved him in return. He had believed that *their* love would never run dry, either.

Blake almost laughed as he recalled his youthful naïveté. He had thought that they shared a bond that would last forever. How wrong he had been. His mouth hardened. It was the first and last time he had made that particular mistake. Not that it had helped much at the time. Back then... Then he had gone quietly insane for a while. Wild, furious, howling pain had been his companion for months. In a duller form, it had dogged his heels for years.

Blake dragged his thoughts back to the present. This was a happy day. He didn't want black memories from his past to shadow it. He only had to look at Grant and Shelby to feel his heart warm and his spirits rise to a normal, even state. He noticed that the people around him were beginning to speak quietly with one another and were looking toward the aisles in anticipation of leaving. Blake stepped forward to kiss the bride as the minister congratulated the groom.

Shelby Marlowe Macklin sighed as she rested her head on her new husband's broad shoulder and gave Blake a radiant smile. "You're next, Blake," she murmured confidently.

He laughed. "Oh no! I've been to two weddings this year, Shelby, having stood by while *both* of my partners joined the ranks of the married. I'm impressed with the glow of happiness all of you radiate, believe me. But one of us has to hold up the virtue of bachelorhood." He tried to look long-suffering but noble about it. "Think how unhappy all those unmarried girls would be if the entire pool of male dates dried up,'' he pointed out.

Blake's memories began to stir again, and he saw a fragment that made his noble grin slip a notch. The girl-woman he had loved had very nearly been his wife. The last time he had seen her, she'd been holding a bouquet. Roses. Wild-strawberry red and hot pink and soft peach and pale orange-white. The roses that were to have been her bridal bouquet. He'd picked them from the thorny vines himself. She'd broken the news then, to his complete shock. She had new plans, and they no longer included marriage to him. A better opportunity had presented itself. He felt a resurgence of the old anger. He'd thought it long dead, but it wasn't. It was only buried. Unfortunately, it had been buried alive, he realized. He grimly clenched his jaw.

Marriage? No, sir, Blake thought with great finality. Not for love, anyway. And certainly not in the forseeable future. He was vastly pleased with his life as it was, thank you. He blinked as he realized rather belatedly that he'd been staring blankly at Shelby while his angry memories had bubbled up within him. He cleared his throat and tried to refocus his thoughts on the present. Shelby was looking at him so steadily that Blake wondered if she had divined what he had been thinking.

"You and Grant are right for each other, Shelby," Blake told her with tender affection. "You've got happiness written in your stars. Both of you."

Shelby laughed, but prodded him gently, asking, "And what's written in your stars, Blake?"

He smiled. "Financial success," he replied easily. "I'll leave the *lucky in love* to you."

Grant laughed but added a heartfelt "Amen to that," and lifted Shelby in his arms. "Let's get this parade on the road, Beauty," he said. "I think our guests are ready to party!"

As Shelby looped her arms around his neck, Grant carried her down the chapel aisle with the confident stride of a very happy man. Her elegant white wedding gown spilled over his powerful arms, and the pale cloud of her veil fluttered over his broad back.

As Blake passed through the chapel's great stone portals and out into the brisk December air, he casually surveyed the wed-

ding guests and wondered how many of *them* had found the
happiness that Grant and Shelby had. Not many, he was willing to bet. Most of them had achieved a peaceful coexistence,
or perhaps a harmony of mutual interests, if they were lucky.
Few of them wore that glow of deep and passionate devotion
that Grant and Shelby possessed. Many looked as if they had
given up hoping for love and had settled for a certain station in
life, or a bank account, or perhaps a threadbare companionship. Blake felt absolutely no urge to join such marital ranks.

Blake watched with an unexpected twinge of envy, however,
as Grant set Shelby on her feet and helped her unwind her
breeze-whipped dress from around his arms and legs. They were
laughing and touching each other's arms and looking like a
couple of kids who'd just won the lottery. Blake couldn't remember ever seeing Grant look so content. Grant could be a
tough SOB when the occasion called for it. A year ago, Blake
would not have believed that he would be standing at Grant's
wedding, seeing the tender look that was on the man's face
now.

"Good luck, old friends," Blake muttered under his breath.

He put his hands in his pockets and hunched up a little
against the chilly winter wind that whistled down his neck.
Wryly he wondered if love could really keep you warm. At the
moment, he would have chosen a good heavy coat instead. Bah
humbug, he thought cynically. Two romantic idealists in the
business were more than enough. He would hold down the role
of the man who knew that love was just an illusion, Mother
Nature's insane way of tricking men and women into propa-
gating the human species.

Or breaking hearts. His eyes narrowed slightly.

The newlyweds climbed into a silver-gray limousine amid a
sudden shower of wild rice. Blake grinned and waved at them
as the long car pulled away from the curb. They were leading
the way to the wedding reception, an intimate affair being held
several miles across town at an elegant private club.

Blake sensed that a couple had stopped at his side, and he
turned to find his other partner, Alex Sutter, accompanying his
wife, Sarah. Another pair of genuine lovebirds, Blake thought.
Alex had been Grant's best man today, as Grant had been

Alex's early last summer, when he'd married spunky Sarah Dunning.

"This looks like our car," Alex was saying, indicating the limousine pulling up in front of them even as he spoke.

Blake nodded and stepped forward to hold the door for Sarah. "Do you think I can persuade Alex to let me have a dance with you, Sarah?" he teased.

She laughed, and her short brown-blond hair rippled in the breeze as she nodded her head. "No problem, Blake," she assured him. Sarah was wearing a loosely cut dress and coat. If Blake hadn't known she was five months pregnant, he never would have guessed.

Alex slid into the backseat next to her and placed a quick, hard kiss on her upturned lips.

"Just don't give away too many dances, Sarah," Alex warned her as he draped an arm possessively about her shoulders. "Save a few for me." He gave Blake a measuring look. "Let Blake find his own wife to dance with, damn it. The man's got money, connections and doesn't embarrass his friends in public. Sooner or later he's bound to find someone who'll put up with him."

Blake, having joined them in the backseat of the limousine, managed to look mildly insulted by his partner's backhanded compliment. "Thanks a lot, Alex," he said dryly.

"Don't mention it," Alex replied equably. "Don't worry, Blake," he added, grinning. "You're too good a catch to escape the matrimonial seas much longer, especially around here. Washington is crawling with pretty women. And they've got some of the profoundest nest-building and husband-acquiring instincts I've ever seen anywhere in the world. Sooner or later, you'll take the bait." Alex's black eyes gleamed like a Caribbean pirate's as he sighted his booty. "Then *Grant* and *I* will have the pleasure of giving *you* away, partner."

Sarah laughed. "Don't tease him, Alex! Don't you remember how much you hated being teased about me before we got married?"

Alex pulled Sarah closer and rubbed his cheek against hers. "No. I've forgotten, sweetheart." After silencing her with an indelicately thorough kiss, he added, "Besides, after we met, I wasn't single for long, if you will recall."

Sarah smiled tenderly. "I recall," she admitted in a soft voice.

Blake sighed and attempted to deflect his friends' matchmaking enthusiasm. "I'm *delighted* that marriage agrees with you two. I'm *ecstatic* that it suits Grant and Shelby," he further conceded. "You all have my blessing and my profoundest admiration." He grinned at Sarah and then added, "Personally, Alex, I think that you and Grant were incredibly fortunate to get two such terrific women to agree to put up with you."

Alex smiled and pulled Sarah a little closer. "You won't get an argument from me on that. Nor from Grant. I'm sure he won't mind my speaking for him, either."

Blake nodded and continued on to his main point. "However, I'd appreciate it very much if you'd forget about planning *my* nuptials," he declared firmly. "I am *not* interested in being a notch on some woman's matrimonial belt. They can dangle bait all they want. I'm not swallowing any."

Alex's eyes narrowed as he stared at Blake. He had detected an underlying vehemence in Blake's position. "Is there any particular reason why you wouldn't care to be a notch on some charming young lady's belt?" Alex asked curiously.

Blake's expression became shuttered. He wasn't interested in going into that. And Blake had known Alex long enough to realize that Alex already had figured out that something serious was behind his comments. Well, he'd just have to speculate, Blake thought.

"I've never met the lady whose notch I'd care to be," Blake demurred, raising his eyebrows. As Sarah giggled and Alex stared at him rather doubtfully, Blake shifted the subject a little. "Having said all that," he went on, "I'd like to point out that I am getting *very* hungry." He lowered his brows warningly as he looked at Alex and Sarah. "And since it ruins my appetite to be the focus of predatory matchmaking, I'd appreciate it if you would find something else to pick on besides me and my sweet freedom at the reception. Pick at the canapés," he suggested.

Sarah laughed again. Her eyes were filled with sympathy.

"All right," Alex conceded. "I won't tease you about your pitiful bachelor status at the party." Alex placed Sarah's hand proprietarily on his thigh. Then he said, "Grant told me that you made a deal with him. He did you a favor, and in return you promised to take some time off. His half of the deal was serving as Shelby's bodyguard when she was having problems a few months ago."

Blake was a little startled. "Yes. That's right."

Alex nodded. "Grant, Shelby, Sarah and I talked it over last night. Grant's going to hold you to the agreement. We want you to take a vacation." Alex grinned and explained. "We all feel guilty."

Blake looked at Alex and Sarah in surprise. He hadn't expected this. "You want me to take a vacation because you're all so happy?" Blake repeated. He started laughing. What a bunch of plotters!

"Exactly," Alex admitted. "We want you to have some fun, too, while you're waiting for Ms. Right to reel you in. You know what they say about all work and no play making for very dull boys.... We don't want you to get so dull that Ms. Right will overlook you."

"I see," Blake said, his humor subsiding a little at the mention of Ms. Right. "I'll try to fit it in." He didn't sound terribly convincing. True, he'd made a bargain. Maybe a day off would do it.

But a vacation held about as much appeal for Blake as marriage did. Work *was* his vacation. He enjoyed it. He found it both stimulating and relaxing. He relished the responsibilities and took pleasure in the creativity it demanded of him.

Furthermore, he couldn't think of a single woman he was interested in vacationing with, and going somewhere alone didn't sound very attractive, either. Play. He wasn't sure he remembered how to play. He relaxed with his friends over dinner or took weekend walks in the parks. Most of those friends he'd met through his jewelry business. Most shared his interests. All of them loved fine jewels, just as he did.

Gems were what fascinated him. They always had. Their shimmering depths, their unexpected colors, their great beauty shown off against gold and platinum and silver. They could be hot or cold, elegantly refined or coarsely rough. Each was unique to him. He'd learned to release their individual beauty with a perfect cut, a carefully placed facet, a delicately molded setting. Everyone he'd known socially for years had crossed his path because of their interest in gems and jewels.

Including that girl-woman long ago.

Blake frowned slightly. Her image flashed before his mind again. A young girl, seventeen, laughing and smiling and hugging him and running through a field of wildflowers, her golden auburn hair flowing behind her like sunlight. Chasing her until he caught her. Holding her lithe body close, feeling her heart beat fast, feeling her lips against his cheek, her arms around his back, her breasts pressed against his chest. The excitement of thinking that she was his, that she wanted him as intensely as he wanted her. The joy. The fascination. She had been a gem. Fiery and ravishing. Ready to be set in fine gold and silver so that her soul-deep beauty could be revealed.

Blake crushed the vision. After all, it had all been a lie. Her beauty had been shallow and fraudulent, he coolly reminded himself. She wasn't a treasure, as he had once thought. No. Elizabeth had been a very clever fake.

"Blake?" It was Sarah. From the slightly perplexed inflection of her voice, it was obvious that she had been trying to get his attention for some time.

Blake snapped back to the present. "Sorry," he muttered, clearing his throat. He felt a little embarrassed this time. The lapses were a disgusting display of weakness. He despised himself for feeling anything at all about that ridiculous affair. Indifference. That was what he should feel now. Nothing at all.

"You seemed very far away," Sarah observed gently.

"Just getting old," he said with a wry grin.

She looked unconvinced, but she didn't press him further.

Blake felt the old bitterness begin to well up inside him as he remembered the girl who had wound herself around his heart so many years ago. She'd been like fire and ice to him. Fire in his blood when he'd held her in his arms. Ice in his heart when she'd spurned everything he'd thought they had. She'd been a battle that he'd lost, and Blake had always hated losing. It angered him that he had never completely forgotten the pain, or the fury. It angered him still that she'd spurned him. And, worst of all, it angered him that it angered him! Hell, he thought in exasperation. He tried to shake off the bitterness and the hatred. He was usually a very easygoing, good-natured man. He told himself to relax and forget it all.

Indifference. He concentrated on it.

Their limousine drew to a smooth stop in front of the baroque architecture of a building that had once been a European ambassador's residence. It had been converted into a private club several decades ago. Blake stared at the ornate, nineteenth-century house where the reception was being held for Grant and Shelby. It was an appropriate setting, he thought. There would be a lot of old money types there, as well as people from several foreign embassies. And then there were the museum people and the art crowd. Blake sighed. Once they'd started working on a list, they'd all been a little shocked to see just how many friends Shelby and Grant actually had. It had made them all pause to consider how much they took friendships for granted.

"We've arrived," Blake observed.

The doorman stepped forward to open the car and help Sarah out, and Alex and Blake followed her inside. Violin music floated through the open doors, welcoming the arriving wedding party for a long evening of dancing, dining and sophisticated revelry.

Blake strolled into the reception, smiling and nodding and greeting people along the way. There had been another category of guest, he recalled rather ruefully. Washington's glitterati. Some of them had pleaded with Shelby to be allowed to celebrate. They claimed friendship through embassy connections or Shelby's Chinese art world or their intimate involvement with the international jewel cartels. In the end, it had been simpler for Shelby to issue the invitations. Besides, Blake recalled, she'd been so happy, she overflowed with the feeling. Shelby had welcomed everyone who wished to share her joy. And Grant, the mysterious man of shadows, had agreed without the slightest resistance. If that wasn't love, Blake didn't know what was. He chuckled.

Blake looked around the room and noticed a number of women he'd seen socially over the years. He had been too busy to wine and dine many of them recently. Business had taken a heavy toll on his time. He'd broken off his last long-term relationship close to two years ago, mostly out of irritation at the shallowness of it and mutual boredom. However, there were several women who'd made it fairly obvious that they would be receptive to a dinner invitation from him. They'd made it clear that invitations of a more intimate nature would also be welcome. And they were perfectly willing to take what little he would give of himself.

So be it, Blake told himself. He'd prowl the night circuit with a few discreet women. With a little luck, his two partners and their charming wives would forget about their matchmaking and leave him in peace to work through the winter. With the contracts he had negotiated in the past six months, he was poised to take Malone's from its current status as Washington's premier jewelry salon to a position in the next decade approaching that of the great jewelers of Paris and New York. Close to a dozen of the world's greatest jewelry designers now sold their most original pieces to him. With the influx of wealthy people and upscale living in the Washington area, there were plenty of takers for the jewels he had on display. Money never seemed to be a problem for his clientele.

It had taken him a mere fifteen years to create the business from the small initial investment he'd inherited from an old mentor. His accomplishment was something of a record, he was often told by envious competitors. He had become a name to be reckoned with in the fine jewelry markets of the world. It certainly hadn't been easy. It had been a long, hard road from his rag-tailed days in Texas and Arkansas and California.

And from that beautiful young girl who had left him for a wealthier, older, more successful man. His eyes cooled. Indifference, Blake, he reminded himself. Indifference.

Blake followed Sarah and Alex into a room where hors d'oeuvres and champagne were being served. He hadn't gone fifteen feet when he noticed the attractive daughter of a popular European diplomat smiling invitingly across the room at him. She wiggled her fingers and motioned for him to join her.

Blake touched Sarah's elbow lightly and murmured, "If you and Alex will excuse me, I think I'll go strike up a conversation with Mr. Louwens' charming daughter, Katrin." He grinned and cocked his head to one side as if listening. "I believe I hear her siren call."

Sarah laughed, and Alex lifted an eyebrow dubiously.

Blake crossed the room to join the young woman who'd been discreetly batting her eyelashes at him. He bowed slightly when he reached her.

"Katrin!" he murmured as he lifted her bejeweled fingers to his lips. "Did you come alone?" He arched one dark brow questioningly.

The elegantly slim blonde gave him a Mona Lisa smile and shook her head, sending her white-blond hair sailing in a graceful arc. Her pageboy cut furled around her ears and cheeks in a soft silky wave.

"No," she admitted with a great, sad sigh. Then, with a dimpled grin, she squeezed her father's arm. "But I don't think that Papa will mind if I leave without him...." she added, laughing.

Blake took Katrin's arm and tucked it through his. Then he bent his head close to hers and inquired, "Would you care for a glass of champagne?"

Katrin eagerly nodded her head. "Oh, yes, Blake. I love champagne. I think I could drink it for breakfast!" She giggled as if embarrassed by her own admission.

Blake laughed. "Spoken like a bohemian, Katrin. Your father would be shocked." Katrin was a charming girl, and her father was an honest, kindly man. Blake liked Katrin. Moreover, he knew she wouldn't push him to be more to her than he was prepared to be.

Katrin giggled and asked him slyly, "And what would I have to do to shock *you*, Blake?"

"I don't know," he admitted. "It's been a long time since anything has shocked me." He caught sight of a waiter bringing around a tray of sparkling drinks, and he steered Katrin in that direction. When they finally had the glasses of champagne in their hands, Blake touched her glass with his and declared, "To a happy end of the year and a very fine year to come."

Katrin smiled and studied him with eyes that were much older than her years. "To a very fine year indeed," she murmured as she lifted the glass to her pink-glossed lips.

The wedding celebration lasted until midnight. Blake drove Katrin home, but he declined her offer to come in for a drink.

He didn't want her to misconstrue his companionship as being more than simply that.

Maybe he was getting old, he thought wryly. Or maybe it was remembering the girl who had gotten away. His face hardened. And so did his heart.

January blew its frigid breath across the monuments and halls of Washington. It was the time of year when politicians were taking or leaving office as a result of the fall elections. Most of the town was absorbed in moving, or forming new political acquaintances, or kneeling in thanksgiving that they'd been given another period of steady government employment.

It was also the time of year when Blake patiently listened to his accountant's lengthy explanations of the business's tax position and cash flow needs for the upcoming twelve months.

Blake leaned back in his swivel chair and stared at the little man across the broad mahogany desk. "Thanks, Albert," he said. "As usual, you make the complicated seem simple to grasp. Let's see if I understood you." Blake ticked off the major points on his fingertips, one at a time. "We've taken in considerably more than we've paid out. We've got large amounts of cash to spare. Our credit is excellent. And I can go on a buying spree this spring in the seven- and eight-figure range without bothering any of our banks for a loan. Correct?"

The accountant looked over his reading glasses at Blake and nodded cheerfully. "Yes."

"Tell me, Albert," Blake asked thoughtfully. "If you had a million dollars to spend, what would you buy with it?"

Albert shrugged. "Something in scarce supply but in great demand, I suppose." The sallow-complexioned man chuckled. "Of course, it's difficult to figure out *what* that *is*. If it was easy, I guess everyone would be rich." He sighed. "Or maybe no one," he amended pensively. Albert glanced at his twenty-year-old wristwatch and clucked at himself for being late. "My wife will be madder than an auditor who can't find his adding machine! I promised her I'd be home early to take her out to dinner tonight," he exclaimed mournfully.

Blake watched the accountant scurry toward the door, shuffling and juggling papers as he tried to make a hasty escape. "Tell Enid hello," Blake said dryly.

Albert nodded. "I will." He was obviously alarmed at facing his wife. "She expected me home forty minutes ago, and with the traffic the way it is downtown, it will take at least forty minutes for me to get there if I leave this minute!"

Blake grinned sympathetically. He reached in his pocket and tossed a set of keys. "These are for the white Cadillac in the basement, Albert. There's a car phone in it. You can talk to her all the way home. Maybe by the time you get there, you'll have everything straightened out."

Albert looked both pleased at Blake's offer and a little dubious that Enid would be so easily soothed. "It won't hurt to try, I suppose," he said with a sigh. "Thank you."

"Any time, Albert," Blake replied, still grinning.

Blake watched in amusement as the harried accountant dashed through the main showroom and straight toward the elevator to the garage. He'd known Albert and Enid for years. Enid would pace and fret and fume, but in the end she'd be happy to see Albert and all would soon be smooth sailing again. Enid was a million-dollar investment for an overworked man like Albert Tinzel. Blake wondered if Albert realized that.

Blake had been too busy all day to read the newspaper, but now his desk was fairly clear. He pulled *The Washington Post* off the top of his correspondence pile, shook it fully open and began to scan the headlines. There were the usual stories of murder, mayhem, double-dealing and manipulation that every day's news seemed to bring. He worked his way through to the Style section without finding anything out of the ordinary.

Then he saw it.

It was a short article on Dorian Rand, an aging and quite famous gem cutter and jewelry designer. He had been living in Europe for many years now, but he was coming to the United States to retire. Rand was leaving Switzerland, where he'd been for the past twenty years, and would soon be arriving in Washington, D.C. He was relocating his gem designing business, and had already been invited to serve as a special consultant and guest lecturer at the Smithsonian Institute. He would be giving a series of lectures next month at the Smithsonian's Museum of Natural History. He was apparently planning on retiring in the Maryland suburbs.

Blake grimly wondered if he was going to be able to tolerate Rand's distasteful presence. He'd avoided business dealings with the man for years. Of course, it was impossible to avoid Rand's jewelry. No world-class jewelry salon was complete without at least one of his pieces. But Blake had always dealt through several middlemen. And he'd always purchased pieces made by one of the younger designers in Rand's employ.

Blake noted with professional interest that Rand was going to sell some of his most famous pieces at auction some time during the next twelve months. They would go to the highest bidder to help finance his golden years. Apparently Rand needed the money. Or at least wanted it. And he was no longer interested in paying the insurance on the pieces. Blake gave a short, mirthless laugh. Money had always been of paramount importance to Rand.

Blake grimly read the rest of the brief article.

"Dorian Rand," he murmured harshly. "You old *bastard*. What a pity you couldn't just stay where you were."

Blake stared at the grainy black-and-white photograph that accompanied the article. For decades, Rand had avoided photographers like the plague. It was a miracle anyone had gotten close enough to snap this shot. It looked as if it had been taken at quite a distance, using a high-powered lens. Rand was using a cane and leaning on it rather heavily. He looked much older than his seventy-odd years. Behind him, in a car, Blake saw two shadowy images. Rand's two traveling companions, waiting for him.

Was that her? Blake wondered, as an icy feeling formed in his gut. Was that smudged black-and-white shadow in the photograph the girl he'd known fifteen years ago? The young girl who'd intoxicated him with her vivacious beauty? The one who'd made a fool of him? The one he'd asked to marry him? The one who had betrayed him instead?

And next to her... Her husband, perhaps? The man whose love she had preferred to his. The wealthy, experienced, older man she had said she loved too much to give up?

Blake crumpled the paper in his fist. The icy feeling turned frigid. The fury, the outrage and the betrayal all came back in a harsh, surprisingly fierce rush. He felt a bitter taste in his mouth and realized that for the first time in his life, he wanted revenge for something. He wanted revenge for the agony she'd inflicted on him. He wanted that as much as any piece of jewelry he'd ever gone after.

Blake pushed the intercom button.

"Yes, Mr. Malone?" his secretary replied.

"Janet, would you come in my office for a few minutes? Bring your notebook, too, please."

"Certainly." Within moments the secretary was closing his office door behind her and sitting down in her chair beside his desk. "What can I do for you, Mr. Malone?" she asked cheerfully.

"I'd like you to conduct a special research project for me, Janet. This will be confidential. Don't discuss it with anyone else on the staff." He added weight to each word. Janet often did confidential work, but he wanted her to know that this would require more than the usual discretion.

"Certainly." She appeared surprised but was professional enough to push her reaction aside and do as she was requested.

Blake tore out the newspaper article and handed it to her.

"I'd like you to follow this story. Get whatever information you can about Dorian Rand. I want to know where he is, when he's arriving here, where he'll be staying, exactly what jewelry he'll be selling, and who will conduct the auction. Everything. Anything." He swiveled the chair and stared across the room at the elegant case of Oriental and Caribbean jewelry.

"Yes, sir." His secretary looked at him expectantly. He didn't seem quite finished with her.

Blake hesitated. He searched for the way to put it without betraying his motives.

"Will there be anything else, Mr. Malone?" Janet asked tentatively.

He turned his chair again and stared blindly at the gleaming surface of the mahogany desk. "Yes. There may be a man and a woman traveling with Rand. I think they're in the car in that photograph. See what you can find out about them." He looked at her. "Discreetly, though, Janet. I don't want them to be aware of our interest in them. And I don't want anyone else aware of it, either.''

Janet was accustomed to doing confidential background research on people and issues, but she looked at her boss curiously, as if she sensed a different undercurrent in his interest in these particular people. ''I'll do my best to be as discreet as possible. Do you know the names of the other two people?'' she inquired.

His face hardened. ''I don't know the man's name. The woman's name is Elizabeth Rossi.'' He gave a short, mirthless laugh. ''It used to be Rossi. I don't know what her last name is now. She'd be about . . . oh, thirty-two, I guess.''

He could see the curiosity flickering in his secretary's eyes. It would just have to flicker, he thought. He wasn't going to explain himself. With rather uncharacteristic curtness, he brought their meeting to a close.

''That's all, Janet. Thanks. Why don't you take an early evening? I'm sure your husband would enjoy having you home for dinner before eight.'' He grinned at her. Her long hours were a constant source of marital friction. He could see that his offer was welcome. ''I'll be here for a while. I'll lock up.''

''Thank you, Mr. Malone,'' Janet said as she rose to leave. She folded her notebook and cheerfully went in search of her coat. ''Have a nice weekend.''

''You too, Janet.''

Blake was barely aware of his secretary's departure a few minutes later. He was lost in his own thoughts.

Elizabeth. He hadn't spoken her name aloud in nearly fifteen years. And the last time he'd said it, it had been a wounded cry of fury, he grimly recalled. *Elizabeth*. The beautiful young girl who had taught him the meaning of fierce desire and sweet longing. Not to mention treachery and betrayal. His mouth twisted bitterly. Ah yes, Elizabeth had taught him a very great deal. He owed her a lot, he supposed, if you looked at it objectively, something he'd been unable to do fifteen years ago.

He spread his hands in front of him and slowly formed them into fists. The knuckles turned white. If he'd been holding a pencil, it would have snapped in two. Objectivity. He could have used that a decade and a half ago. And indifference. How he could have used indifference.

"Elizabeth, my dear," Blake murmured coldly. "It appears that our paths may be about to cross again." He sat back in the polished wooden chair and let it swivel from side to side. "I wonder if you've been happy? What have you done with your fifteen years, Elizabeth? Have you loved the man you left me for? Has he given you the pleasure that you expected?"

He found he couldn't quite bring himself to think of her having children. He wasn't sure why. Whenever he tried to conjure them up, they wouldn't materialize. Damn it, she still bewitched him, he thought angrily. He forced his emotions to bend to his mind's command. He would feel only indifference for Elizabeth Rossi, or whatever her name was now. Indifference, he told himself grimly.

But in his thoughts, he hissed her name.

Elizabeth.

Chapter 2

Elizabeth Rossi's eyes were bleak as she surveyed the property.

Dorian had purchased it largely with money that she had earned for him. That stung her. For nearly fifteen years she had designed jewelry for Dorian Rand. Exquisite pieces that had fetched handsome sums. She, however, had received only a small fraction of the money. Dorian had always managed to pocket the lion's share. He was always clever about it, claiming that business expenses ate up a lot of their earnings, that he wasn't getting rich, either. Of course, some of those "business expenses" financed his elegant life in Europe. Dorian had a taste for aristocratic companions and all the costly accoutrements that went with them. He'd had a town home in Zurich, an apartment in Paris and a country retreat in Gstaad. Not to mention the servants to keep all those homes running, and lavish dinner parties intended to bind his clientele to him emotionally as well as financially. Dorian was very cunning. Very shrewd.

Elizabeth slowly looked around again, bracing herself against the depressing sight. She knew that Dorian had been spending beyond his means for several years and had used up quite a bit of his operating capital. For a long time she had been expecting him to sell his residences in order to replenish his bank accounts. The quiet sale of his homes in Paris and Gstaad, therefore, had not come as any surprise to her.

But to leave their comfortable work environment in Zurich for this? Elizabeth still wondered why it had been necessary to go to such an extreme. It was even more appalling now that she saw exactly what he had done. Extensive renovation would be needed to make the building suitable for their jewelry design business, not to mention the work the house needed simply to be lived in comfortably.

For a brief moment Elizabeth wondered if Dorian's judgment was beginning to fail. He wasn't a young man anymore. Perhaps he was losing control of his faculties. No. It was hard to believe that. It was more likely that this was another example of Dorian's perverse and domineering arrogance.

Elizabeth angrily squeezed shut her eyes. Tears suddenly threatened to overwhelm her, and she fought to keep them at bay. *Dorian would not bring her to her knees,* she vowed fiercely. For years she had been virtually an indentured servant to Dorian Rand. He knew a terrible secret about her family, and she had bought his silence by being his faithful—and extremely lucrative—jewelry designer. In the first few months and years of working for him, she had been wild to escape his control. At times she had thought she might actually go mad, so deeply did she despise being enslaved by him. Only her love for her aging father had kept her going when despair and frustration began to swallow her.

There had been one other thread that had held her sanity intact. It had been her ardent hope that in the end, somehow, she would find a way to escape and keep the awful secret unrevealed at the same time. Rand had bruised her spirit and her hopes repeatedly over the years, but he had not succeeded in destroying them. *And you never will, Dorian,* Elizabeth swore. *You never will.*

She got a firm grip on herself again and sensed that she'd transcended the urge to cry. She blinked her eyes and stoically focused her attention on her new "home." She was standing at the bottom of a great, stone staircase that rose in a semicircle to the front door of a dun-colored brick mansion.

Well, it certainly wasn't new. The building had obviously seen better days, Elizabeth thought. The dark humor of the situation brought a faint smile to her lips. We've all seen better days, she had to admit. At thirty-three, she was increasingly aware of her own mortality and the relentless passage of time. She had once thought that she would be married and have three or four children by this time in her life.

The thought of children conjured up another image. It was a man's face. He had dark hair and smiling eyes and a firm, honest mouth. She felt her heart begin to ache a little, as it always did when she thought of Blake Malone. Elizabeth frowned and tried to push the memory away. There was no point in torturing herself about her long-lost love. He had forgotten about her eventually, she reminded herself unsympathetically. She'd seen his picture in the society columns occasionally, and she knew from her business connections that he was doing very well financially. Blake no doubt had all the comfort and companionship that he wished. She knew it was foolish to pine for a love that she herself had destroyed, but it was hard not to yearn for what they had once shared. Warmth, tenderness, sweet-hot love. And happiness. Sweet dreams of forever.

"No," Elizabeth whispered to herself, ordering herself not to give in to her sadness. She bit her lip and pressed her fingertips to her forehead. *This is now. This is here. I have to deal with the present. The past is gone. Dead. Buried.*

Perhaps that was the problem, she thought. It wasn't dead and buried. Blake Malone was alive and well, and closer to her than he had been in over a decade. *Damn you, Dorian,* Elizabeth thought.

She heard the movers grunt and laugh, and she looked up in time to see them heave her dearest possessions onto the threshold. The men had been struggling under the bulky weight of her two large steamer trunks, but they stepped lightly now that they'd reached the top of the climb. She watched them pass through a pair of huge open doors and disappear into the three-story house, bearing her worldly goods.

Elizabeth relaxed almost imperceptibly. She was very glad they hadn't stumbled or lost their grip. She didn't want to lose what little she had. They weren't the kinds of things that others might have worried about, she supposed, just a few old snapshots, some professional equipment that had sentimental value, clothes that made her remember happier days long ago. Her eyes clouded over again a little. Those trunks held her lost dreams.

Elizabeth stared up at the sprawling house. Stairs. A house this size obviously had to have lots of stairs. That was going to make things difficult for her father, she thought unhappily. Her eyes softened tenderly. Somehow, they'd find a way to manage in spite of his wheelchair. It wouldn't be the first time. And it probably wouldn't be the last. Not as long as Dorian was around.

Personally, Elizabeth would have preferred a small rambler with just enough dirt around it for grass and flowers to grow in the spring. Something one-story would have been wonderful. That would have made it easy for her father to get in and out. And rather than something old and crumbling, she would have delighted in almost anything fresh and new. A little home like that would have had an aura of hope about it, she thought. And she needed hope.

Dorian, of course, hadn't even considered anything smaller than a three-story house with a double garage, a guest house and two acres of land. Dorian always had measured success in numbers, she thought distastefully. The bigger, the better, as far as he was concerned.

She hoped that her father had been carried inside very quickly. He had always preferred living in cottages with character, surrounded by gardens, where nature could grow wild. The neglected stone and withering plants must have appalled him, she thought. They appalled her.

Alongside the curving staircase, the mangled bushes that had once been planted in an effort to spruce up appearances were now stripped bare of leaves, making it look as if the place were dying. The few scraggly oak trees that had survived on the otherwise barren grounds were now a dismal shade of grayish-brown thanks to a steady drizzle that had been soaking the area for several days.

Fortunately for Elizabeth, the rain had exhausted itself forty-five minutes earlier, just before she arrived. At least she was dry, she thought in grim amusement.

Dorian's seventy-year-old "retirement" home in the Maryland suburbs of Washington was a far cry from his well-kept residences in Europe. Even under the best of circumstances, this would have been a depressing sight, Elizabeth thought, but the decaying atmosphere of the place was being magnified by the miserable weather. Gray clouds smeared across the dismal sky, and the cold was chilling her to the bone. It was a perfect match for the pitiful appearance of the mansion and its grounds, she thought wryly.

And then there was the depressing fact that she would be living in the same city with Blake Malone. Blake...

She hadn't wanted to come back to the United States. Not to this part of it, where Blake lived. She'd been careful not to be too obvious about her reluctance, however. She didn't want Dorian to know how desperately she wanted to avoid having to see Blake again. Somehow he would have found a way to use her desire to avoid Blake to force her to do what he wished. She wasn't a fool. She would not reveal a new weapon for him to use against her. He had more than enough power over her already.

Elizabeth couldn't even try to pretend that Blake might not know she was back home again, either. With the publicity that Dorian had so smoothly arranged, only a man in a coma would have been unaware of their arrival. Dorian Rand's retirement to the outskirts of Washington had been a topic of gossip among gem dealers worldwide. And the newspapers had all dutifully covered it, as well. Including *The Washington Post.* Elizabeth was grateful that the photo they'd run with the story had been too poor for anyone to make her out clearly. She and her father had been sitting in the back of Dorian's car, waiting for him, as usual, when a particularly aggressive paparazzo rushed forward with his camera. Since Dorian was notoriously camera-shy, the snapshot had been run in more than a dozen papers within the first week.

Elizabeth couldn't help wondering what Blake's reaction had been when he'd heard the news. Silly to wonder about it. What difference would it make, anyway? He probably had not given it more than a moment's notice at best, she told herself critically. Why, Blake might not even know that she had been working for Dorian all these years. He probably thought that she was living in the lap of luxury with her "older, wealthier husband." If he thought of her at all.

He had probably forgotten her years ago, Elizabeth thought sadly. Since she was going to be so close at hand again, perhaps it was just as well that he had. The last time she had seen Blake, he had been angrier than she had ever believed him capable of being. He had shouted at her, and it had sounded like the roaring of a fiercely-wounded male animal. To this day, the memory of his incredible fury held her transfixed. She had never seen him like that before. It had seemed so completely out of character at the time. He'd always been an easygoing, laid-back kind of guy. Until she'd told him they were through.

She remembered standing there that evening, fifteen years ago, holding the roses he had given her in her arms, watching in a silent agony that she could not let him see as the fire of love in his eyes had slowly turned to hatred. Elizabeth shivered. She never wanted to see that look again, but that had been her punishment. For fifteen years she had seen his face like that every time she thought of him. His beloved face. Hating her. Something inside her had shriveled and died that night in the face of his howling pain. She had loved him desperately. She had lied when she had denied it the night she sent him away. It might not have broken his heart, but she knew it had broken hers.

Blake had left a short time later. She had never really known how he had taken their parting, once he had recovered from his initial surprise and anger. She was certain that he hadn't recovered overnight, though. After all, he had loved her enough to want to marry her. Blake had been a serious man. Elizabeth knew that he had not made the proposal lightheartedly. He had never been the type of man to trifle with a lady's affections.

A bittersweet smile haunted her lips. Knowing that Blake had truly loved her was one of the few things that had sustained her during the many times that her life had seemed unbearably bleak over the years. How she had cherished that tender memory.... Now, remembering the terrible night she'd told him that she was leaving him, the heartbreaking pain of it came back to haunt her.

"I'm sorry, my love," she whispered. Her voice was husky with tortured emotions that she had hidden from prying eyes for years. "I'm so sorry...."

Her lips felt cold. Vaguely she realized that the temperature had dropped. In a way, she welcomed it. It distracted her.

Elizabeth stared fatalistically at the weathered ocher and biscuit colors of the mansion and its staircase. She'd always worried that someday she would face Blake again. She had often wondered what they could find to say to one another. Dorian had hinted at the possibility of seeing Blake for over a year now. Malone's had become a prominent and prestigious name in the world of gems and fine jewelry, and Dorian was well aware of it.

Dorian Rand never missed an opportunity, Elizabeth thought in disgust. And he didn't care who got hurt. She flushed angrily and clenched her hands. Dorian was up to something. Unfortunately, she wasn't certain exactly what it was yet. From a couple of sly innuendoes that Dorian had made about Malone's, she was sure that Dorian was planning to involve her in taking advantage of Blake. She hated being used as a pawn. And she would do anything in her power to avoid hurting Blake again. And, of course, it would give her great satisfaction to foil Dorian.

Elizabeth felt the sting of tears forming in her eyes, and she rapidly blinked them away, embarrassed and a little dismayed at being overcome by her feelings. She wasn't usually given to tears. She'd learned to be strong a long time ago. But this dismal place, the years of entrapment, and thinking about Blake...

An aging male voice snapped her rudely away from her introspection. "Crying, Elizabeth?"

Elizabeth lifted her chin with an aristocratic gesture that made her look both elegant and dignified. "No, Dorian," she denied huskily. "It's the chilly air. The cold wind bites."

Dorian Rand looked at her with the same detached curiosity that an experimenter might use on a prize strain of laboratory animal. "I never noticed the cold bringing tears to your eyes when we went skiing last winter," he observed mildly.

A sudden breeze lifted the hem of her coat. The cold air caressed her like a ghostly hand. Elizabeth shivered and drew the wool material tightly around her. She should have remembered how raw the days could be here in winter. Funny. Ever since Dorian had dropped the bombshell about coming back, all she had thought about was how warm and wild and wonderful it had been in the States.

The wind slithered across her ankles and calves, and Elizabeth shivered again.

"Cold, my sweet?" asked the white-haired man with the cane in his hand who stood solicitously at her side.

"Yes," Elizabeth replied softly. "I'm cold inside and out, Dorian."

"Perhaps you should stop resisting my plans, my dear, and simply go inside?" he suggested. He was using the smoothly oiled voice that he employed when he wished to manage her without an argument. "It's warm inside, Elizabeth. You know that I always keep a fire going in the main halls of my homes." He tapped the tip of his cane against one of the stone steps. The step was cracked. Under his prodding, it broke a little more and began to slide apart.

Elizabeth turned slightly and stared at him. She let the silence string out between them until it was taut, icy and unforgiving.

"If there is *one* thing I've learned about your homes, Dorian," she said coolly, "it's that they are cold no matter how many fires you light." She pushed the shattering stone step apart with her toe and added, "I've also noticed that you enjoy destroying things almost as much as you enjoy trying to enrich yourself."

Dorian chuckled and made an amused, clucking sound with his tongue. "My, my, Elizabeth," he murmured in mock dismay. "You have a gothic imagination, I must say. How can you say that about your partner, my dear? We share a business. We live under the same roof. We are a most formidable family unit . . ." He hesitated, then, with a conciliatory shrug, he conceded, ". . . even if our ties are not those of blood or marriage."

His eyes narrowed slightly, and his bushy white brows arched. He pointed a bony finger at the house and added, "You could make it warmer, Elizabeth. You have no one to blame but yourself for the coldness you find. I told you years ago that I would use the information I had to destroy your father without a second's hesitation and that you might as well adjust yourself to that fact and learn to live with it. A practical woman would have made the best of the situation. A reasonable woman would have found a seat by the fire and warmed herself, made a life for herself. Why, I even suggested that you marry my son! I offered to tie my family and yours together in blood as well as in legal documents, mutual interests and business deals." He stared harder. "A practical woman would have acquiesced, Elizabeth, but you treated my offer as a vile insult!"

Elizabeth flashed him an angry look. "It *was* vile. I *was* insulted. I didn't love him, and you knew that!" But the fire in her eyes wasn't just for Dorian's failed matchmaking. It was for the love he had forced her to destroy. "I prefer to marry a man of my own choice," she said stiffly.

Dorian laughed. The sound was like leaves being rustled by the winter wind.

"My dear Elizabeth," he said, as if he couldn't believe she might still be clinging to her youthful dreams, "you aren't still angry because I interfered with your elopement, are you? Why, from the sparkle in your eyes, I can almost believe that's it. And I thought you'd forgotten about it." He shook his head. "Love! That wasn't love, my dear. It was sexual chemistry that sent you, flushed and eager, flying through the woods to see him at night." He chuckled indulgently. "If I had let you marry for love fifteen years ago, you would never have become the designer that you are!" He snorted disgustedly. "Why, you should thank me, my sweet. And if that does not soothe your long-ruffled feathers, consider what my interference did for your would-be husband. Surely you don't believe that Blake Malone would have worked as single-mindedly as he did if he had married you then? Why, half the hours he used building up his business, he would have spent in bed with you!"

Elizabeth blushed angrily but refused to be drawn in. Dorian seemed to find that even more amusing, and he continued.

"Can you imagine him acquiring the investment capital that he did if he'd had a wife and children to provide for? Paying medical bills, saving for college, family vacations?" Dorian looked skyward and then shook his head, as if it were all a horrible nightmare. "Why, if it weren't for me, my dear, Blake Malone would still be a minor gem cutter, working forty hours a week to support the small army of babies he seemed poised to give you fifteen years ago! And you would be designing family dinner menus on a budget, instead of jewelry fit for a queen to wear!"

Elizabeth stared at the gnarled, white-haired man lecturing her with such insufferable arrogance. He always knew her weak spots, she thought, and he'd struck home again. It wasn't the part about her jewelry designs being bought by royalty. It was what he had said about Blake. Would marrying her have held him back? They'd been so young . . . and it was so hard to start a business. Especially his kind of business. But she didn't want him to know how close to the mark he'd come, and she brushed off his remark.

"That's all ancient history, Dorian," Elizabeth pointed out quietly. She shrugged her shoulders delicately. "What I've always resented is your dictating terms to me. You know that." She hoped he'd swallow that and stop talking about Blake. She hated hearing his name on Dorian's lips. It brought out her protective instincts, she realized.

"You are a stubborn, unyielding young woman," Rand complained with a frustrated sigh. He reached out and lifted a soft strand of her auburn-gold hair, and he fingered it like a connoisseur might handle a delicate treasure that he much admired. "If I had been twenty or thirty years younger, my sweet, I might have tried to win you myself instead of encouraging you to accept my son." He sighed and let go of her hair, enjoying seeing the silky strands float like gossamer on the chilly breeze. "Just do not forget, my dear. We are partners."

Elizabeth's eyes flashed angrily. "Partners? When one is held hostage through blackmail? That's not my definition of a partnership, Dorian."

The movers had begun pulling dollies of boxes and trunks up the steps. As they passed Dorian and Elizabeth, they glanced over at her with obvious male interest. Elizabeth smiled back at them, silently thanking them for their admiration, yet gently discouraging anyone thinking of making a real pass at her. The men's stares acquired a shade more respect, as if she'd been transformed into a sister-figure.

Elizabeth gathered the folds of the coat and turned to climb up the steps. "If you'll excuse me, Dorian," she said coolly, "I think I'll go inside and see how my father is doing."

"Of course, Elizabeth," Dorian murmured. "I'll see you both at dinner. Mrs. Einer says it will be served in the dining room at eight." The white-haired man chuckled. "That is, if she can find the crockery she needs."

Elizabeth nodded and began climbing the stairs.

Dorian controlled a great many things in her life, but there were a few areas that belonged solely to her. Her memories, for example. Dorian couldn't control them, and he couldn't destroy them. She was grateful for that. At least she had those to treasure.

And they were treasures, she thought as she ascended the crumbling stone staircase. They were sweet, warm memories of a love that had once been everything to her. Everything.

Elizabeth found her father in a second-floor bedroom, the one closest to the house's aging elevator. He was sitting in his wheelchair, staring daggers at his nurse who was lecturing him on the dangers of wheeling himself down the hall to the bathroom alone. The young woman wagged her finger at him reprimandingly, unaware of Elizabeth's arrival.

"... and if you'd gotten stuck in there, Mr. Rossi, no one would have known about it, and you could have had an awful experience. Besides, I'd have gotten into a lot of trouble, so I wish you'd tell me when you want to go, sir!" The nurse inhaled deeply to regain her wind and sailed into her patient one last time. "I don't want to get fired, Mr. Rossi, and you know darn well that I'd get blamed if you fell or got hurt or anything. Please, promise me you won't do that again?"

Karl Rossi, sitting straight as a Prussian officer, gave his anxious attendant a malevolent look and firmly closed his eyes, as if to say he couldn't hear a thing she was saying and never would.

"Mr. Rossi!" the nurse wailed in frustration. She literally pulled at her hair. "No wonder your daughter has to hire a new nurse twice a year!"

Elizabeth sighed and walked into the room. Her father's pride was difficult to work around. He refused to admit the limitations imposed by the stroke he had suffered years ago. He doggedly attempted to take care of himself, spurning the efforts of his hired help without even the hint of an apology for his lack of cooperation.

The young licensed practical nurse turned when she heard Elizabeth's footsteps on the bare wooden floor, and her face lit up. "I'm so glad you're here, Miss Rossi," the young woman exclaimed in relief. "Maybe you can make Mr. Rossi listen."

Elizabeth took off her coat and hung it on a brass coat rack standing beside the bedroom door. Her father had opened his eyes and looked at her the moment he'd heard the nurse say her name. He looked like a small boy who was determined not to give in to the authority figures in his life, she thought. Proudly disdainful and yet a little bit abashed to be in the position he was. She went over to him, bent down, and gave him a hug and a kiss. He seemed to relax a little, she thought as she straightened. Unfortunately he was still giving a dark and nasty look to the poor young nurse hovering halfway across the small room from him.

"What have you been doing to poor Miss Smithson?" Elizabeth asked her father gently. "She's a very nice young woman. You told me you liked her when we interviewed her last week. You know she's only doing what the doctor told us she should do. . . ."

The man in the wheelchair looked furious at the mention of his doctor. His cheeks reddened, and his left hand gripped the wheelchair hard. He struggled and concentrated and tried to get out the word that he wanted to say. His mouth worked, and his tongue and teeth twisted, and finally the sound came out, a little garbled but understandable. "Fool," he croaked.

The poor nurse looked at the ceiling in exasperation. Elizabeth stifled a laugh by putting her hands in front of her face for a moment.

"The doctor is a fool?" Elizabeth asked, trying hard not to giggle and encourage her father's delinquent behavior.

Karl Rossi stuck his lower lip out and tightly pressed his upper lip down onto it, as if closing himself up like a clam. He gave a quick hard nod of his head. He thought his doctor was a fool. He didn't like the medical advice he was getting. And he clearly wasn't going to cooperate with the nurses assigned to help him along on a daily basis. He was the picture of a very proud man entrenched in denying that he had a very big problem.

Elizabeth sighed and gave the young nurse an apologetic smile. "I'm sorry, Cassie. He's a man of firm convictions."

The nurse rolled her eyes. "That's an understatement."

Karl looked as if he would have thrown her out of the house if he could and was furious that he couldn't.

Elizabeth made placating gestures to both of them and decided the best thing might be to separate them for a while. Like fighting cats.

"Every new relationship goes through a period of adjustment," Elizabeth said soothingly. "I'm sure you'll work through it. Besides, we're all a little tired today, with the moving. Moving can be disrupting, don't you think?" She looked optimistically at the nurse, who seemed doubtful. She looked at her father. He was staring at her as if she'd grown a dragon's tail. "Look, Cassie," she suggested, her optimism fading. "Why don't you go downstairs and have a nice cup of tea or soup or something? You've had a long morning. I'll stay with my father for the next hour."

The nurse perked up a little. "Thank you, Miss Rossi." She gave her patient a friendly smile. "Can I bring you anything, sir?"

He shook his head and frowned at her fiercely, as if advising her to stay wherever it was she was going and not come back.

The young nurse wasn't that inexperienced, however. She didn't take his recalcitrance personally. "Nothing? All right. Maybe later. I'll be in the kitchen if you need me, Miss Rossi." She pointed to the second of six buzzers on the wall beside the door. "If you push that one, the intercom goes on and I can talk to you."

Elizabeth nodded and said, "Thanks, Cassie." She waited until the nurse left before she turned back to her father. "Father," she said, imploring him to try to cooperate, "please try to get along with Miss Smithson. She's a very nice young woman. And you know that you're supposed to have someone with you. Please? Try? As a special favor to me?"

Her father stared at her, and the granite stillness of his angry face began to erode. He looked down at his hands, and tears began to fill his eyes. He blinked them away, but they began to fall anyway. His right hand lay twisted and clenched in his lap. He gripped it with his left, trying to spread the unresponsive fingers. Tears spattered on his age-spotted skin.

"No good," he said, struggling to get the words right and to get them said. "I'm . . . no . . . good. . . ."

Elizabeth knelt in front of him and put her arms around him as best she could.

"You're very good," she said vehemently. Her own eyes filled with tears as she saw the agony he was in. "It's not your fault that this happened to you. . . ."

He grew very angry. His eyes flashed. "My fault. My fault." Guilt was plain on his aging features. Tremendous, agonizing guilt. "My fault," he choked out again.

Elizabeth grasped his good hand between hers, wishing she could tell him it wasn't so. Unfortunately he was right, in a way. Her tragedy and his were rooted in a mistake he had made thirty years ago. If he hadn't forged several pieces of gold jewelry to raise the money he needed to try to save her mother's life, Dorian would have nothing to hold over them. Dorian would not have been able to blackmail them fifteen years ago. There would have been no awful secret to hide. Then Elizabeth would not have had to send Blake away, as Dorian had ordered her to do. And Karl Rossi might not have suffered the crippling stroke when he'd discovered the price that Elizabeth had paid to keep him out of jail. If . . . if . . .

Tears ran down her cheeks, and she laid her face close to his.

"We have to stick together, darling," she told her father huskily. "It doesn't do any good to blame ourselves or wish that life had been different. We can't undo what we have done." She pressed a gentle kiss to his quivering jaw. "We have to go on from here."

They sat together in silence for a long, painful time, while the gray light outside the bedroom window slowly darkened into night.

Finally Elizabeth pulled away and found a lamp to light. Her father looked wilted and very tired now, she thought.

He raised his haggard eyes to hers and seemed to beseech her to accept his apology.

Elizabeth rejoined him and took his outstretched hand. Smiling, she nodded. "It's all right. Forget it. I know it's hard for you, being trapped inside your body, not being able to tell us your thoughts." She squeezed his hand affectionately and managed a smile. "Of course, you always make it clear what you *don't* like!" She laughed softly, trying to cheer them both up.

Her father smiled wanly and shrugged. Then he nodded, as if to say, *Yes, I always try to make my dislikes known as clearly as possible. I suppose that is something, anyway.*

The intercom buzzed softly, and Elizabeth went to answer it. "Yes?"

"Miss Rossi? This is Cassie. I'm with Mrs. Einer in the kitchen. We're discussing the dinner menu. I wonder if we could try a new fruit for Mr. Rossi tonight. The doctor has it on his list, but Mrs. Einer says she's never fixed it for him in the past."

"What is it?" Elizabeth asked curiously.

"A stewed prune compote."

Karl Rossi rolled his eyes and made a gagging sound. Elizabeth, accustomed to his tantrums, grinned and disregarded his theatrics.

"I'm sure my father would be delighted to try it. He's promised to be very gracious tonight. He wants to make amends for the worry he caused you this afternoon."

There was a startled silence at the other end of the intercom. The nurse cleared her throat and said, "Why, that's wonderful. Tell him I've already forgotten all about it."

Elizabeth eyed her mildly irate father and said, "I will, Cassie." She turned off the intercom and gave her father an innocent look. "You were always an old-world gentleman, Father," she explained smoothly. "Always very gracious to the ladies. I was only saying what you'd want me to, wasn't I?"

Karl Rossi gave his daughter a severe look. Then his face softened, his eyes warmed, and a smile slowly lightened his features. He shrugged as if to say, *Have it your own way, my dear. I'll go along with it, if it makes you happy. I suppose I can still be a gentleman, in spite of everything.*

Elizabeth smiled at him tenderly. "Thank you, Father."

He nodded, and his affection for her warmed his old, tired eyes. He concentrated and pursed his lips. "Welcome," he struggled to reply. Then, grimacing, "Prunes!"

Chapter 3

Blake sat alone in his office, rocking back slightly in the heavy wooden chair behind his desk. The lamplight shone on its highly polished, dark cherry arms, making them gleam... except where a shadow was cast by the manila folder he was holding in his hand.

In it was the information that his secretary had compiled on Dorian Rand and Elizabeth Rossi in the past ten days. There were many facts and figures. Lots of newspaper clippings. A few notes Janet had jotted down after discreet conversations with several people. He was tempted to smile when he thought of how careful she'd been to appear to be talking about things other than Dorian and Elizabeth. Janet had done her usual conscientious job on this assignment. His brows knitted in a frown, and he lightly tapped the file against the palm of one hand. She hadn't uncovered much, but what she had, wasn't what he had been expecting.

He heard someone moving around in the main salon display area. The last customer leaving for the night, he presumed. Then Janet came to his door and rapped softly.

"Come in," he said.

She stuck her head inside and asked, "We're closing up, Mr. Malone. Will you need anything else before I leave?"

He shook his head. "No, thanks, Janet. You've got everything so well in hand that I'm still catching up with you." He smiled at her. "Give me a few hours to come up with some more work."

She laughed. "I guess I'd better work more slowly." She dipped her head as a way of saying good-night and left.

After she'd gone, Blake stared at the bone-colored folder, wondering what he should do next. And when. He hadn't expected the situation to be what it was. Some of his original ideas were going to have to be trashed.

For one thing, financially besting Elizabeth's husband wasn't going to make much sense. Elizabeth didn't have one. Apparently she never had. Janet hadn't even run across any notices of an engagement. Elizabeth skiied and had been mentioned occasionally in a few socially prominent charity events in Zurich. If she'd had a hot love affair, he presumed someone might have been aware of it and enjoyed gossiping about it. But Janet had found nothing there, either. No publicly acknowledged, or privately rumored, love affairs. Hell, he thought irritably, she hadn't even appeared as the "close personal friend" of anyone. That was really hard for him to believe. She must be a virtuoso at disguising her personal life, he thought. She *couldn't* have lived a life that socially quiet, that devoid of romantic attachments. His face hardened. He refused to believe it.

She'd told him flat out that she was leaving him for another man. So who had he been? What had happened to him? Why hadn't she married him?

Blake rapped the file sharply against the rounded brass edge of his mahogany desk, and his eyes narrowed as he considered the possibilities. It didn't take much imagination to come up with a few of the more obvious ones.

Perhaps the man had been seriously injured or killed in an accident before a formal engagement had been announced. Or maybe he'd fallen ill and suffered a lingering incapacity of some sort before she could marry him. It was also possible that the man's relatives had intervened and somehow convinced him to break off with Elizabeth before they actually got to the altar.

That was a strong contender, Blake thought, since the man had been older and wealthy, and his family might well have resented a young woman moving in to snap up all his worldly goods.

Then Blake's eyes grew hard. He shouldn't overlook one of the most common possibilities of all, of course. The man might simply have seduced Elizabeth, plying her with promises of wealth and status, and then later abandoned her, presumably after he'd had all he wanted of her. From his observations, that kind of thing happened with breathtaking regularity.

Blake wanted to feel some sort of primal satisfaction at that last scenario. He wanted to feel avenged. He wanted to relish the possibility that Elizabeth had been dumped as she'd dumped him. To his consternation, he realized that he didn't feel particularly triumphant. True, there was a small taste of vengeance satisfied. However, mostly he felt as if his emotions had gone to war with one another. Conflicting feelings roiled inside of him, battling for supremacy.

On the one hand, it appealed to his sense of irony and justice to think that she might have gotten her just desserts. On the other hand, he couldn't imagine any sane man walking away from Elizabeth Rossi. Especially if she'd gone to bed with him. To his disgust, he realized that he was actually rather irate on her behalf. How dare some aging lothario behave with such irresponsible cruelty? Elizabeth had claimed that she loved the man, for God's sake. Blake's surge of outraged and protective feelings for her suddenly made him furious. What in the hell was wrong with him? He should know better than to feel chivalrous toward a woman who'd sliced his heart in two without more than a teary apology.

Unfortunately his feelings didn't seem particularly inclined to pay any attention to his logical thinking. The feelings were there, whether he liked them or not.

Blake ran his hand through his hair and cursed his idiotic reaction. Thinking up hypothetical explanations like this was obviously getting him nowhere. If anything, it was driving him crazy, and that certainly hadn't been his goal. It obviously wasn't productive for him to speculate about what might have happened to Elizabeth's aged, former fiancé. He needed more facts.

Since his secretary, who was an excellent sleuth, had only
been able to unearth the scantiest information, he concluded
that there might be only a few people who would be able to
answer his questions.

One of those people, of course, was Elizabeth herself.

He filed the folder in the cabinet beside his desk and locked
it. Then he got up and walked around his office, rubbing his
forehead tiredly.

Elizabeth. Perhaps the direct route would be the most productive in the long run. He would simply ask her what had
happened. When they finally met, he supposed that it would be
a natural enough question for him to ask, considering their
previous relationship. After all, he told himself bitterly, it
wasn't as though he were still carrying a torch for her. If anything, he thoroughly disliked her. Elizabeth was probably
expecting that and wouldn't misconstrue his query as some sort
of . . . personal interest in her.

He gave a short, harsh laugh at that idea. It wasn't as if he'd
spent the years pining away for her.

Blake came to a halt in the middle of the room and thrust his
hands into his trouser pockets. All right, that was it, then. He
would ask her himself when the opportunity arose. That
shouldn't be long, either.

From the information that his secretary had gathered on
Dorian Rand, Blake was certain that he would be running into
Elizabeth very soon indeed. Dorian was planning on displaying the jewelry he was auctioning off. Most prominent jewelers in the country would be sending a representative to examine
the items and pick up a sales catalogue. Malone's would be receiving an engraved invitation to the event, no doubt. All he
would have to do was accept and go.

Apparently Elizabeth would be there, serving as Dorian's
personal assistant. Since Blake was a prime potential customer, she would be obligated to give him all the time that he
wished.

He smiled cheerlessly. What an ironic twist of fate, he
thought. He'd lost her—in part, at least—because he had been
next to broke. Now he had the upper hand, because Elizabeth's pockets were nearly empty.

He heard a church bell chime outside, and he noticed that i
was quite dark now. He walked past his desk, intending to leave
the office, but his eyes fell on the filing cabinet, and he re
called something else that his secretary had discovered. It wa
something that had made him feel pity and sadness, more than
anything else, however.

It had been the sketchy biography of Elizabeth's father, Karl
Rossi. According to Janet's sources, Karl had apparently suf
fered a crippling stroke and hadn't worked productively fo
years. Blake was genuinely sorry to hear that. He had been Karl
Rossi's apprentice for six months in Arkansas, fifteen years
ago. He'd learned a great deal about the faceting and design of
diamond jewelry from Karl. The man had had a genius for us
ing the various colors of gold with precious and semiprecious
gems, and for seeing the angles to slice a stone to its best ad
vantage. Karl had an instinctive feel for precious gems that was
unrivaled, in Blake's opinion.

It had been in Karl Rossi's workshop that Blake had first seen
Elizabeth. Shy, virginal Elizabeth, who had loved the glitter
ing jewels as much as Blake and her father did. She'd showed
promise as a jewelry designer herself. According to Janet's in
vestigation, Elizabeth worked for Dorian, but her responsibil
ities had been difficult to pin down. She seemed to live in his
shadow, well out of the limelight. Blake couldn't help wonder
ing if she'd continued designing. He couldn't recall having seen
any work attributed to her. He frowned as he considered that.
She must have quit. There were easier ways to earn a living, he
thought cynically, but somehow he hadn't seen her as a quit
ter.

Damn her anyway. She'd been so breathtakingly beautiful,
so fresh and untainted by life, when he'd fallen in love with her.
He still couldn't understand how she could have so thoroughly
deceived him. Angrily, he ran a hand through his hair.

Elizabeth had obviously been one hell of an actress. And he
had been a pathetically besotted young fool. Blake stared into
his bitter past for a long, painful moment. Indifference was
proving difficult to achieve. Damned difficult, to tell the truth.

He brushed aside his memories of Elizabeth and forcibly
turned his attention to the reality of his office. He needed to
make sure the vault built into his office wall was locked for the

night, and he moved to check it, as he did every night before leaving.

As he did so, his thoughts were drawn to his old mentor, in spite of his determination to concentrate on his present surroundings. There were magnificent pieces of jewelry locked in that vault. Pieces that only the Karl Rossis of the world could create.

What a pity, Blake reflected, that instead of realizing his gifts, Karl had been crippled and prevented from using them. That was a great loss, not only to Karl, but to the world. He wondered how Karl had adapted to that shock. It must have been very tough.

Blake remembered Karl's face as it had been years ago.... His gray eyes had been the texture of antique pewter, hard when he needed to be, but occasionally softened by a rare patina of genuine human kindness.

Next to Elizabeth, Karl's work had been his entire world. The sun had risen and set on his beloved daughter. In his eyes, she could do no wrong. Blake's mouth tightened into a sardonic smile. He had felt the same way himself at the time. Two blind fools. Blake wondered if Karl still was blind when it came to Elizabeth.

On the other hand, no piece of jewelry that Karl had made ever completely pleased him. He had been a perfectionist, always trying to create a flawless masterpiece, perpetually chasing a dream that just eluded his grasp. Blake thought it ironic. For Karl's designs had been utterly exquisite. Perfect in every way. But Karl had never seen it. He had been blind there, too.

And now he was crippled. Dependent on others. Robbed of his art. Of his dreams. Blake toyed with the idea of going to visit Karl, out of friendship. Karl Rossi had treated him more like a son than an apprentice. If it hadn't been for Elizabeth, they would probably have been close friends, personally and professionally, for the last decade and a half. But after Elizabeth's betrayal, Blake hadn't wanted to stay. Seeing her was more than he could stomach at the time. So he had left to pursue another opportunity. Anything had seemed better than being near her and not touching her, having to see her face light up in gladness at the sound of another man's voice, waiting for her to leave to marry someone else.

Blake's anger surged anew in spite of his effort to suppress it. He had the feeling that she must have been a big disappointment to her father. Poor Karl. The man had surely had more than his share of suffering, Blake thought. Karl had been grooming Elizabeth to become a master jeweler, even though she'd been only a teenager. To others, Karl had often been abrupt or taciturn, but never to Elizabeth. Even when he was angry at the way some piece of work was progressing, he softened and became more tender when Elizabeth was there. She had been the center of the stubborn old jeweler's universe, Blake recalled grimly. And she had disappointed him, apparently. Just as she'd disappointed Blake.

What had Karl gotten for all his years of sacrifice? Blake wondered angrily. A daughter who turned down love when money was waved under her nose? A daughter who apparently was too lazy to use her own gifts and her father's training to become the best she could be? A daughter content to be the assistant to one of the slipperiest jewelers in Europe? That was the final insult, Blake thought. How could she prostitute herself to the likes of Dorian Rand?

Dorian Rand. Now there was a man that Blake had never fully trusted. He might have outstanding taste in jewelry and impeccable credentials as a jeweler, but Rand was principally concerned about feathering his own nest, no matter what the cost. Rand had never had any brushes with the law, as far as Blake knew, but Blake was not fully convinced of the man's honesty. Men like Rand were more concerned about whether they could successfully sidestep a law than whether there was anything fundamentally wrong with evading it to begin with.

Thinking of Dorian Rand brought to mind another fact, and Blake drummed his fingers on his desktop as he considered it. Rand would be attending a tea at the Smithsonian this weekend. He was giving a brief talk and then fielding questions about the upcoming auction of his jewelry.

There had been no mention of Karl Rossi being in attendance, but Blake couldn't envision the arrogant and aristocratic Rand going anywhere without some sort of entourage. The man relished grand entrances and publicity. And who better to dance attendance on the old coot than the beautiful young woman who served as his assistant?

"I've never gone out of my way to attend teas in this town, Elizabeth," he murmured softly, "but in this case, I will make an exception." Because, through her, he might locate Karl.

The smile in his eyes was cold and unfriendly, which was just how he felt about Elizabeth Rossi. Indifference wasn't coming easily to him at all. Not where Elizabeth Rossi was concerned.

Mozart's "Quartet in F" was being piped in over the public address system in the conference room in the basement of the Smithsonian's Museum of Natural History. Close to fifty people had come to sip English tea, munch on freshly baked crumpets and be seen by their colleagues. As they circulated, careful not to muss their silk dresses or fine suits, they smiled at each other vacuously, murmuring about how exciting it was to have Dorian Rand in town, what an immense publicity boon his upcoming auction would undoubtedly be to the local upscale jewelry market, and how amusing it was to hear the anecdotes the man was famous for.

Elizabeth Rossi was standing next to one of the museum's up-and-coming gemologists, Jerome Elbertson. Jerome was regaling her with tales of his latest acquisitions for the gemological exhibit upstairs.

"...Of course, everyone comes to see the Hope Diamond," he admitted with a laugh. "We've always got a line around it, and the other famous gemstones in the room with it." He shrugged philosophically. "I don't mind. At least it gets people into the exhibit. Perhaps a few kids will be fascinated by the crystals, the colors, the variety."

Elizabeth nodded in agreement, but her eyes wandered from his earnest face. She felt as if she were adrift in a sea of strangers. Nowhere could she find a familiar face.

Dorian had allowed himself to be carried off by some blue-haired dowager ladies to the far corner of the room. He had left her to the tender mercies of poor Jerome Elbertson. The museum had arranged for Jerome to drive them to the tea. Elizabeth decided he had more or less been assigned valet duty. He was pleasant, but completely overawed by Dorian.

Jerome was chatting amiably, quite comfortable with Elizabeth's wandering attention, not in the least offended. Elizabeth managed to say *um hmm* and *oh?* at all the right moments, as she casually perused the crowd.

"Would you care for a cup of tea now, Elizabeth?" Jerome inquired.

"That sounds lovely, Jerome. Thank you," she murmured pensively.

"Do you take lemon or milk?" He leaned toward her, an earnest expression on his freckled face.

"Lemon, please." She smiled at him, feeling genuine sympathy for the man. He was wiry and tall, but very youthful looking. With his old-fashioned manners, he seemed the most harmless of men. She touched his shoulder lightly, as she would have touched a younger brother. "Would you like me to go with you? It might be too much to carry with this crowd."

Jerome fairly beamed at her concern. "No, no. It will be no problem at all. You just, uh, wait right here. I'll be right back." He began backing away, bowing a little. Then he blushed, having realized that he must look like an overawed schoolboy. He cleared his throat and straightened his face into a more serious expression. "It will just take me a few minutes."

Elizabeth's smile softened further as she watched him stumble through the milling crowd. Poor man. He obviously spent more time with stones than with women, she thought sympathetically.

"It looks as if you've made another conquest, Elizabeth."

Elizabeth whirled to face the man who had just spoken to her. Her smile was frozen on her face, and she raised a hand slightly, as if she were reaching out for help. She would have recognized his voice anywhere, even though it had been fifteen years since she had heard it.

"Blake," she whispered. His name came out as an aching caress. She couldn't help it. She had been caught unprepared, and her feelings burst forth before she could do anything about them. "Blake..."

He was standing in front of her, looking much the same as he had, although perhaps a little more filled out, a little more mature. He was still unbelievably handsome. He was smiling slightly, but there was a hardness in his eyes that seemed at war with the curve of his lips.

He reached out and took her hand, lifting it to his lips to kiss. When his mouth brushed the back of it, his fingers tightened ever so slightly.

Elizabeth felt the blood begin to rush through her chilled body, bringing her back to life. It had been so long since she had seen him. So long since she'd felt his hand on hers. Felt his lips. She stared at his dark hair, wishing she could reach out and touch it, as she had years ago.

He raised his head and looked at her steadily. "It's been a long time." He released her hand, appearing somewhat amused at her shock. He smiled a little, without warmth. "You look as if you've seen a ghost, Elizabeth," he observed.

"I think I have," she said, barely above a whisper. She searched his face, seeing the man he had become. There were small wrinkles at the corners of his eyes. She let her gaze roam over him, trying to do it quickly, lightly, the way people do when they haven't seen each other in a long time. It was difficult, though, for she wanted to linger. He looked as if he'd put on ten or fifteen pounds, all muscle. "You haven't changed a lot," she said at last. "If anything, you've just improved with age, like a good wine." She made an effort to smile, but she didn't really feel like smiling, and it came off as a weak and ambivalent glimmer. "I wasn't expecting to see you here," she admitted honestly.

"No?" He raised a brow in surprise. "Why not? Did you think I'd be nursing old wounds, hiding from you?" he asked, as if it were the furthest thing possible from the truth.

Elizabeth was a little confused by his question. There was a hard glint of amusement in his eyes, she thought, as if the idea of his nursing wounded feelings for her was quite ridiculous. And yet there was an undertone in his voice that seemed like anger to her. She wasn't sure which message to believe. Perhaps she was projecting her own feelings on him, she thought. She swallowed her discomfiture and tried to nurture her limp smile into a more convincing variety.

"No. I'm sure you haven't been nursing a wounded heart for fifteen years," she replied. She was looking into his eyes, and it was heavenly, even with that mystifying hard amusement she saw in them. "I just meant that I didn't think a man as successful as you would have time to drop in on a tea like this."

He dipped his head in acknowledgment of her compliment. "I'm flattered you're aware of my small accomplishment."

Elizabeth's smile radiated a genuine warmth. "You're becoming quite well-known," she assured him. Her eyes glowed then, as she thought of how proud she was of him. "It hasn't been easy to do, I know."

Blake shrugged. "I had some help," he said easily. He glanced around at the people in the room and pointed out, "I sell jewelry to a lot of people who are here today. Your arrival is an event. I come to affairs like this periodically." He grinned. "It's good for business."

"Yes, of course," Elizabeth hurried to agree.

So he hadn't particularly cared whether she was there or not, she thought. Funny how that hurt. It didn't make any sense, of course. She had no right to expect him to seek her out. She'd certainly made sure to avoid *him* for years, but that had been to protect herself, and him. It had been because she had no choice. She knew she was being perverse, but how she wished that he had treasured some small fondness for her. Enough to come to a tea to see her again.

Blake had been watching her face, his own expression as opaque as an uncut gem.

"Of course, there was another good reason to come," he added carefully. "I haven't seen you in years. You know, you've grown into your coltish bones, Elizabeth." He slowly ran his gaze over her from head to toe. There was grudging admiration in his voice when he added, "You've become a beautiful woman."

Elizabeth felt her breath catch and an ache form in her heart at his words of praise. Her smile faded, and a look of such longing filled her eyes that the people near them who noticed it blinked in surprise.

"I never thought I'd hear a kind word from you again, Blake," she admitted in a low, soft voice. "Thank you." She took his hand in hers and covered it, holding it like a pledge. She could feel tears from the years of loneliness threaten to fill her eyes.

Blake stared at her, but it was difficult to know what he was thinking.

"Fifteen years is a long time," he pointed out dispassionately. "Wouldn't you agree?"

Elizabeth's throat ached with the effort not to cry. "Oh, yes," she whispered. An incredibly long time, she thought sadly. God, she hadn't expected to be so overwhelmed. She had known that it would be difficult to see him again, but she had never dreamed that it would affect her this strongly. Somehow she had to push her emotions back into their cage. Otherwise, the situation could become disastrous. It wasn't just that she was likely to make a fool of herself, staring at this man with her heart in her eyes after all these years. No. The problem was that Dorian would see it. And she mustn't let that happen.

A movement by her side offered her a welcome excuse to drag her gaze away from Blake. She released his hand and turned to see Jerome returning with their tea. From the expression on his face, he had guessed that Elizabeth and Blake were not engaging in the usual frothy tea party conversation. His freckles began to melt as an embarrassed blush stole across his cheeks.

"Uh, here is your tea, Elizabeth," he muttered uncomfortably. He held her cup out to her, jingling it on the saucer in his nervousness.

Elizabeth took the cup and saucer from him, and this time she managed a fairly credible smile. Her initial shock upon seeing Blake began to wear off, and she tried to rise to the occasion gracefully.

"Do you know each other?" she inquired of the two men.

"Aren't you Jerome Elbertson?" Blake asked, holding out his hand and firmly shaking the nervous museum gemologist's.

"Yes, sir. And you, of course, are Mr. Malone."

"Please call me Blake."

"Why, thank you!" Jerome's freckled face lit up like a Christmas tree at Blake's casual offer. He stretched out his hand, offering Blake the untouched cup of tea that he had brought back for himself. "Would you care for this? I'd be more than happy to get another cup for myself." He laughed awkwardly. "I haven't touched it yet."

Blake gave him a relaxed grin. "No, but thanks, Jerome."

The museum gemologist took a hasty swallow of his tea and looked from Blake to Elizabeth. "Have you two met previously?" he asked innocently.

Blake looked at Elizabeth and slowly nodded. In a voice soft and compelling he replied, "Yes, Jerome. Elizabeth and I are . . . acquainted."

There was something in the narrowing of Blake's gaze that made Elizabeth wonder if perhaps he *had* thought of her in the past fifteen years. And not with particular fondness, either.

"Well, well, what have we here?" asked a familiar, raspy-voiced man, as he merged from a nest of talking women off to Elizabeth's right. "If it isn't Blake Malone! I have heard great things about you, Blake. But I must confess it's a surprise to see you here. Frankly, I was not expecting you."

Elizabeth stiffened and turned to face Dorian Rand. "Funny you should say that, Dorian. I just told him the same thing."

Dorian's sharp-eyed gaze raked over Elizabeth, taking in her now cool, stony face. A calculating smile played on his thin lips. "I happened to look across the room and see you talking a few minutes ago, Elizabeth. You had the most . . . *enraptured* . . . look on your face. Did you know that?" He chuckled as Elizabeth's cheeks darkened in embarrassment and anger. "Hah! You didn't know, did you?" He turned to study Blake, then slowly nodded his head. "I hope we will be seeing you in the future, Blake. I have some jewelry that might be of interest to you. Of course, I'm certain you have heard about that already."

Blake smiled and dipped his head slightly. "Yes. I have."

Dorian chuckled and gave Elizabeth an affectionate glance. "And then, it's good to see the roses return to Elizabeth's cheeks. Whatever did you say to her?"

"Dorian," Elizabeth interrupted, trying to laugh off his telling comments. "Blake isn't interested in your teasing, and surely I am old enough to be spared it, aren't I? If my cheeks are red, it's undoubtedly because of the hot tea." She looked around, wishing desperately that the formal proceedings would begin. "Shouldn't we be taking our seats now?"

Blake, who had been listening with no discernible reaction, lightly touched Elizabeth's elbow and pointed her toward the front row of seats. "That sounds like an excellent idea," he said. "Do you mind if I join you?" He raised his brows questioningly and looked at Elizabeth, then at Dorian.

Elizabeth glanced up at him rather sharply. He hadn't been asking, merely mouthing the formalities, while beginning to move her gently in the direction that he wished. She heard Dorian chuckle, and she felt even more uncomfortable.

"Mind?" Dorian exclaimed. "Of course not. Elizabeth would be delighted to have you join her, wouldn't you, Elizabeth?" He paused, forcing Elizabeth to voice a reply.

"We'd be delighted, naturally," she reluctantly agreed.

Blake murmured. "You don't sound delighted, Elizabeth."

Elizabeth glanced at Blake, wondering uneasily why his lightly spoken words somehow sounded as sharp as diamond drill bits. However, she was distracted as, behind her, Jerome began clearing his throat and trying to get a word in.

"Uh, would you like me to take your cup, Elizabeth?" Jerome asked, as he hovered uneasily near her shoulder. "That is, if you're all through with it?"

Elizabeth slowed enough to hand him the teacup along with an understanding smile. "Thank you, Jerome. It's very kind of you. I'll save you a seat. All right?"

Jerome was wreathed in smiles as he balanced both cups and turned to plow a path through the chattering crowd. "Thank you. Uh. Thank you," he stuttered.

"I see you haven't lost your touch," Blake observed, as he watched Jerome disappear into the crowd.

Elizabeth looked at him in confusion. "Lost my touch?" she echoed blankly.

"With men," he explained. "You can still manage them quite effortlessly."

He was speaking in a mild conversational voice, and yet he made it sound like an insult, she realized. This was neither the time nor the place to pursue that, so she silently followed him to the front row, wondering uneasily what would come next.

In all the times she had imagined meeting Blake again, she had never envisioned anything like this, she thought. She had an awful feeling that this was just the beginning.

Chapter 4

Elizabeth was sitting between Blake and Jerome, and Dorian was smiling down at them from his seat on the dais. A Smithsonian board member introduced Dorian in glowing terms. Then, amid the politely enthusiastic applause, Dorian held forth on his favorite subject: the creation of beautiful jewelry and the transformation of it for wealth of a more exchangeable variety.

Elizabeth forgot about Jerome after the first few minutes. The poor soul more or less blended with the chair and his surroundings. Not so the man on her left, however. She was acutely aware of him. She wished that she could feel as relaxed as he appeared to be. He was lounging back in his seat, his jacket open, his legs crossed casually at the ankles and one arm stretched out along the back of her chair.

After thirty minutes of listening to Dorian, she began to move restlessly. She wished that Dorian would begin taking questions and finishing up.

Blake, noticing her movements, leaned over and whispered in her ear, "Getting bored? You must have heard all this a hundred times."

She felt his warm breath brush across her cheek as he spoke, and she half closed her eyes at the tantalizing sensation. How long had it been since she had felt a tender caress? A man's kiss? She couldn't remember. Not even the most innocent one. She felt the warmth from Blake's nearness and realized he was waiting for her reply. What had he asked? Oh, yes. Had she heard Dorian's comments before?

Blake had straightened up again by the time Elizabeth was ready to answer. When she turned to reply, she was forced to lean toward him. Since he was taller, even sitting in a chair, he bent his head slightly to hear what she had to say. She hadn't expected him to be moving closer to her, and her lips lightly brushed his ear as she whispered back, "I must have heard him say this a *thousand* times, at least!"

His blue-green eyes seemed very dark and distant, she thought, as she gazed into them for a long, silent moment. When she had brushed his ear with her lips, she'd thought he had flinched. Perhaps that was just her imagination, though. She knew she was oversensitive where he was concerned. Maybe she had accidentally tickled him. She tried to be sensible and shake off her fanciful thinking. Then he was bending close to her again, and she felt a strange giddiness scamper through her heart.

"Have you enjoyed working with him?" Blake whispered.

Elizabeth lowered her eyes for a moment and tried to remain composed. How could she answer, for heaven's sake? She didn't want to lie to Blake, but she couldn't tell him the truth, either. She raised her eyes and found him watching her with unnerving steadiness.

"I have learned a lot from Dorian," she whispered in reply. A slight frown formed on her brow. "More than I ever thought possible."

Blake's eyes held hers for a silent moment. He seemed to be searching for the answer to an unasked question. Then he settled back in his chair. His profile gave no clue to his thoughts. His face was utterly expressionless.

People were asking questions about particular pieces of jewelry they had seen in catalogs over the years, pieces that had been designed by Dorian Rand's jewelers. There were inquiries about the upcoming auction and the pieces that would be going on the block.

It was forty minutes later when the Smithsonian board member finally stepped back up to the podium, asked everyone for a final round of applause for their guest of honor and adjourned the meeting.

Jerome popped out of his seat like a jack-in-the-box and declared, "I'll run out and get the car. Shall we meet at the Mall entrance, where I dropped you and Mr. Rand off when we arrived?"

Elizabeth nodded and smiled at Jerome. "That would be fine, Jerome. I'll tell Dorian." She felt a little guilty for having ignored Jerome for the past forty-five minutes. To compensate, she put her hand on his and impulsively offered, "And you must come in and talk with us when we get home."

Jerome looked as if he'd been offered a ten-carat emerald. "Thank you, uh, Elizabeth." He couldn't quite get used to using her first name. He grinned at her and Blake, and excused himself.

Blake seemed quite amused. "You've reduced him to a stammering boy."

Elizabeth looked at Blake curiously. "That's the second time you've made a comment like that."

He shrugged, as if it weren't particularly important. "So it is," he agreed. He saw Dorian slowly making his way through the glad-handers and heading in their direction. "I take it you're living with Dorian?"

Elizabeth didn't like the way it sounded when Blake said it. As if she weren't just living with him, but perhaps sleeping with him. She stood a little straighter and lifted her chin in a pridefully defensive gesture.

"Yes," she admitted. She had no choice about it, though. She couldn't afford to live anywhere else, and Dorian kept it that way. Unfortunately, she couldn't tell Blake that. She looked straight into his eyes and asked, "Do you live in Washington?"

"Yes."

She wondered if he lived alone, but she was reluctant to pry. It would have been a rather personal question, and they hadn't been exactly "personal" with one another for a very long time.

Her curiosity would just have to wait. From the look in his eyes, it was apparent that Blake was about to ask *her* something, anyway.

"How is your father?"

Elizabeth's face softened, and a sad, tender light filled her eyes. "He's doing as well as can be expected." She hesitated, not sure what Blake knew. Gently, she explained, "He had a stroke years ago, and he hasn't been able to use his right side very much. He's wheelchair bound."

As Blake nodded, she realized that he must have been aware of her father's condition. He hadn't looked shocked or surprised. She wondered how he had found out. People in the business, perhaps, she thought. A friend of a friend might have mentioned it. Still . . . it didn't quite seem to fit. She felt a little puzzled. Actually Blake hadn't looked surprised to see her, either, she recalled. Of course, he had had time to recover from his surprise before he approached her. Still . . .

"Did you know about Father's stroke, Blake?" she asked.

"I had heard he was crippled." He didn't elaborate. "Is he living with Dorian and you?" he asked casually.

Elizabeth hated the way it sounded again. As if she and her father were parasites sucking on Dorian for a living. She blushed as she realized what a poor opinion Blake would have of that. She stubbornly tilted her chin. "Yes. We're both living with Dorian."

"I'd like to see Karl some time."

Elizabeth hadn't been expecting that. She stared at Blake in surprise. He didn't look too pleased by her gaping.

"Would that be a problem for him?" Blake demanded coolly.

Elizabeth shook her head. "No," she murmured. "I don't think so." Then she had a vision of her father seeing Blake. Her father who felt guilty for having been the cause of breaking up their love affair. What if he tried to tell Blake what had really happened? Elizabeth paled.

Blake saw her loss of color and misconstrued its cause. "Would my visiting him be a problem for *you,* Elizabeth?" he asked. His voice was deceptively soft. There was nothing soft about his eyes, though.

Elizabeth sensed the steel beneath the softness. She racked her brains for a way to avoid another catastrophe. "No. Of course it doesn't bother me," she denied, laughing nervously.

"You seem less than eager to have me visit," he observed dryly. "Would you mind telling me why?"

She said the first things that that came to mind and hoped she wasn't digging a new grave to fall into. "He tires very easily, so we're very careful about visitors. He doesn't have too many, and they never stay long."

Blake shrugged. "There shouldn't be any problem, then. I can accept that."

"But..."

"But what?"

She saw the determination in Blake's eyes. He was going to see Karl Rossi, and nothing was going to stop him. If she blurted out that her father might be upset by his visit, Blake would probably demand an explanation. Then what would she tell him? More lies? More half-truths? What if she forgot what she had already made up? She didn't want to be caught in a tangled web of deceit. And she desperately didn't want to lie to Blake. Not again.

"But *what,* Elizabeth?" Blake repeated in the steely soft voice that was quite unlike his usual tone.

Elizabeth smiled sadly and laid her hand on his arm, as if in apology. "Nothing, Blake," she told him quietly. "We'll find a way to work something out. Just...give us a little time to get settled in, all right?"

He seemed to relax a little and nodded his head in agreement.

Elizabeth saw Dorian trying to slip away from the conversational grasp of two particularly tenacious museum patrons. It wouldn't take him long now, she thought. She would be leaving in a matter of minutes. She turned back to Blake and extended her hand to him.

"I'm glad you came tonight," she told him, trying to sound cheerful and in control of herself. She thought she succeeded fairly well. And even when he took her hand, she managed to keep her smile in place. She was quite proud of that.

"So am I," he murmured. Then he reached for her left hand and held it up for his view. There was no wedding ring on her finger. He touched the spot where it should have been and lifted questioning eyes to hers. "You're no longer married?" he asked, as if it were of only mild interest to him.

Elizabeth felt her cheeks heat. "No," she said, pulling her hands free of his. "I'm not married."

She looked anxiously toward Dorian, who was still approaching at a snail's pace. It was hysterical, really. Here she was actually welcoming Dorian's arrival, hoping it would save her from having to answer Blake's questions. Or having to lie to him.

"There must be a story behind that," Blake said, stroking her fingers with his. "I'd like to hear it some time."

"Really, there's nothing to tell," she said hastily.

Dorian, his cane firmly in hand, joined them, grinning broadly. "Are we ready to leave, my dear?" he asked genially.

More than ready, she thought with a sigh of relief. "Yes. Jerome should be waiting for us by now." She turned toward the door, praying that Blake wouldn't pursue his last line of questioning. At least, not until she had decided how to handle it. She needed time to think.

"Will you join us for drinks at the house?" Dorian asked Blake.

Elizabeth's heart sank. The old fox scented her flight and wanted to keep the hound on her. Dorian gave her a sly look, and she knew this was only going to be the beginning. She looked him straight in the eye and smiled. She wouldn't give him the satisfaction of seeing her panic. Damn him.

"I'm sure that Elizabeth would enjoy renewing your acquaintance," Dorian said smoothly. He chuckled. "And I certainly would be pleased to have a visit from you myself."

Blake looked at Elizabeth for a moment, as if turning over something in his mind before replying. "Would you enjoy renewing our acquaintance, Elizabeth?"

What could she say to that? she wondered desperately. Yes or no, either way, she would have problems. She drew in a breath and mentally crossed her fingers. "I'd be delighted, of course." She glanced at Dorian. "Besides, Dorian would never forgive me if I alienated a potential customer, would you, Dorian?"

Blake's eyes narrowed in displeasure at Elizabeth's innuendo that she was primarily receptive because of their potential business relationship. However, Elizabeth didn't see his expression. She was locked in silent battle with Dorian.

Dorian chuckled and herded them toward the exit. "Elizabeth, my dear, how tactless of you! I really can't believe you said that." He patted Blake on the back in avuncular fashion. "Never mind her tongue. I think she's still suffering from a little jet lag. Besides, it's past her feeding time. She is always more charming when she's been wined and dined."

"I'll remember that," Blake said tightly. "Well, perhaps another time." He ran his eyes over Elizabeth in a cool, distant fashion. "Give my regards to Karl, will you?"

"Of course," she replied softly.

He nodded curtly to her and bid them goodbye at the base of the steps outside the museum. Then he walked briskly across the grassy Capitol Mall to the metro stop near the Freer Gallery. He never looked back.

Elizabeth watched him until he disappeared from view down the metro's steps.

"My dear, is that your heart I see in your eyes?" Dorian inquired curiously.

Elizabeth shook her head. "No, Dorian. Just some old memories. My heart died a long time ago." Jerome was holding the car door for them, and she got in. When Dorian had joined her and Jerome was rushing around the outside of the car to get into the driver's seat, she calmly told Dorian. "It was certainly an eventful afternoon. Wouldn't you agree?"

He studied her thoughtfully. "You're still a mystery when you want to be, Elizabeth, my dear. I am never truly certain that I know what you're thinking." He put two gnarled fingers under her chin and tilted her head toward him.

She smiled at him icily. "I'm delighted to hear it, Dorian."

He grunted. "Yes. I can see that you are."

They were interrupted by Jerome as he slammed his door shut, fastened his seat belt and cheerfully announced, "Here we go!"

Blake shoved his farecard into the slot and passed through the metro system's turnstile. He did not need to think about which way to go. He rode the metro frequently. It was a good thing, too, because at the moment, he wasn't paying the slightest attention to the direction he was going. He was still thinking of Elizabeth Rossi.

Well, he had seen her again, he told himself sarcastically. And it had hit him like a knockout punch. When he had entered the conference room at the museum and scanned the crowd for her, he had thought himself mentally prepared to meet her again.

Prepared! He could not have been more wrong.

Blake laughed out loud and shook his head slightly, still a little dazed at his own unrealistic optimism. He had been no more prepared for her than he would have been to dig diamonds with his bare hands.

She had been standing there with that boy Jerome, giving him a gentle smile and listening to undoubtedly boring patter. The moment he'd seen her, Blake felt as if all the breath in his body had been sucked out. For a minute he'd literally forgotten how to breathe. She still had that special something, he thought bitterly. He wished to hell he knew exactly what it was that made him react to her so violently. Even across a crowded room. And fifteen years too late.

He'd shaken hands with a few people, murmuring the polite things one had to say, as he slowly made his way to her side. He had used that time to get a firm grip on himself. It had not been simple. He had been staring at her pale, golden red hair, the delicate shape of her woman's body beneath the simple cream-colored suit, and the glimpses of her face he caught from time to time. There had been an unsettling air of sadness about her that disturbed him. Then he'd reminded himself that he was there for revenge, not solicitude, and he'd hardened his heart against her.

He had believed himself more than ready to come face-to-face with her, and he had made the first comment that came to mind. To his annoyance, it had revealed his own irritation at her ability to bring men to her feet. And what had the beautiful, elusive witch done? She had turned around and stared at him as if she would have given the rest of her life for that moment.

For a split second he'd forgotten everything that had come between them and could only remember the vivid pleasure of loving her. But only a split second. He was no green boy now. He was a man. And he had refused to be bewitched by her again.

Blake ground his teeth in fury. What kind of a fool did she think he was? Surely she didn't think she could wrap him around her finger the way she could the Jeromes of the world. She didn't think him such an idiot that he would have forgotten how she had treated him fifteen years ago, did she?

The worst of it was that the heartbreaking look he had seen in her eyes had touched a part of his heart that hadn't been touched in years. Not since she had touched it.

Silently, Blake swore. He stood at the empty trackside, waiting for the train that would take him back to Malone's, wrestling with the bitterness that he had thought he'd put behind him.

He had intended to be cold and cavalier with her when he had taken her hand and kissed it. Instead, he had rediscovered how incredibly soft her skin was and how much he enjoyed caressing it. Then, when he had whispered in her ear, he had inhaled her scent. That had been another big mistake, he thought cynically. He didn't know if it was the same. After all these years, he couldn't remember. But she smelled like an aphrodisiac to him, unfortunately. It might have been a different scent, but it seemed to be just as effective! She was wearing a touch of perfume now, something more expensive than when they had been younger. He had felt an incredibly strong urge to lean closer to her and sweetly savor the experience.

Hell's fire! Becoming intoxicated by the woman all over again. This was not what he'd had in mind at all, he reminded himself grimly. Hadn't he mentioned the word *indifference* to himself over and over? Apparently to little avail, he thought in disgust.

That brush of her lips had not helped, either, he recalled with a grimace. It had only made him want to lower his mouth to her skin and see if she tasted as intoxicating as she looked and smelled. *Intoxicating* was undoubtedly the correct word for it, he decided. She was deadly poison to him. He must not forget that.

The soft rocking clatter of an approaching subway train drew Blake's attention. In a few moments it had quietly stopped in front of him. He and the few other passengers embarked, and the doors slid closed. He held on to a pole near the doors and watched the white-tiled subway walls flicker by, faster and faster, then turn into blackness.

He didn't feel like sitting. He felt like pacing. Pacing like a caged cat. He gripped the pole more tightly in frustration.

He had debated whether to accept Dorian's invitation for drinks. It would have been convenient. He might have maneuvered them into letting him see Karl, however briefly. But it had angered him that Elizabeth suddenly seemed hesitant to have him come. She herself had invited that Milquetoast Jerome to join them. Why had she turned cool to him? Blake wondered angrily. Her attitude had brought back the bitter fury he had felt fifteen years ago, the last time she had rejected him. His spine had stiffened, and he had wanted nothing more to do with her for the time being.

He had never felt such white-hot anger toward a woman in his life as he had toward Elizabeth Rossi. That bothered him. He didn't want to feel that teeth-grinding animosity toward a woman. It seemed fundamentally wrong to him. He had a reputation for being a gentleman with the ladies, and he wished to keep it.

Blake stood, his legs spread for easy balance, rocking gently with the motion of the train, wondering if he was making a mistake seeing Elizabeth again. He didn't want to turn into one of those men he read about in newspapers. The ones who lost control and did despicable things to the women they had thought they loved.

Normally he would not have considered himself inclined to such unconscionable loss of control. But he had never felt such fury as he had with Elizabeth, he thought darkly. Probably because he had never felt such passion or love, either. He seemed incapable of neutrality or indifference where Elizabeth Rossi was concerned. It simply was not possible for him. He would have to accept that fact, he thought grimly.

Through the bright lights and dark caverns beneath Washington, try as he would to forget it, Blake kept seeing Elizabeth's face and the incredible look of longing and joy that had lit it for a few brief seconds when she had seen him for the first time in years. It was slow torture to him, but he couldn't seem to free himself of it. It was the expression that he would have given *anything* to have seen on her face fifteen years ago. The look that had not been there when he had needed it. So why had she chosen to wear it for him today? She couldn't have come up with a more clever attack on him if she'd spent every waking hour for the last year thinking about it.

"Elizabeth," he whispered tiredly. "I wonder if God put you here to drive me mad." It was a distinct possibility, he thought grimly. "Damn you, anyway, Elizabeth. Damn you."

Elizabeth was grateful that her father was not having dinner with them that night. It spared him from having to hear about Blake from Dorian. She went up to see him on her way to bed, hoping to break the news as gently as possible. She was not looking forward to broaching the subject, and the worry must have shown in her eyes as she walked into Karl's room, if the questioning expression on his face was any indication.

She sat down on the bed next to him and took his good, left hand in hers.

"I came by to kiss you good-night, darling," she told him.

He nodded and muttered, "Umm hmm." She usually came by. That was normal. He cocked a shaggy brow upward a little more. He could see she had something special to say.

Elizabeth managed a weak smile. "You know me very well, don't you?"

He nodded contentedly. "What?" he asked, meaning, What was bothering her?

She looked down at his hand in hers and murmured, "I went to the tea with Dorian today."

"Hmm." Karl nodded. "So..." he prodded her, his voice unsteady and singsong.

"I saw someone we know.... Someone you know. We haven't seen him for a very long time." Elizabeth ran her tongue over her upper lip. It was a nervous gesture she'd had all her life.

Karl looked at her and frowned a little. "Who?" he asked, having had to strain hard to get the right word out.

Elizabeth swallowed and looked at his face. "It was Blake, Father. Blake Malone."

The old man's eyes seemed to go blank for a moment, as if he had withdrawn into himself in surprise. Then he focused on Elizabeth and leaned forward. His whole body radiated intensity. "How . . . ?" he said, forcing the word through lips that seemed unconnected to his mind.

Elizabeth knew her father well and tried to fill in the rest of the question for him. "How is he?" she guessed.

Karl nodded. His eyes were riveted to Elizabeth's.

Elizabeth smiled a little more warmly. "He's fine. He looks, well, he looks like the old Blake, but he's a little more manly." She laughed nervously. "You would recognize him, I'm sure."

Karl studied her closely. "You?"

Elizabeth sighed. "How am I?" she guessed.

He nodded again.

She patted his hand. "I'm fine. It's been fifteen years, Father. Everyone gets over things in time. And that's a very long time, for me and for Blake." She tried to be philosophical and lighthearted. "He's done a wonderful job with his business. He's gone on to other things. He has his own life. He said he lives here in Washington. . . ."

Karl tried to get a word out, but he couldn't quite find it, and he began to get angry at his inability to communicate what he wanted. Elizabeth patted his hand reassuringly.

"There is one other thing I wanted to tell you about Blake," she told him gently.

Karl stopped searching mentally for what he wanted to tell her. He waited expectantly.

Elizabeth lifted her chin a little and told herself this would all work out somehow, she just had to get through it. "Blake would like to come and see you sometime."

Karl looked thunderstruck.

"You don't have to see him if you don't want to, darling," she hurried to reassure him. She leaned forward and gave him a quick hug. When she sat back, he looked as if he were trying to think of the implications. She could see the wheels going round in his faraway eyes.

"Tell him," Karl said, with great effort and a very great deal of conviction.

Elizabeth paled. "Tell him the truth?"

Karl nodded his head and clutched her hand with his one good one. "Tell him." It sounded like a raspy croak, but there was no missing his meaning.

Elizabeth shook her head. She freed her hand and gripped his shoulders firmly. "No. And that is what I came here to talk about. He must not know that I lied to him. If I let him come and see you, you must promise me not to tell him."

Karl frowned, and it made him look positively fierce. "Why?" he demanded in a guttural burst. He began to look anxious, and he searched her face. "Love? Wo...wo..." He couldn't get the word out, and he cursed in a garbled way that would have been funny if it hadn't been so tragic.

Elizabeth put her arms around her father and patted his back soothingly. "I don't understand you, darling," she admitted regretfully. "But I imagine you're trying to talk me out of my position. If that's what you're up to, don't try. You must believe me.... We must not tell Blake what really happened in Arkansas." She kissed her father's cheek and pulled back to look at him. "We can't tell anyone. We've come too far to go back. We have nearly all the gold jewelry that you forged. There's only one piece left. When we have it, we'll be free."

He seemed a little confused, but then his expression cleared and he managed to ask, "Then? Tell then?"

Elizabeth bit her lip. "You want me to tell Blake the truth after we have all the jewelry back?"

"Yes." He nodded his head.

Elizabeth frowned. "I don't know...." She gave him a gentle smile. "Blake doesn't love me anymore, Father. What would be the point? And perhaps he would get into trouble if we told him what you'd done." She frowned. She had no idea whether Blake could be considered an accessory after the fact if they told him about Karl's actions.

Karl gave a great, unsteady sigh and rubbed his face with his good hand. He shook his head helplessly.

"I know, darling," Elizabeth murmured sympathetically. "It's very confusing for you."

He pushed his lower lip out and nodded. But the look in his eyes was not particularly confused.

Elizabeth was never sure how much her father understood. Sometimes she thought he understood everything that she said to him. The big problem was getting out what he wanted to say. The stroke had damaged the communication network going out more than it had the one going in, it seemed. Other times, he seemed genuinely confused. He just didn't understand.

She leaned forward and kissed him on the cheek. This had been more than enough for him to handle at one time, she thought.

"Go to sleep," she told him affectionately. "We'll deal with Blake some other time." She brightened. "Perhaps he'll forget about us, and we won't have to argue about what you should and shouldn't say to him."

Karl sat up a little straighter in his bed and gave her a sharp look. He obviously didn't appreciate having his offspring dictate what he should or should not do.

Elizabeth decided to quit before he dug in his heels and refused to pay any attention to her wishes at all. She rose to leave the room, turning off his light as she left. At the door, she turned to blow him a final kiss.

He was sitting there staring at her intently. Elizabeth had the uneasy feeling that he was plotting something. Just so long as it wasn't spilling the beans to Blake, she thought. Anything but that.

Chapter 5

Elizabeth was not surprised when Dorian spoke to her about Blake over breakfast the following morning. She took a sip of her juice and listened to him very carefully. With Dorian, one always had to read the fine print. His most innocent suggestions invariably concealed ulterior motives.

"Seeing Blake Malone yesterday was certainly fortuitous," he declared enthusiastically as he helped himself to a chocolate croissant and a dishful of strawberries. He had the pleased look of a man whose plans were coming together nicely. He glanced at Karl, who had been wheeled in to join them for the meal. "Good morning, Karl. Did Elizabeth tell you that we saw Blake at the tea yesterday?"

For once Elizabeth wished that Dorian wouldn't try to include her father in the conversation. Dorian had always treated Karl as if he were fully present and able to participate in their discussions. Until now, that had been the one thing about Dorian that Elizabeth had appreciated.

Karl gave Dorian a grumpy look and a sharp nod in the affirmative.

Dorian smiled broadly. He put a teaspoon of sugar in his cup of coffee and stirred it with a dainty silver spoon. "I'm sure that you would enjoy seeing your old student again, wouldn't you, Karl?''

Elizabeth stared at her father, pleading with him silently to say no. The slice of melon on her fork was suspended halfway to her mouth as she awaited his answer. Karl looked at her for a long moment, obviously considering how to respond to their crafty partner. With Dorian, one never knew which way was safe to jump.

Karl shrugged, conveying that seeing Blake again was not a matter of tremendous importance to him. Then he made an affirmative sound and nodded his head. ''All right,'' he said, with the usual gargling sound. Seeing Blake would be all right with him.

''I'm glad you are agreeable, Karl,'' Dorian remarked easily. He lifted the silver coffeepot and let the spout hover over Elizabeth's cup. ''Would you care for your coffee now, my dear?'' he asked solicitously.

''Yes, please. Thank you.'' She stuck the melon in her mouth and munched on it stoically. If it wasn't for the distasteful conversation, it would have been delicious.

Dorian poured the coffee and then resumed thinking aloud. ''Perhaps we should invite Blake for a weekend stay here.''

Elizabeth was swallowing her food and nearly choked when she heard that.

Dorian was the picture of concern. ''Are you all right, my dear?''

She cleared her throat and touched her napkin to her lips. ''Perfectly.''

He chuckled. ''Perhaps my suggestion was hard for you to swallow?''

''Very funny Dorian.'' She couldn't afford to appear upset about being around Blake, so she shrugged as if it really didn't matter to her particularly. ''If you want Blake to spend the weekend, go right ahead and issue the invitation. I certainly have no objection.'' She looked at the shabby wallpaper and said pointedly, ''Frankly, I'm surprised that you would want anyone to see the house.''

Dorian sipped his coffee and took another bite of his croissant. ''It may be advantageous for people to feel that I've come down a few stations in life,'' he responded. He was completely dispassionate about it. "It's really very generous of you, my dear, to be willing to have him under the same roof, though." He looked at her through narrowed eyes. "I know it must be difficult for you, seeing him again."

"Not at all." She spoke lightly. She even smiled credibly. "I've never forgiven you for forcing me to break off with Blake, but that doesn't mean I'm still in love with him, Dorian."

Dorian seemed to be considering whether to believe her. "You seemed quite delighted to see him yesterday," he reminded her.

Elizabeth laughed softly. "Well, of course. He's a handsome man. I have very fond memories of him. It was delightful seeing him again after all these years."

Dorian nodded. "I suppose," he agreed, although he looked unconvinced. He finished his coffee and leaned toward her conspiratorially. "It's fortunate that you're so levelheaded about him."

Elizabeth knew that tone of voice. He was about to try to manipulate her into doing something she probably would not like. She stared at him, waiting for the ax to fall. "Really? Why?"

He smiled. "I would like your assistance in a rather delicate matter, and it involves your Mr. Malone."

She met his gaze steadily. "He's not *my* Mr. Malone," she reminded him. "For all I know, he's married or engaged or living with someone. You seem to have doubts about how thoroughly I've gotten over Blake, but surely you don't believe he still feels anything for me?"

"Oh, I think he feels something. Perhaps not love anymore, but . . . something."

"Perhaps you're seeing what you wish to see, Dorian," she suggested carefully. "I certainly didn't sense anything." That wasn't quite true. She *had* sensed something. But it had been close kin to anger.

Dorian steepled his fingertips and explained. "I need to learn more about Blake's business. Specifically, my dear, I need to know how much money he might be likely to bid for that special piece of jewelry I'm going to be selling in a few months."

Elizabeth frowned. "I don't see that I can help. He's not likely to tell me. He's certainly not a fool when it comes to business, Dorian."

Dorian chuckled and nodded in agreement. "No. He's not a fool when it comes to business, my dear, but he might be a fool when it comes to you."

"I think you're wasting our time," Elizabeth protested, careful not to sound heated or overly concerned. "He might have cared for me once, but he's certainly not going to make that mistake twice." She made no effort to conceal her bitterness on that score. Dorian knew she would never forgive him for that.

Dorian was not the least moved by her opinion. "Nevertheless, I would like you to renew your friendship. Do the best you can."

Elizabeth stared at him in angry disbelief. She doubted that Dorian was simply urging her to befriend Blake. She glanced at her father, concerned that he might become irate at the implication in Dorian's comment. She could see the fury in her father's eyes. Burning like fire in his gnarled and aging face was the impotent rage of a man who desperately wanted to free his daughter from the control of a hated enemy.

Elizabeth bit back the scathing rejoinder she was tempted to make to Dorian. Arguing would only further inflame all of them and drag out this unpleasant scene. She didn't want that. If she blurted out to Dorian that she wasn't about to play the whore in his newest game, she feared that her father's dangerously rising blood pressure might result in another devastating stroke. Karl would burst a blood vessel for sure. Worried, she firmly clamped her mouth shut on all of her unspoken words and prayed her father would calm down.

Dorian smiled at them as if nothing in the least out of the ordinary had been mentioned. "Why don't we drop in at Malone's and look over his store one day this week? That would be natural enough, don't you think? And then . . . we'll take it from there."

Karl shoved his wheelchair away from the table and moved toward Dorian, his gray eyes the color of darkening thunderclouds. "Leave . . . her . . . 'lone . . ." he croaked threateningly.

Dorian looked quite startled. "Don't worry, Karl. Nothing bad will happen to Elizabeth. You know Blake would never do anything to hurt her. Elizabeth will be in complete control." Dorian looked at her for confirmation. "Isn't that right, Elizabeth?"

She got up from the table and went around to Karl. Taking hold of his wheelchair and pulling it away from Dorian, she said, as calmly and confidently as she could, "That's right. I won't do anything that I don't wish to do, and I'm sure that Blake will be a perfect gentleman. He always was," she added softly. Her eyes narrowed. "Unlike you, Dorian."

Dorian managed to look slightly wounded by her low opinion of him.

Elizabeth gripped the handles of the wheelchair a little harder. "If you'll excuse us, Dorian, I think we'll go into the shop. I'm working on a design, and I want Father to see it before I get any further along."

He waved them off and poured himself a second cup of coffee. "Go right ahead, my dear. We'll talk more about this another time."

Wonderful, Elizabeth thought sarcastically. She was seething at her powerlessness. Just a little longer, she promised herself. Then she would be free. Just one more piece of jewelry and Dorian would no longer have anything to hold over them. It was so close . . . so very close.

It was the ides of March when Blake saw Elizabeth and Dorian walk into Malone's. An appropriate date, he thought, as he walked over to greet them.

"Are you looking for something in particular?" he asked dryly. "Or is this a scouting trip to check out your competition, Dorian?"

Dorian chuckled and wrapped his gnarled hand more tightly around his cane handle. "A little of both," he replied genially. "I hope you don't object?"

"Not at all," Blake said easily. He looked at Elizabeth, and his expression become more speculative. "And what about you, Elizabeth? Is this visit business or pleasure?"

She could see that he was remembering what she had said to him on the steps of the museum about being nice to him because he was a potential customer. She was surprised that he was still thinking about it. She had intended to put him off, of course, but she hadn't realized that he would be that sensitive. She noted with relief that he didn't appear particularly angry with her. However, there was definitely a coolness in his eyes as he waited for her to reply to his casually phrased question.

"Dorian thinks of it as business, but to me, it's a pleasure," she told him, quite truthfully.

Blake dipped his head in acknowledgment of her comment and murmured, "Thank you." He glanced at Dorian in amusement. "Although I wonder if your employer feels equally grateful for your words."

Dorian sighed like a long-suffering uncle. "I told you she has an independent tongue." He chuckled and looked from Elizabeth to Blake, a shrewd light in his eyes. "More so, I fear, than when you knew her." He paused and waited significantly, as if inviting Blake to reminisce about his former love.

"We all change," Blake said smoothly.

From his tone, it was difficult to know whether he meant for better or for worse.

Elizabeth was thankful that Blake had so easily finessed Dorian. She prayed he would continue to ignore the bait being cast in his direction by the shrewd old jeweler. She glanced around the elegant interior of the main showroom, making no effort to disguise her genuine admiration. Malone's lived up to its reputation, she thought. It really was impressive.

"I've often wondered what Malone's looked like," she confessed, smiling at Blake. It was a more relaxed smile than those she'd nervously managed to wear at the museum. Of course, she was past her first shock at seeing him again. And Blake was meeting her more than halfway, she thought gratefully. He was being courteous and diplomatic at every turn.

"If you're interested, I'd be more than happy to show you around," he offered.

"Wonderful!" Dorian declared. He tapped the tip of his cane on the floor. The thick wall-to-wall carpeting muffled the sound completely. "I would love to see the secrets of your success, my boy."

Blake had been looking at Elizabeth, however, when he had made the offer, and he was clearly waiting for her to accept.

There was something gripping about his relentless gaze, and Elizabeth wondered why she should feel that. Her heart beat a little harder, and her hands suddenly felt cool and damp. Nerves, she thought uneasily.

"I'd love to see it, Blake," she told him. There was just the faintest touch of honest humility in her voice as she added, "It would be an honor."

His eyes darkened ever so slightly, she thought, and she wondered why on earth that would be so. Surely it didn't irritate him that she had said she'd be honored to see the salon? But if not that, then what? She was still staring into his eyes when he turned aside and gestured for them to go through the doors discreetly placed along the far wall. Elizabeth followed him silently. Once again, she wondered just how much anger simmered beneath the surface in Blake. She shook the question away. She was being fanciful again, she thought tartly. She still felt guilty about what she had done to him, and as a result, she was oversensitive, even a little paranoid, perhaps.

It was easy to forget that little niggling worry, because Blake was ushering them into a large workroom and briskly sketching out his operations. She concentrated on what he was saying as she followed him around for the next forty-five minutes. Dorian engaged Blake in small rounds of question-and-answer, leaving Elizabeth free to admire and listen without interruption. If it hadn't been for Blake's occasional questioning glance in her direction, checking to see if she wished to ask him anything, she might have thought they had forgotten about her.

Elizabeth's first reaction was that the workshop was certainly a dramatic contrast to the main showroom.

The showroom had plush carpeting and soundproof walls with elegant wallpaper. Serene opaline grays, dark and muted earthtoned pinks, and elegant gold fixtures gave it an opulent feel. The display cases were set apart from one another and lined with black velvet. Special lighting softly spotlighted the gemstones nestling in their expensive settings. Two men and a woman, tastefully dressed and gracious, were working as salespersons. Comfortable chairs were assembled in a small knot around a coffee table, and there were fine china cups, a silverplated carafe of coffee, antique silver spoons, a sugar server and a small silverplated creamer. Soft classical music soothed any nerves that might still be on edge, although Elizabeth wondered how anyone could have felt nervous here. The store welcomed the visitor with an aura of sophisticated but genuine hospitality.

The workshop had a different purpose entirely.

It was fortunate that the walls were soundproofed, because the two jewelers there had equipment that would have jarred the sensibilities of the clientele on the other side. The older of the two, a balding man who by all appearances was well into middle age, glanced up at them as they passed by his workbench. He was wearing a plastic headband with a set of magnifying glasses attached to it, and he pushed the lenses upward so that he could see them without enlargement.

Blake smiled at the man and introduced them all. "This is Jon Tabor, our expert in repair and resettings. Jon has done some very fine designs, as well, but he's in such demand to rescue damaged pieces that he doesn't do as much as he could." Blake indicated the other man, younger and a little less sure of himself than Jon Tabor. "And this is Jon's brother, Griffin."

Dorian extended a bony hand and said, smiling toothily, "I didn't realize it was such a family business, Blake." Dorian cast a fond look in Elizabeth's direction. "I have taken the same route myself," he added, obviously referring to Elizabeth and her father. He ignored the chilly reception in her eyes and blithely observed, "It makes for very close working relationships, wouldn't you agree?"

Blake had seen Elizabeth's expression ice over. Apparently she was less than thrilled with her association with Dorian, Blake thought. He was surprised and curious to know just how discontent she was. And why. Remembering how close that relationship had been for years, he spoke with a slightly sarcastic edge when he replied to the man's question.

"I suppose the relationships are more complex when they involve relatives who are also colleagues," Blake agreed. "However, there are only two related people here at Malone's," he pointed out dryly. "The rest of us are simply friends."

"Friends," Elizabeth murmured enviously. "How very lucky for you all."

Blake's brow furrowed slightly, and his eyes narrowed. "Aren't your colleagues friends, Elizabeth?"

She smiled slightly. "Some are."

"That's a rather evasive answer."

"No it's not. It's an honest one."

Dorian cleared his throat and shot a silencing look at Elizabeth. "My dear, your *old friend* will think you've been unhappy in your work if you don't sound more enthusiastic," he chided.

Elizabeth shrugged and ignored his warning to be silent. The way Dorian had emphasized *old friend* had offended her. He was trying to stir dead embers by reminding Blake of how he had once felt about her. She absolutely hated that.

"You wouldn't want me to lie, would you, Dorian?" she challenged softly. She was pleased when he looked startled by her rejoinder. He was surprised that she hadn't simply cooperated with him, surprised that she had openly, albeit discreetly, broken with him. And he couldn't very well advise her to lie! Not when Blake was listening, anyway, she thought in amusement. Got you this time, Dorian.

Dorian, his options limited under the circumstances, chose to laugh it off. "No, my dear. I certainly wouldn't want you to lie," he agreed. "I have always had a high regard for the truth."

Elizabeth struggled to keep from rolling her eyes at that blatant falsehood. She couldn't go too far, however, without facing serious reprisal. Somehow, she managed to keep a straight face.

"No one knows your regard for truth and honesty better than I do, Dorian," she said, looking him straight in the eye. She had the satisfaction of seeing a moment of doubt shadow him. He wasn't sure what she would do next. How delightful.

Blake watched the camouflaged barbs fly and wondered precisely what was going on between Dorian and Elizabeth. It was a subtle conflict. If he hadn't known Elizabeth so well, he might have thought it was just teasing banter between two friends. But he did know her. Or he had, he reminded himself. And he was certain that the tension between them was a personal power struggle.

He had no idea what it was over, of course. It could have been a small, specific disagreement, something they'd come to loggerheads over this morning or earlier in the week, still unresolved. Perhaps she had wished the business to do one thing and Dorian had wanted it to do another.

On the other hand, it could be a more ongoing battle of wills, the latest in a long-term wrestling match between two independent people whose goals were not quite in harmony. Since he hadn't had any direct dealings with either of them for years, he wasn't in a position to tell whether they got into these veiled duels on a regular basis.

His curiosity was piqued, and he wondered how difficult it would be for him to find out more about Elizabeth and Dorian and this peculiar tension between them. He wasn't particularly surprised to discover that he relished the possibility that they had actively disliked one another for some time. It gave him pleasure to think that Elizabeth might have been at odds with the man she had taken as her boss. It certainly would have served her right, he thought vengefully. She couldn't have picked a more treacherous man to work with this side of a prison cell if she'd made a concerted effort to do so.

Dorian's gesturing drew him out of his dark thoughts.

He was pointing with his cane, indicating an empty work station across the room from them. Dorian obviously wanted to change the subject, Blake noted with interest, as if he were trying to conceal the subtle conversational rift that had occurred between himself and Elizabeth. Blake narrowed his eyes thoughtfully.

"And who works over there? At the third workbench?" Dorian was demanding.

"I do," Blake replied.

"Ah hah!" Dorian exclaimed triumphantly. He marched toward Blake's work and excitedly tapped his cane on the floor. "I wondered if you were still keeping your hand in, Blake!" He grinned broadly and leaned hard on the highly polished hickory stick. He pinned Blake with sharp eyes. "Diamonds?" he guessed.

"Mostly," Blake conceded. He turned toward Elizabeth, preferring to find out more about *them* than they discovered about *him*. "What about you?" he asked her, being deceptively casual. "Do you still make jewelry yourself?"

Elizabeth lowered her eyes to the tools spread across the work table. It made her feel closer to Blake, being where he worked. She ran a fingertip lightly over a saw. He had obviously been working with it the last time he had sat at the bench. She lifted her eyes to Blake's, and for an instant they were standing in another workshop fifteen years ago. Her heart ached, and her throat felt tight, and she felt the yearning that had plagued her for years.

Blake murmured, "This is like old times, isn't it, Elizabeth?" His eyes were the dark, cool blue-green of a winter sea. The sardonic lift of his brow made his smile appear to be one of mockery. He waited for her to reply, seemingly oblivious to Dorian's shrewd regard.

"Yes," Elizabeth answered, speaking much more softly than she had intended. She tried to infuse her next words with a little more strength. "And, yes, I still make jewelry occasionally." She waved a hand, indicating the extensive equipment and supplies that Blake had: gold and silver in every conceivable shape and thickness; a small furnace; diamond drills; jeweler's saws; metal stamps and hallmarks; soldering equipment; a wide selection of knives and hammers and tongs. "I have to content myself with designing, at the moment. We have nothing like this at our house in Maryland."

"Not *yet*," Dorian amended quickly.

"Then you intend to go back into business?" Blake asked Dorian with mild surprise. "I must have misunderstood. I was under the impression that you were retiring."

Dorian chuckled. "You didn't misunderstand, my boy. I am indeed retiring."

Blake lifted a brow in question. "Then . . . ?"

"The workshop, when we've gotten everything in place, will be for Elizabeth. After all, Elizabeth will still need to earn a living. She is *far* too young to retire!"

Blake turned to Elizabeth, a half smile on his handsome face. "So you're going to be my newest competition?" he teased her softly, looking her over as if examining his adversary for the first time.

Elizabeth felt the blood rush to her skin everywhere his eyes roamed. When at last his gaze returned to her face, there was a becoming blush on it and a wary look in her eyes.

"You'll be much easier on the eyes than most of my competition," Blake murmured.

"Thank you," Elizabeth said stiffly, upset by his slow perusal.

She was an excellent jeweler and a highly successful designer. Of course, Blake probably didn't realize that, because she had been careful to keep hidden in the background. At the moment, she would have loved to have seen the light of recognition in Blake's eyes. Along with a touch of admiration and respect, perhaps.

"Elizabeth has done quite a bit of designing over the years," Dorian offered.

Elizabeth blinked and looked at Dorian in surprise.

Blake saw the interchange and murmured, "Has she? I didn't know."

"Of course not. She's very modest. Always wanted to keep out of the limelight, said she preferred anonymity to publicity." Dorian went on, obviously in an expansive mood now that he had decided to break his silence on the subject.

Elizabeth was still staring at him, wondering what on earth had possessed him. What trick was this going to be? And that nonsense about her preferences! She nearly laughed out loud. She had never been granted the right to decide whether to be publicly known for her work. Dorian had chosen to control the designs—and the money they earned him—from the start, and he had not wanted people to know how much of the jewelry created by Rand, Limited came from her fertile hands. Elizabeth had been so concerned about earning back that fraudulently stamped gold before someone discovered her father's crime that she hadn't fought back against her "anonymity."

Blake watched the shadow cross Elizabeth's pretty brow and wondered what in the devil she was thinking. He obviously couldn't find out in this short tour of Malone's. He would have to find a way to get her alone for a while. Away from Dorian.

"I'd be interested in seeing your work," Blake told her. He smiled at her, a warmer, more inviting smile than the others he had given her. To his pleasure and surprise, her eyes widened and her lips softened in response. She wasn't indifferent to him, he thought, as angry satisfaction warmed his icy veins. That could be useful. For a lot of things.

Dorian, seeing that Elizabeth wasn't going to say anything, filled the breech with a sudden offer. "Why don't you come out for dinner this weekend?" He paused, allowing the offer to sink in for a moment before broadening it. "You would certainly be welcome to see the pieces that Elizabeth hasn't chosen to sell as yet. And perhaps some of her equipment will be in place by then. What do you think, Elizabeth? Most of it should be unpacked by then, shouldn't it?"

Elizabeth swallowed hard and tried to think of a reason to refuse. Stalling for time, she stammered, "I—I suppose most of it will be up then...."

She didn't want him out there, Blake thought coolly. She was racking her brains to come up with a reason to beg off. That angered him and goaded him on. He had let her off the last time she had reacted like this, when they had parted at the museum tea. He'd be damned if he would let her do it again. He didn't care why she didn't want him going out there. That garbage she had spouted about tiring Karl had been a bunch of tripe, and she knew it. Too bad, Elizabeth. You'll just have to steel your tender self and prepare for my arrival.

Blake flashed his teeth in a predatory smile and bent his head in acknowledgment of Dorian's invitation. "I'd be delighted to accept."

Dorian beamed and reached into his suit pocket to remove a small notepad and paper. He jotted down the address and handed it to Blake, who folded it and slipped it into his own pocket.

"Dinner at eight on Saturday? And plan to stay for Sunday brunch." Dorian had returned to his brusque, take-charge self.

"Thank you. I'll look forward to it," Blake said. He looked at Elizabeth, standing pale and still as a statue, and he added, softly, "I think we'll find a great deal to discuss."

Elizabeth felt his probing gaze and went warm and cold at the same time. Blake obviously was not going to restrict himself to business talk, she realized. He had some personal items on his agenda. And he would also expect to see Karl, she thought grimly.

Blake's eyes were darkening, and there was a slight edge to his voice as he asked, "Do you mind, Elizabeth?" He dared her to say she did.

She had the feeling it would be futile. Blake was obviously intent on seeing them in their natural surroundings, although she wasn't sure why. Curiosity, perhaps. Naturally Dorian was only too willing to play go-between and jovial host! She managed a smile of sorts and said, as convincingly as she could, "No. I don't mind." She cast a critical sideways glance at Dorian. "However, I do think that Dorian is being a little rash inviting you to spend the night. The place needs quite a bit of fixing up before guests will be comfortable."

Blake didn't seem put off. He shrugged. "It's good enough for you," he pointed out reasonably.

Elizabeth gave him a slightly acid smile. "Yes, but *we* are in the rooms with the ceilings that don't leak."

Dorian coughed noisily. Blake looked taken aback.

Elizabeth ran her finger along the smooth work surface and wandered toward the door that led back into the showroom. "Don't say I didn't warn you," she shot back over her shoulder.

Blake regained his aplomb and straightened his features. "All right," he agreed. He grinned, then, and added, "I'll bring along a few pots to catch the water, if you like."

Elizabeth looked into Blake's eyes as he teased her, and for a moment, she was tempted to run into his arms. There was a flash of the man she had known before in that humor. The Blake who had always been ready to listen to her, to comfort her, to encourage her, to tease her. How he had teased her, she recalled. Her eyes softened with the memory.

Blake saw it, and something twisted in him, a sweet pleasure from years ago. His gaze dropped to her lips, and he wondered what it would be like to kiss her now. He felt his blood heat at the possibility...and at the memory. What an exquisite delight it had been kissing her fifteen years ago. His body urged him to recall the sensations in detail, and he vividly envisioned where the kissing had led them toward the end.

He lifted his gaze and found Elizabeth staring at him, her eyes wary and slightly alarmed. Like a doe seeing a stag in the rutting season, he thought in angry amusement.

Perhaps if she had looked at him like that fifteen years ago, he wouldn't have ended up demonstrating just how wild he was for her. And he wouldn't be standing in the workshop of his own store in the middle of the day becoming aroused at the memory of making love to her in those hurried, stolen moments in the middle of the night.

"Why don't I show you the rest of the place?" Blake said tersely. He walked by Elizabeth without a glance and held the door for them. "We have a garden you might find interesting," he said briskly.

"Really?" Dorian exclaimed in surprise.

"It's a classical stone garden designed by a Japanese acquaintance of one of the members of the firm. It's up ahead and over to your right, through those shoji doors. Then we can spend a few minutes in my office, if you like."

"Wonderful," Dorian said, his wizened eyes gleaming at the possibilities coming to mind.

Wonderful, Elizabeth thought dismally, as she tried to forget the memories that had come rushing back at her in the past few moments. Blake might feel indifference or dislike for her, but she had no doubt at all that his body remembered hers . . . and that hers most vividly remembered his.

It was going to be a long weekend, she thought tensely. A very long weekend . . .

Chapter 6

Standing in the foyer of Dorian's "retirement home" on Saturday evening, Blake almost wished that he *had* brought a couple of pots to catch leaks in. Through the lead-framed glass that bordered the heavy front door, he could still see the dark and threatening skies. There was a faint roll of thunder, and the March wind began to whip the air with a fury. He could hear the rafters creak from the buffeting. He frowned slightly as he wondered why in the devil Rand had purchased this crumbling mausoleum. Either Dorian was a lot worse off financially than he had thought, or the old swindler was losing a battle with senility.

"Charming, isn't it?" asked an amused feminine voice from the hallway.

Blake turned to watch Elizabeth enter the vestibule.

"'Charming' wasn't the word that came to mind," he admitted dryly. He took in her black silk evening pants, her elegant crimson blouse with its ruffled cuffs, and the fine strands of her twisted gold necklace. "Very nice," he murmured.

Elizabeth laughed nervously and clapped her hands together, as if she couldn't believe his comment.

"Very nice?" she exclaimed, nearly choking in her disbelief. "You mean you *like* this place?"

She had intentionally misread his compliment, he thought, curious as to why. Nerves, perhaps? The corners of his mouth lifted ever so slightly, and his eyes narrowed a shade. He couldn't say that he was exactly sympathetic with any nervous anxiety she might be suffering at the moment. If anything, he found it gratifying. He had suffered a certain amount of ambivalence himself about coming here for the weekend. Hell, he still wasn't sure it was a good idea. The possibility that she was a little apprehensive actually made him relax, he discovered. The ghostlike smile haunting his mouth became a little more hearty.

"I wasn't referring to the house," he pointed out as he walked over to join her. In a low voice he added, quite clearly, "I was referring to you." He held her eyes with his, daring her to pretend she didn't understand him this time. He saw the flash of uncertainty in hers, and, to his surprise, something that resembled fear. He frowned slightly.

Elizabeth smiled weakly and murmured, "Thank you."

She wished that he wouldn't look at her that way, as if he were trying to read her soul. It made her feel quite vulnerable. She couldn't dissolve in a puddle at his feet, she told herself stoutheartedly. So she strengthened her smile and indicated he should follow her into the adjoining room, one that served both as a living room and as a reception area for visitors.

"Did you have any difficulty finding us?" Elizabeth asked lightly.

"No."

She looked at him in admiration. "You're one of the few," she said, laughing a little. "The roads are so convoluted, and they cross one another so many times, that it could take *years* to learn your way through the maze!"

"Years or a decent map," Blake pointed out reasonably.

She laughed again and said accusingly, "A map! That's cheating!"

He looked surprised and a little amused by her teasing rejoinder. They were standing in the middle of the large, sparsely furnished room, staring at one another. It was the first time they had been alone in years. He saw the realization come to her just a moment after it hit him.

"No. It's not cheating," he said, his voice low and edged with an old memory of warmth. "I had no intention of driving in circles. I wanted to get here." His mouth curved into a slight smile. "Tonight, not tomorrow morning."

Elizabeth couldn't help staring into his warm, steady gaze. There was something mesmerizing about Blake, she thought hazily. Absolutely mesmerizing. She remembered feeling that way before, as if she could drown in sensation just looking at the man.

"I'm surprised you accepted the invitation," she said huskily. She couldn't help the blush that stole across her cheeks. "After what happened to us..." She couldn't quite say it, though, and the sentence trailed off into nothing.

Blake noted the blush with a certain amount of satisfaction. She *should* be embarrassed about the careless way she had given him the brush-off, damn it. *No one* should encourage another to love them and then toss that love back, as if it had merely been a temporary convenience. He deftly curbed his anger, keeping his expression courteous and reasonably interested, and carefully chose his words.

"I'm a *man,* Elizabeth, not a *boy,*" he reminded her. "What happened between us was over and done with years ago."

Elizabeth searched his face, wanting to believe that he no longer held that awful night against her, that he had gotten over it without deep emotional pain. He seemed relaxed, although there was a disturbing intensity in his eyes. Of course, that could just be her oversensitivity again.

Shrugging indifferently, he added, "You certainly weren't the first woman in history to tell a man that she was no longer interested in his attentions." He smiled wryly. "The male of the species is built to take it, believe me. The initial shock wears off. Eventually the bruised ego heals." His smile became more private, as if he were recalling a number of highly pleasurable stops on the road to recovery. "And there are always sympathetic women willing to soothe the wounded breast."

When he got to the part about other women soothing his wounds, jealousy sank its teeth into her. He didn't have to tell her that! Gentlemen didn't kiss and tell, and he darn well knew it! Heaven knew she didn't enjoy hearing about it. However, with a gentle smile firmly on her face, Elizabeth suffered in silence. She knew it was ridiculous to wish that he hadn't found sympathy or compassion from other women, but she did. She yearned for him to have been faithful to her, at least in some quiet, emotional corner of his heart. As she had been to him...

If he only *knew* the fantasies that she had nurtured about him! He would probably laugh himself sick, she thought. At times those fantasies had been the only dike holding back the seas of despair in her life. While *he* had been basking in the eager sympathies of those other women, *she* had been clinging blindly to fairy tales, promising herself that someday everything would magically be righted again. That the look of hatred she had seen in his eyes would be transformed back into a tender expression of love and friendship.

Elizabeth repressed a sigh. She knew her fairy-tale visions were preposterous and would never actually materialize, but her heart had stubbornly clung to the fanciful dream. She had always known that Blake's real life would be far different from her wistful imaginings. However, it would have been very nice if he had kept his reality to himself instead of sharing it with her. She wasn't eager to know just how far he had strayed from the role of devoted hero.

"You look a little shocked, Elizabeth," he said, curious and a bit amused. "Surely you didn't think I took holy orders or swore off women?"

She laughed uncomfortably. "Of course not."

"After all, you were leaving *me* for *another man*," he reminded her. "It's normal for the rejected lover to pick up the pieces of his heart and find new playmates when that happens."

From the easy way he said it, it didn't sound as if it had taken long for the pieces to mend, she thought, dismayed at how that hurt her.

"I'm happy you didn't have any trouble getting over it," she said, finding it difficult to keep her feelings out of her voice.

His ease at talking about getting over her shook her confidence for the first time since the night she had broken up with Blake. She frowned a little and stared at him pensively, wondering if perhaps his feelings for her *hadn't* been as strong as she had always believed them to be. Surely he should feel some trace of bitterness, some wellspring of anger, if he had loved her as deeply as she had thought? She would have gladly absorbed the brutal lash of his anger. It would be easier to endure his animosity than to face the cool hollowness of this indifference. At least hatred was a strong emotion, something to cling to. His sophisticated neutrality offered nothing but emptiness.

His description of the way she had broken off with him had held a hint of bitterness, though, she thought. Searching for a place to connect with him emotionally, she went back to it.

"I don't believe that I said I was no longer interested in you...." Elizabeth murmured.

"Telling me that you loved another man more than you loved me was *hardly* the way to convey your undying affection," he pointed out dryly. Dubiously, he lifted an eyebrow for added emphasis.

"No. It wasn't," Elizabeth guiltily had to agree. "I wish there had been some other way...." She had to be careful what she admitted. After a quick consideration, she decided to plunge ahead. "I'm *sorry,* Blake. I've wanted to tell you that for years. I'm so *very* sorry."

A blind man could have seen the honest regret in her eyes. Unfortunately, Blake was worse than blind where she was concerned. Instead of regret, he saw pity, and it was bitter gall to his pride.

Sorry? She was *sorry?* Just as he had begun to believe that he had overcome his penchant for erupting in anger at her, he felt rage boiling up within him. It was very difficult for him to conceal the fury that her apologetic words had inflamed. With diamond-hard determination, he smothered the dangerous emotions, cooling his temper through sheer force of will.

He wasn't interested in Elizabeth's pity! From the warm, pleading look he saw in her eyes, he assumed that she wanted him to forgive her for her ancient cruelty. It would be a cool day in hell when he did that! he vowed silently. He rarely held a grudge, but in Elizabeth's case, he would cheerfully make a lifelong exception. If he was lucky, someday he would be able to forget what had happened between them. But forgive her? Not likely. Not bloody likely.

He gave her a mocking look. "As I recall, you told me at the time that you were sorry, Elizabeth. If you wanted to apologize further, you could always have picked up the phone," he pointed out. The teasing in his voice softened the biting words, making it difficult to tell if he was serious.

"I...suppose..." Elizabeth agreed in confusion. Blake looked strange, she thought. That dangerous glitter in his eyes didn't go with the smooth, humorous tone in his voice. Was he laughing at the old disaster, or was he still offended?

"I'm more interested in talking about the present than the past," he told her casually. "When the maid answered the door and ushered me in, she gave me Dorian's apologies for not greeting me in person. Something about an unexpected call from Zurich?"

"Yes," Elizabeth murmured. "He shouldn't be much longer."

"Will Karl be joining us?" he asked carefully.

Elizabeth looked away from him. "For dinner."

"You still seem uneasy about my seeing him," he pointed out.

"I'm sorry," she said apologetically. "Perhaps I've become overprotective of him." She smiled ruefully at Blake. "I've told him you would be here. He's looking forward to it."

Blake was surprised she had admitted it. He motioned toward the couch and said, "Why don't we sit down?"

"Of course."

He lightly touched her elbow and drew her over to the settee near the cold, empty fireplace. It had been laid with logs and kindling, but no one had thought to light it.

They sat down, half-facing one another. The settee wasn't particularly large, so they were close, although not so close that they had to brush against one another. Blake leaned back comfortably and stretched his arm behind him. Elizabeth knew it wasn't intended as a form of intimacy. It was simply a comfortable way for a man as tall as Blake to relax on the relatively small divan.

"So tell me, Elizabeth, how long do you intend to stay with Dorian now that he's retiring?"

She nervously crossed her legs and tightly wrapped one foot behind the other. "I'm not sure. Dorian and I haven't discussed that," she hedged.

Blake's eyes gleamed in amusement at her fortresslike position. She had drawn up her bridges.

"I've often wondered how you and Karl ended up with Dorian," Blake mused aloud.

"Dorian had always wanted my father to design exclusively for him," she explained reluctantly.

"How did Dorian persuade him?" Blake asked curiously.

Elizabeth managed a tight smile. "He made us an offer we couldn't refuse."

"What did he offer you? Riches beyond measure?"

Elizabeth wondered if you could put a price tag on your freedom. "Yes. I guess you could say that's exactly what he did offer," she murmured.

Blake sensed an undercurrent in the conversation and wondered what it was that she wasn't telling him. His eyes narrowed thoughtfully.

"What riches did he offer, Elizabeth?" he demanded softly.

She stared at him, wondering what she could say that would be honest and yet not the literal truth.

Dorian's arrival spared her the trouble. Having obviously overheard Blake's question, he interjected, "Wealth and fame for Karl, and the hand of my moneyed son for Elizabeth. That was what I offered them. Who could have refused such jewels?" Dorian demanded with a jovial chuckle.

Blake rose to his feet and courteously shook Dorian's hand. It was done out of habit. Under other circumstances, he would have crossed the street to avoid shaking hands with the old snake.

Dorian noticed the dead fireplace and went to the doorway to bellow. A uniformed maid, the one who had answered the door and ushered Blake into the house, appeared almost immediately. She looked quite alarmed that her employer was displeased and was murmuring apologies as she followed him to the cold andirons.

Blake sat down again and settled his gaze on Elizabeth.

"Dorian's *son* was the man you were going to marry?" he asked incredulously. "I don't believe it!" he muttered sarcas-

tically. He stared at her, as if horribly fascinated to have discovered a woman capable of such repulsive behavior. "Dorian's
son had a reputation on *three* continents. He went through
wives and girlfriends like chocolates!" Then, as if this might be
of special interest to a gold digger such as herself, he added,
"And he *wasn't* known to be *generous afterward,* either!"

He couldn't have made his poor opinion of her any clearer
if he had put it in lights on Broadway.

Elizabeth bristled defensively.

Of course, she knew that Blake was right. No sane woman
would have willingly consented to marry Dorian's charmingly
irresponsible son. The man was terminally self-absorbed. When
she had been forced to socialize with him, he had been tolerable company...up until the end of the evening. Then, each
time, he had used every trick at his disposal to try to seduce her.
Conquest had been his goal, and he had pursued it as tena-
ciously as a terrier shaking its favorite bone. Her subtle, persistent refusals never wore him down. He simply assumed he
should try harder the next time. When he had finally accepted
the fact that she would never love him, never respond to him
sexually, he had been much easier to get along with. He'd
treated her like a casual sidekick. That had amused Elizabeth
and infuriated Dorian.

What really bothered Elizabeth was that Blake had immediately believed the worst about her. The minute Dorian had
hinted he had thrown his wealthy son at her, Blake had been
willing to swallow it. She knew that she was reaping the seeds
she had sown fifteen years ago when she had portrayed herself
as a gold digger to drive Blake away from her. She had only
herself to blame for his jumping to the wrong conclusions,
especially with the misleading comment Dorian had made!

But she blamed Blake anyway. Surely he should be able to see
the *real* her in spite of everything, shouldn't he?

"You don't believe that I could have such poor taste in
men?" she said in a dangerously icy voice as she carefully re-
phrased his accusation. Seeing his dark, condemning expression increased her irritation, and she tried hard to avoid getting
angrier. "I'm delighted that you have the good sense not to
believe it!"

His expression went from distasteful to perplexed. "Is that so? Why?" he asked suspiciously.

"Because I *didn't* marry him," she said with a chilly smile. She folded her arms protectively and lifted her chin a notch for good measure. "Your faith in my taste in men is justified. Wouldn't you agree?"

Blake frowned. He didn't think she had been married. Janet had found no record of it. But it was possible. And, of course, Elizabeth could have gotten involved with that pig without actually going through the legal formalities. *That* was the real bone in his throat. The vision of Elizabeth rolling around in bed with another man severely worsened his already marginal temper. He glanced quickly in Dorian's direction, relieved to find him still lecturing the poor maid on the proper way to light a fire. Then he turned a third-degree frown on Elizabeth.

"But Dorian just said—" he whispered harshly.

"That he *offered* me his son in marriage," Elizabeth interrupted, angrily whispering back.

Blake still thought it bizarre that a grown man could be bartered in marriage like that, and he didn't bother to conceal his contempt. At least she'd had the sense not to take the oaf, he thought. She would look guilty if she wasn't telling him the truth, and she didn't look guilty at all. *Mad* was how she looked. So Dorian had tried to get her interested in sonny boy and she . . . "But you turned him down?"

"Exactly."

Blake stared at her, surprised at how relieved he was to hear her deny it all. The residual disgust in him unraveled a little more. It was damn hard to hold on to it when her eyes looked the way they did. Fiery sea-green. Glittering like a tropical sea on a late afternoon, the hot sun painting it in iridescent colors.

"You know, I had nearly forgotten how your eyes looked when you got angry," he said softly. His voice sounded as if it was coming from a long way away. As if his mind had warped into another dimension for a second. Damned peculiar sensation.

Elizabeth saw the darkening intensity in his eyes and felt so faint that she wondered if she had forgotten to breathe. Dizzy. Light-headed. Where had all the oxygen gone, anyway? And where was everything else, for that matter? Could you fall into another dimension by looking into the mysterious depths of a man's gaze? Making the rest of the world recede until it wasn't there at all? That was what it felt like to her. As if there were only the two of them, and they were locked in a separate universe, imprisoned by an invisible, magically charged net that emanated from themselves. Odd. And a little scary.

Blake's arm, which he had draped behind her on the settee, lowered. She felt the touch of his hand on her shoulder. Tentative. As if knowing this was a risky thing to do. Risky for both of them. His strong fingers touched the silky fabric of her blouse. Lightly. The warmth easily crossed the fragile barrier. His warmth to her. Her warmth to him. His palm flattened against her, and he slid his hand downward a couple of inches. But slowly. Very slowly.

Elizabeth's anger completely dissolved, mellowing into another dark emotion. She knew that emotion, that strange sensation. It was a haunting feeling, one that she hadn't felt in an achingly long time. It was coming back to her, though. Stronger than ever. It had been one of those treasures that Dorian had never been able to touch. But it had been a long time since she'd felt the real thing, and memory had dimmed. Had it always started this way? Warmth and a swirl of giddy anticipation somewhere in the pit of her stomach? Blake's slow caress, the tightening of his arm around her shoulder, brought it all back to her. She almost sighed.

"Why didn't you marry him?" Blake murmured, coaxing her to give him the truth, searching her face for it.

His husky whisper sent a distinctly pleasurable sensation shivering down her spine, and Elizabeth succumbed to the desire to give him what he wanted.

"I didn't marry him because I didn't love him," she whispered. She was staring at him hypnotically. His satisfaction at her reply was easy to see. He relaxed slightly, and his mouth lost some of its hardness.

Blake's satisfaction ebbed, however, as he replayed her answer in his mind. She hadn't married *him,* either, he recalled. She hadn't loved *him,* either.

He moved his arm away from her. The warmth between them chilled a little.

Elizabeth wondered why he had withdrawn, but she wasn't as lost in the haze as she had been a few moments before, and she wasn't about to ask him. She folded her arms protectively and tilted her chin up. The precious warmth had gone away. She was alone again.

Dorian, having finally supervised the fire into existence, rejoined them.

"It's time for a little refreshment, I think," he said with relish. The maid scurried out of the room, returning with a silver tray bearing filled champagne glasses and hot canapés. Mrs. Einer hurried in behind her with the ice bucket, champagne bottle and an assortment of small decorative napkins.

"Please excuse our casual hospitality," Dorian said as they were being served. "We haven't completely settled in as yet."

Blake lifted his champagne in a low salute to Dorian. "To your upcoming retirement," he said easily. Then, turning to Elizabeth, "And to your future successes."

"And to yours," she said softly.

Elizabeth touched her glass to his, but she found herself wishing that it had been their lips that touched instead. The crystal was smooth and cool against her mouth, and the champagne's icy froth slid down her throat like sparkling magic. She welcomed the chilling sensation and took another deep swallow. Being with Blake was doing peculiar things to her nervous system. Disturbingly *familiar,* peculiar things. She prayed that she would find the strength to keep her distance from him. She could see it was not going to be easy. She held the glass a little tighter.

Dorian gave her an unexpected respite as he engaged Blake in a wide-ranging discussion of the state of the international jewel market and effectively ignored Elizabeth. Gradually, however, Blake began directing questions toward her and coaxing her into the conversation, progressively drawing her out on specific issues as they worked their way to the bottom of the champagne bottle.

It was soon obvious to Blake that Elizabeth had indeed kept up with the business over the years. She wasn't simply a pretty administrative figurehead for Dorian. She knew what had sold well and to whom. She knew where the market had gone soft and why. And she also expressed very intriguing observations about the quality of gemstones being set in several well-known firms in New York and Belgium.

Grudgingly, Blake realized he would have to discard his suspicions that she had probably disappointed her father and failed to develop her potential. While it was still not clear to him what she had accomplished, he could already tell that she had been working very hard in those backroom shadows that she had apparently haunted.

He was frowning at her, wondering what else she had done with her life that he didn't know about, when the maid timidly reappeared in the doorway and silently motioned to Dorian.

Dorian put his empty glass on the table nearest to him and, smiling smoothly, rose from his chair with heavy reliance on his cane.

"I believe dinner is about to be served," he announced in the genial voice of a veteran host. He motioned toward the now empty doorway. "Shall we go?" He began walking toward it, leaning a little more heavily than was usual on his cane. "How I despise growing old," he complained wryly. "The spirit is still eager and hot," he said with a bitter laugh. "But, alas, the body weakens and cannot keep pace."

Blake wondered cynically if the note of regret in Dorian's voice was real or contrived. If anyone other than Dorian had made that remark, he would have murmured some expression of sympathy. With Dorian, however, it seemed wiser to keep his sympathy on a short leash. Blake thought Elizabeth was thinking pretty much the same thing. Her shoulders were braced a little too firmly, he noticed, and she looked as if she had heard Dorian sing this refrain many times before. From the wary expression in her eyes, he surmised that on some previous occasion when Dorian had tried this disarming tactic, the result had been unpleasant.

They rounded a corner, and Dorian tossed back at them casually, "Karl should already be there, I believe."

Blake walked a little more purposefully. This was one of the main reasons he was here, and he made no effort to hide the fact. Beside him, he observed Elizabeth begin to lag a little, as if she were walking to an execution rather than a dinner party.

"Did you forget something?" he asked her, wondering what was causing this renewed reluctance on her part.

She immediately picked up her pace and put a stiff smile on her face. "No," she assured him. "I don't think I've forgotten a single thing." She superstitiously crossed her fingers and hoped her optimism would be borne out. If her father just remembered—and honored—his promise, everything would be fine.

As they entered the dining room, Blake's attention was immediately drawn to the figure sitting in the wheelchair at the far end of the long, linen-covered table. The room was softly illuminated by the ornate chandelier overhead and four braces of candles evenly spaced along the table. Four places were set at one end, where Karl had been left by his nurse to await them.

The closer Blake got to Karl, the more clearly he saw him. He had been preparing mental images of his old friend and mentor for weeks now, but, in spite of that, he was shocked at the dramatic changes that the years had wrought. Karl sat hunched up and withered, like a shrunken copy of the man he had once known. His hair was now wispy and silvered, and his once skilled right arm now lay protectively close to his body. Only his eyes reminded Blake of the old Karl. They were still piercing and direct.

When Blake reached Karl's side, he realized that there were tears glimmering in the old jeweler's eyes. He became uncomfortably aware that there was a lump forming in his own throat. There had once been a time when he had prepared himself to think of this dignified old man as his future father-in-law. Two lifetimes separated them now, one Karl's and the other Blake's. Karl's life had dwindled into a thin trickle, while Blake's had flooded into a powerful river.

Blake took the good left hand that Karl was holding out to him in an obvious gesture of welcome, only to be startled by the strength of Karl's grasp. He squatted down so that they would be closer to the same eye level, remaining silent for an emotional moment.

"Hello, Karl." Blake's voice sounded embarrassingly rough to himself. He cleared his throat. "It's been a long time."

"Long...time," Karl managed to get out. He squeezed Blake's hand harder and nodded.

"It's good to see you again," Blake said softly. He squeezed the gnarled hand clutching his like a lifeline, trying to send a silent message of empathy.

Karl blinked his pale gray eyes and nodded some more. "Good," Karl agreed. Then he smiled awkwardly. "Blake." He said the name, as if in welcome. He meant, *Everything will be better now that you're here, Blake.*

Blake frowned a little, wondering why Karl would be looking at him as if he were Sir Galahad bringing in the Holy Grail. He glanced at Elizabeth, who had moved to Karl's other side and placed a comforting hand on his shoulder. She looked worried.

Blake rose and, as Karl reluctantly released his vicelike handshake, sat at Karl's right. As he looked around the table he was struck by the wide variety of emotions evident among them. Elizabeth seemed strangely tense, Karl profoundly relieved and anxious, while Dorian was smiling with satisfaction, a calculating gleam lighting his eye.

Blake shook out his napkin as the first course arrived in the brisk hands of the maid and Mrs. Einer. Then he turned his attention to Karl Rossi.

Chapter 7

Blake had to admit that Dorian was handling the evening with the smoothness of an experienced stage manager. First had come the aperitifs in the living room and time alone with Elizabeth, which in retrospect had obviously been intended to whet his appetites—the one for food, and the other most compelling appetite that came to mind. Dinner had apparently been designed with an eye for deepening that arousal. Dorian had blatantly encouraged the sharing of memories in an effort to strengthen the emotions being cultivated, with Karl joining them primarily as an enhancer.

Strong feelings broke down reserve and made a person more vulnerable, and Dorian had clearly been playing on that fact all evening long.

Now they had reached the after-dinner stage of the play, and Dorian's plans for the final act were rapidly being unveiled. Blake was tempted to applaud the elaborate effort being made on his behalf. Cynically, he wondered why he was the target of all this attention. He presumed that it probably had something to do with money. That was usually the root of the matter when Dorian was involved.

So, curious to see what would come next, Blake stood by the fireplace, gently swirling his brandy in its snifter, lazily watching as Dorian finally stood up to take his leave.

"I think I should join Karl," Dorian exclaimed with a chuckle. Karl had already retired to his room for the night, having been taken there by his nurse, Cassie, a short while earlier.

Elizabeth quickly stood up and started to speak.

"No, no, my dear," Dorian admonished her before she could utter a word. "Don't get up. I wouldn't think of cutting short *your* evening."

"It wouldn't be . . ." She tried to protest.

Dorian limped over to her and patted her shoulder in a show of affection. "I'm certain that you two aren't the least bit ready to retire yet. It's quite early for young people such as yourselves."

She glanced at the antique grandfather clock. "Ten-thirty isn't really early." She cast a quick look in Blake's direction. "And I'm sure that Blake has heard more than enough for one evening."

Dorian laughed and shook his head. "Elizabeth, my dear, the man is still drinking his brandy."

She could hardly argue with that.

Blake took a leisurely sip and watched as Dorian touched Elizabeth again, his gnarled hand tightening on her arm in some sort of unspoken message. He thought Dorian's eyes hardened a little, but it was difficult to be sure in the dancing firelight.

Elizabeth stiffly moved away from Dorian and deliberately put her own empty brandy snifter on a silver tray.

Dorian limped slowly toward the door, turning just before he left to say, "I wish you good night. And I look forward to asking you more about that dealer in Stockholm tomorrow over brunch."

Blake gave the old fox a slight smile and lifted his brandy in a farewell salute. "Good night, Dorian."

Dorian pressed a final word of advice on Elizabeth, who had not moved from her position next to the brandy decanter and its silver tray. "I imagine that you and Blake will also be up earlier tomorrow morning than either Karl or I will be. Why don't you show him your workshop then, my dear? And perhaps some of your designs? Then meet us for brunch in the dining room at, say, ten-thirty? Does that sound like a good plan?"

Elizabeth stared at Dorian. "Yes. Of course."

"Wonderful. Again, good night. Until tomorrow..."

Dorian moved away, humming to himself happily.

Blake took another sip of his brandy and watched Elizabeth, speculating about what she would do now. She had become increasingly uneasy as the evening had come to a close, and now that Dorian had neatly retired all the other players from the field of battle, she was left alone with him. That had obviously been the plan all along.

He had to admit that his appetite had been whetted for her. Unfortunately for Dorian, however, desire had not dulled his memory. It would take far more than the usual circumstances for him to want to fondle and kiss Elizabeth Rossi again.

The sound of Dorian's cane had faded away, and the room was deadly silent, except for the rhythmic ticking of the grandfather clock and the slow hiss and crackle of the smoldering fire.

"Does he always do this, Elizabeth?" Blake asked dryly, as the lengthening silence between them became strained.

She had been looking into the fire, but at his question she lifted her eyes to look at him. "Does he always do what?" she asked uncomfortably.

Blake produced a cynical smile. "Let's not pretend we don't know what he's doing, Elizabeth."

"All right," she agreed cautiously. "But what is it that *you* think he's doing?"

He laughed. "Throwing us together."

She considered denying it, but she could see that it would be pointless. Blake wasn't blind. At least, not in this instance. She sighed and poured herself another brandy. "Would you like another?" she asked.

"Please."

She joined him at the mantle and poured him another drink, settling the crystal decanter on the stone lip afterward. She lifted her drink to his and offered a small toast. "To honesty," she suggested.

He didn't look completely convinced that she was capable of it, but they clinked glasses, and he drank in unison with her, offering her the benefit of the doubt this time.

Elizabeth rolled the glass between her palms and stared into the undulating flames. It was easier than seeing the disenchanted and cynical expression in Blake's eyes.

"You're right," she admitted. "Dorian *is* intentionally 'throwing us together,' as you put it."

"Why?"

"Because he wants to know more about you."

Blake laughed humorlessly. "What does he want to know?"

Elizabeth bit her lip. "He wants to know more about your business...."

"I got the distinct impression that he has been pumping me quite directly on that subject, starting that afternoon when you paid me that visit at Malone's," he pointed out. "And this evening he launched a continual barrage of questions, following up on it. Why would he now turn over the interrogation to you, if I may ask?"

"He wants more...."

Blake looked at her quizzically. "What else does he want to know? My net worth? My projected income this year?" He laughed softly. "What am I being screened for, Elizabeth?"

She blushed. This was harder than she'd thought it would be. She didn't know if she had the nerve to tell him what Dorian's orders to her had been.

He drained the brandy and put it down on the mantle beside the decanter. "You're blushing, Elizabeth," he observed, mildly amazed. "Now, *why* would that question make you blush, I wonder."

"It's just the fire. And the brandy. They make me warm...."

A log fell apart, and a shower of red embers erupted in a hiss.

Blake watched the light bathe her face in a golden glow, painting her in its multifaceted hues, and another old memory worked its way painfully to the surface. He had stood with her like this once before, he recalled. On a Christmas eve, in Arkansas, a long time ago. Maybe it was the long-buried, poignant memory that made him reach out then, or maybe it was just that he'd been wanting to do it for a very long time. He wasn't sure. It didn't really matter, he supposed. He had been wanting to touch her again ever since he'd seen her at the museum, ever since he'd caressed her shoulder lightly on the settee.

He reached out, slowly, allowing her time to step back if she wanted, letting her see what he was going to do. When she didn't move away but simply looked at him with big eyes veiled in worry and confusion, he lightly touched her cheek with his fingertips.

"You're not blushing because of warmth from the fire," he told her softly. "You're embarrassed about something." He caressed her soft skin, slowly and very gently. "Surely there is nothing left for you and I to be embarrassed about. Remember me?" he teased softly. "I'm the guy you left behind. Surely you can be honest with *me?*"

His touch was so sweet she could have cried. And his voice...so kind and coaxing...There was a hypnotic pull in the way he was inviting her to confide in him. And she was lonely, so lonely, and she had been so hungry for tenderness for such a very long time.

Elizabeth closed her eyes as tears gathered on her lashes. They glistened like liquid gold and glimmered in the dancing firelight.

Blake's eyes narrowed suspiciously. Were the tears real, or had she manufactured them for a purpose? He fought his initial, instinctive reaction: to soothe her and tell her it would be all right, to hold her comfortingly in his arms and kiss the molten drops away. He couldn't trust her, he brutally reminded himself.

"Why the tears, Elizabeth?" he pressed her, using that same soothing, compelling voice.

She sucked in her breath. "Dorian wants me to seduce you."

"What?"

Elizabeth's eyes flew open, and she stared at Blake. He looked thunderstruck, and he was frozen in place.

"Surely you were beginning to guess?" she said, feeling terribly awkward.

He blinked and, realizing that he was still touching her cheek, withdrew his hand. "Seduction was a little more than I was expecting," he admitted dryly.

Elizabeth swallowed. "Oh?" She felt the heat flooding her cheeks again and miserably wished she could disappear through the floor.

Blake recovered and managed to laugh. "Oh, yes. I thought I was being plied in a very pleasant way, of course. You were obviously being left to have a final, intimate tête-à-tête," he acknowledged. "But a full-blown seduction..." He looked at her, and for a moment they were locked in silence. "I'm flattered," he murmured.

Elizabeth felt awful, and she started blushing again. "That's a very kind way for you to respond," she said, laughing nervously. "Thanks for not putting some cruder connotation on it."

He stared at her in silence. Then he asked curiously, "You still haven't told me why I was to be, uh, seduced."

Elizabeth slid her fingers through her hair in desperation. How much truth could she yield to him? She was already walking a tightrope in telling him what she had.

"He thinks that a man would talk in bed...."

"He's quite right," Blake said in amusement.

Elizabeth blushed. "Not *that* kind of talk," she muttered testily.

His grin widened. "Yes. *That* kind of talk," he retorted softly.

Elizabeth glared at him. "If you want me to explain, stop arguing with me!"

"All right," he agreed, still amused. "So what kind of talk were you to elicit from me, once you had thoroughly seduced me and we were suitably relaxed in bed?" he inquired, quite interested.

Elizabeth looked at him steadily. "I was to find out how much you might be willing to pay for the jewelry he will be auctioning sometime in the next few months."

He studied her thoughtfully.

She wondered what he was thinking. What would she have thought if their positions had been reversed? That she was prostituting herself for Dorian. Elizabeth felt a little ill. There was no love burning in his eyes now. She could discern no hate, either. Instead, he was studying her as one might study a diamond in the rough, just before deciding where to strike in order to cleave it. She felt a coldness slide through her insides as she wondered what he would say. Please, not that look of fury, she prayed. The one she had seen burning in his eyes the night she had driven him away. She thought she could take anything but that.

"All right," he conceded, sounding unconvinced but willing to accept her assertion for the sake of argument. "Tonight was to be the beginning of a long-term . . . relationship?" He used the word reluctantly.

"Yes."

"I see." He paused for a moment, then asked curiously, "Why are you telling me this?"

Elizabeth sighed and looked at the ceiling. The root of the problem, after all, involved her father's crime, and she couldn't breathe a word about that. Without that explanation, how could she begin to make him understand? "I don't know if I can explain it to you," she said unhappily.

"Try."

She glanced at him. The hard, ironic twist in that single word was unmistakable. "You don't trust me, do you, Blake?" she said, barely above the level of a whisper.

He looked at her in surprise. "Would you expect me to?" He reached out and pulled her left hand into view, turning it to reveal her ring finger without a wedding band on it. "You told me at the museum that you weren't married. That was a rather evasive answer, wasn't it?"

"I . . ."

"You never got married, did you?"

"I . . ."

"Did you?" He tightened his hold and moved a little closer to her. "You offered a toast to honesty at the beginning of this little conversation. Do you intend to honor it? Or are you going to wiggle out of it just like you freed yourself of our unwanted engagement fifteen years ago?"

She searched his face for some trace of tenderness but found only steely determination and what looked like heavily banked anger. Her heart ached a little, but she told herself that anything was an improvement over indifference. She swallowed hard.

"No," she answered honestly. "I have never been married. I've never been engaged . . . to anyone but you, Blake," she added softly.

He stiffened and frowned. "I've tried to forget that little mistake," he told her, quite truthfully. "I wouldn't speak of it in such soft and dulcet tones, if I were you."

Was that pain he saw in her face? And was it real or synthetic? he wondered angrily. Well, he needn't further humiliate himself by letting her see that it still bothered the hell out of him even to think about their breakup. He forced himself to release her hand, forced himself to relax. He even managed a bitter smile.

"You wanted to know why I'm telling you all this," Elizabeth reminded him quietly, picking up the threads of the conversation.

He nodded. "Obviously."

"I thought it might be better for both of us if I simply laid my cards on the table." Up to a point, anyway.

His expression was neutral. "Go on."

"Well, you see, if I had simply refused to cooperate with Dorian, he could have made things very difficult for me." She could see from the flicker in Blake's eyes that he was going to want to know what she meant by that, and she hurried on, before he could ask. "So I agreed to be friendly with you. I've never agreed with Dorian's more rapacious business instincts. And usually I've been able to avoid getting involved. As he told you, I have been doing some design work, so I've been able to excuse myself from his plans by pointing out that I'm making money for the business elsewhere."

She paused, trying to gauge whether he believed her at all. She couldn't tell.

"What makes this time any different from the others?"

She smiled sadly. "Well, for one thing, this time the person is *you,* Blake. It isn't a stranger, or a competitor, or a client. It's you." She couldn't help breathing the word. It just came out with that ache from deep inside her heart. She could see the cynicism in his eyes, and her heart broke a little more.

"I appreciate your concern," he said dryly.

Elizabeth sighed. "I know that you'll find it difficult to believe this, but, I've always felt . . . connected to you."

He remained silent, but he didn't try to conceal his doubt.

She stubbornly lifted her chin. "I didn't marry you," she pointed out. "But that doesn't mean that I stopped liking you, or respecting you." *Or loving you.* She blinked to try to keep it from showing.

Blake laughed. "So you respect me in the morning, huh?"

Elizabeth's cheeks turned a charming shade of pink again. From the sardonic gleam in his eyes, she was afraid she knew what he was thinking of. They had never completely consummated their relationship fifteen years ago, but they'd gone as far as it was possible to go without technically taking her virginity.

His amusement gradually passed, and he rubbed the back of his neck as he decided where to take this conversation.

"I'd still like an answer to my first question," he said seriously.

She frowned. "I don't remember what it was."

"Does Dorian do this to you often?" he repeated, frowning himself.

Elizabeth laughed bitterly. "He's hinted that he wouldn't mind my being a good listener with a number of people, but he's never asked me to seduce anyone before."

"I'm relieved to hear that."

"Are you?" She sighed. "You were always a gentleman, Blake."

"Was that the problem?" he asked, his voice a little lower, a little rougher, this time, as he stared at her intently.

She looked at him, letting her eyes roam over him with tender affection and poignant regret. "No. It's one of the reasons I decided I could trust you with the truth about tonight. I know you wouldn't use the information to hurt me." She moved a little away and wrapped her arms around her middle. "That wasn't the problem...."

He moved closer and cupped her chin with one warm hand. "Who was he?" he demanded softly. "I used to wonder who it could have been." He smiled a little. "Surely it doesn't matter anymore?"

She stood still, treasuring the wonderful sensation of his lean, strong hand on her face. Regret filled her voice as she said huskily, "I can't tell you his name."

Blake's expression became grim. "It doesn't really matter," he said coolly. He withdrew his hand, assumed a crisper tone and asked, "What will happen to you if your *seduction* fails?"

Elizabeth shrugged. "Nothing. What *could* he do? Tie you up and demand that you respond to me?"

Blake's brows lowered. He doubted that anyone would have to tie him up to force him to respond to Elizabeth, but he could see her point. "You said that if you had just refused to go along with his plan that he could 'make things very difficult' for you."

Here it comes, she thought fatalistically. "Yes."

"What did you mean by that?"

She looked at the parquet flooring. "I can't answer that." Was that the fire hissing or a sharply indrawn breath of masculine distrust? She was afraid to look at him and find out.

"That's very convenient," he said sarcastically.

She looked up at him and saw the cynicism in his eyes. "It's the truth, Blake," she whispered. "I wish I could answer you, but I can't. I think that if you were in my position, you'd understand and sympathize with my dilemma." She flinched at the dubious lift of his brow. "I know it must be hard for you to believe me...."

"Hard?" He laughed bitterly. "Only a moron would swallow that line, Elizabeth." Angrily he ran a hand through his dark hair. "You must really think I'm a fool," he muttered tightly.

Beneath his anger she heard the pain that lay deeply buried. Her heart melted her embarrassment and the fear that she was making a fool of herself by being so honest with him. She wanted so badly to ease his pain that she ached with it. Instinctively she moved closer to him and touched his arm in a gesture of gentle warmth and compassion.

She made no effort to hide her emotions this time, as she told him, "I don't think you're a fool. I never thought that, Blake. I've always thought that you were one of the finest men I've ever had the privilege of knowing, one of the kindest, the strongest, the best men I've ever met."

He could feel her hand, warm and firm, through his sweater and shirt, and memories whispered across his skin of other times when she had caressed him, of the rich heat of that almost forgotten pleasure.

Everything about her was pleading for him to believe her, to trust her, from her clear, worried eyes to her body leaning slightly toward him. If it had been any woman but Elizabeth, he would have trusted her. However, it *was* Elizabeth, and because of that, he couldn't be absolutely sure of her.

Because it was Elizabeth, unfortunately, every masculine fiber of his body was demanding that he stop talking and start touching. He looked at her lips and murmured in a low voice, "For a woman who's admitted she isn't seducing me, you're doing a remarkably effective job."

He put his arm around her and pulled her close, ignoring her startled expression and the slight stiffening of her body. Gently, he ran his hand through her soft hair, sliding his fingers through the silky strands until they delicately cascaded free.

"Do you remember that night at your cottage in Arkansas?" he murmured. "Christmas Eve..."

She stared at him, so shaken by his closeness that she couldn't think for a moment.

"We were standing in front of a dying fire, like this one," he reminded her softly. His night-sea eyes roamed her face as if rediscovering it with reluctant pleasure. "I remember thinking that your hair looked like gold-and-copper filigree, shimmering in the light."

"We'd put presents in the stockings," she whispered, remembering with a soft smile. She slid her arm up around his neck and laid her head on his shoulder, closing her eyes in pleasure, feeling as if she had at long last come home. "I remember," she murmured on a sigh.

He bent his head and kissed her softly on the cheek, letting his lips brush across her skin in a feathery caress. That night had been a revelation to him. Her father had gone to sleep, and they had been left alone. It had been the night he'd first made serious love to her, finding her bare skin and secret places, patiently coaxing her into putting aside her shyness and caressing him in return. His blood heated at the memory.

"Was this setting intended to bring back old memories, Elizabeth?" he asked dryly.

"No," she said, hurt that he might think that of her. She lifted her head to look into his eyes, and her own eyes softened tenderly. "To tell you the truth, I hadn't thought of that night until you mentioned it."

He gently slid his fingers into her hair again, anchoring her head firmly in his grasp, holding her captive. His eyes glittered dangerously as he demanded of her in a low, taut voice, "So... you've forgotten...."

She knew that he was accusing her of forgetting what they had felt for one another, and she tried to shake her head in denial, but he wouldn't let her move.

He smiled bitterly and lowered his mouth, rubbing his lips sensuously over hers in a seductive caress. He envied her, in a way. He would have been spared years of quiet torture if he'd been able to forget.

"Never mind, Elizabeth. I'll give you a fresher memory," he murmured harshly. Then he pulled her fully against him and kissed her.

How much better to feel the reality of his embrace than the mere memory of it, she thought hazily, as she felt herself enfolded in his warm strength. She felt as if he were bringing her to life again by the masterful insistence of his magical kiss. Had he always been this tall? His arms this strong? His body this hard and enticing? And had his mouth always been this incredibly addictive? His taste such an elixir of desire? How could he be so much better than she had remembered, when in her memories, he had been everything she'd ever wanted in a man? Somehow, he was now even more.

Blake felt her relax into him, her arms lock behind his neck, her lips part to welcome him, and he wasted no time in pressing his advantage. Her lips were silky smooth, and he felt her tremble as he began to caress them with his tongue. She felt as fragile in his arms as the most delicate flower, and as untutored in the ways of love as a young girl with her first real beau. He knew that couldn't be the case, because he'd taught her about the basics of love himself fifteen years ago. All the same, he felt an intoxicating rush of male satisfaction at the delicacy of her reaction to him. It made him feel like a conqueror, like a welcome lover being greeted by his faithful mate. It was so close to his own lost dream of what she once was to have been to him, that it rejuvenated his anger and despair.

Elizabeth felt some of the coaxing drain out of him, then sensed the deliberation that seeped in to take its place. He kissed her persuasively, arousing her with the skill of a man determined to bring her pleasure and well able to do it. She wanted to resist, because she knew his hurt and distrust were the driving force now, but she had been alone too long, had yearned for him in her dreams too often, and she found that she didn't have the will to pull away.

His hands slid down her back in long, smooth strokes, making her warm and pliant and relaxed. His mouth moved warmly against hers, sending dainty tingles straight down to her toes. He murmured something dark and unintelligible, and she felt her heart begin to slam in slow, painful strokes against her chest. Then he was kissing her neck and lightly caressing her breasts through her blouse, and she heard a soft moan, barely recognizing it as her own.

"You've become even more beautiful than you were years ago," he murmured huskily, caressing her with words, with his voice, with every movement that he made. He kissed her ear and breathed against it gently, smiling against her as she shivered in pleasure. "Still like that?" He ran his tongue lightly around the whorls, smiling as she pressed more tightly against him and made an inchoate sound of appreciation.

Elizabeth slid her hands across his shoulders, savoring the sensation of touching him again after all these years. His firm, compact muscle and bone, neatly packaged, warm and hard wherever she roamed, was different from her memories. He was stronger, more solidly muscled, even more exciting than he had been before, and she would never have believed that possible until now.

His head was bent, and she realized he was loosening the neck of her blouse. Part of her cried out to slow down, that this increasing awareness and intimacy could only lead them both to more pain, and she feared that *her* pain might well be irreparable this time. Then she felt her blouse being pulled loose from her slacks and his hand caressing her bare skin, and all she could do was suck in her breath in pleasure.

"Smooth as silk," he murmured. He found the curve of her breast and slid his hand up underneath it, enjoying the pleasure of holding her again like this. He slid his thumb lightly across the surface, heard her softly moan and felt his body tighten in response to her obvious pleasure. She was wearing a bra, so he caressed her breast through the barrier, but he could feel her nipple harden beneath the filmy nylon without any difficulty at all. He smothered a groan.

He found her mouth again and kissed her, only he wasted no time with delicate preliminaries. His invasion was thorough and absolute, his tongue sweeping through in masterful strokes, increasing the pressure until she moaned in satisfaction and he began to feel the familiar pooling of blood in his groin. If he didn't slow down, he would have to take her to one of their rooms for the next level of exploration. He was a little too old to enjoy heavy petting in a living room, not to mention making love.

Elizabeth sank her hands into his hair, luxuriating in the closeness and intimacy between them, telling herself it was enough that *she* knew the truth of what lay between them. At least he still cared enough for her to want this, even if the strongest emotion he was feeling was the offspring of sexual desire and the remnants of a love that had turned to hatred.

She felt him slowly relax his hold on her and withdraw from the kiss, until their lips were barely touching anymore. He was staring down into her glazed and slightly confused eyes. He seemed distant, and she released her hold on him a little, allowing her arms to rest lightly on his. She wondered what he was thinking, but he was as unreadable as the Sphinx.

"Tell me, Elizabeth," he said with quiet intensity. "Did you let me kiss you, did you kiss me back, because you wanted to, or because Dorian expects it of you?"

Her head jerked back as if he had slapped her, and the pain that filled her eyes checked even his cynicism for a moment. She swallowed painfully and stepped back out of his arms. With as much dignity as she could muster, she said, "I kissed you tonight for the same reason that I kissed you fifteen years ago. Because I wanted to." *And because I love you.*

He sighed in frustration and ran a finger around his loosened collar, feeling very tired all of a sudden. The problem was that a part of him wanted to believe her. Damn it. Why did she have to look so sincere, anyway?

Elizabeth felt tears begin to fill her eyes, and she fought against them angrily. She'd never been a weepy woman, and she hated looking like one, especially now. She knew Blake would assume that it was another manipulation, another attempt to soften him. She turned away, trying to hide the damning evidence from his probing gaze.

"You don't trust me," she said, as calmly as she could. "I understand why. If I was in your shoes, I would feel the same way." She drew a steadying breath and jerkily reassembled her blouse with stiff, uncooperative fingers. "I guess I've said everything I wanted to say to you tonight, and it's really getting rather late, so, if you'll excuse me, I think I'll retire." She'd begun moving away from him, heading toward the door, and she walked a little more rapidly as she got farther away from him. "I know it's not very polite to leave a guest alone, but there's no one else down here to stay with you, and, under the circumstances, I'm sure you'll forgive me this little lapse in etiquette."

She was nearly across the room when she felt his hand on her arm and heard him murmur in frustration. "Wait, Elizabeth. We can't leave things like this."

She slipped from his grasp. It wasn't difficult; he didn't really try to restrain her. Without looking back at him, she hurried down the hall, nearly breaking into a run as she reached the stairs in the dark.

"Elizabeth!"

His voice merely spurred her on, and she ran up the stairs as fast as she could. She didn't stop until she had reached her room, slammed the door and locked it after her. She leaned against it, the tears falling hotly down her cheeks, her sobs muffled and broken as she fought to contain them. She heard his footsteps, heard him stop on the other side of the door and whisper, "Elizabeth . . . I want to talk to you."

She held her breath and kept absolutely still, but she knew he was aware of her presence. She felt him as surely as she felt the hard wood of the door beneath her flattened palms and cheek.

She heard what sounded like a sigh and a shifting of weight on the floor on the hall side of the door, as if he had stepped away and then hesitated again, undecided whether to press her or let it drop.

"Good night, Elizabeth," he whispered. "I'll see you tomorrow morning."

Elizabeth listened until she heard his door close. Then she slid down to her knees and wept. She still loved him. So very, very much. And she still wanted him. Desperately.

Chapter 8

Blake stood in the warm morning sunlight that was streaming through his bedroom window, wondering how much time he would have alone with Elizabeth in her workshop before the others joined them. He had slept restlessly, and he wasn't in the best of moods. Lost sleep and prolonged frustration made an unpleasant combination. He wanted a quick end to both, although he wasn't certain how he was going to accomplish that. First, he needed facts.

There were a few questions he wanted answered, starting with one that Elizabeth had already refused to reply to: How could Dorian make things "uncomfortable" for her if she failed to do his bidding? That claim had startled him. It had also concerned him. He didn't care for the sinister overtones. Elizabeth might have been fickle and untrustworthy, but he didn't want to see her turned into a prostitute by that old snake. He was surprised at just how fiercely he didn't want it, damn it.

Then there was that other burning inquiry that she had sidestepped: Who was the man she'd left him for, and what in the hell ever happened to the son of a bitch? He had told her that it didn't make any difference at this point, but it did. He didn't need to see the man, or know his name, but he did need to know what kind of man had supplanted him in her affections. That still gnawed at him. Blake cursed his irrationality, but it did no good. He couldn't free himself of the urge to uncover the truth.

Blake stalked across the room, running a hand through his hair in irritation, determined to go knock on Elizabeth's door and get things moving. If she wasn't awake yet, it was just too damn bad. He was getting sick and tired of being driven crazy by Elizabeth Rossi's mysteries. He wanted to cleanse his heart and soul of them, once and for all.

He jerked open his door and strode into the hall, only to halt in surprise within a few steps. He saw Elizabeth rounding the corner, pushing Karl in his wheelchair. She was chatting amiably with the nurse. Then, sensing his presence in the hallway, she looked up at him.

For a moment Blake felt the old familiar bond between them surge to life. It was as strong as it had been fifteen years ago when they'd been meeting in their secret glade in the woods.

He didn't want to feel that mystical bond tighten around his heart again, damn it all. He resented the attraction beginning to burn inside him again for her. He'd never made a fool of himself over other women. Why, then, was he tottering on the brink of making a pathetic idiot of himself a *second* time with *this* woman?

He should feel pure distrust and displeasure at seeing her, he knew, but instead he felt a strong surge of concern join his irrational sense of bonding. She looked pale and fragile as she pushed Karl's wheelchair toward him. Her eyes had the bruised appearance of one who hadn't slept well, and, with her tousled champagne-and-copper hair, she looked like an angel who'd been pushed from heaven's heights by an evil Lucifer.

His eyes fell to her lips, and his urge to offer sympathy was thoroughly drowned by an incredibly urgent need to pull her into his arms and kiss her senseless. He could have strangled her at that moment, so furious was he that she could so completely bewitch him.

The wheelchair squeaked slowly to a halt beside Blake.

"Good morning," Elizabeth said, trying to sound cheerful. It required an effort to smile, but she did her best. "Did you sleep well?"

"As well as could be expected." He smiled thinly and looked straight at her, saw color wash across her cheeks, and his smile twisted a little in bitter pleasure. At least he wasn't the only person here losing sleep. "You look as well rested as I feel," he observed, with as little sarcasm as possible.

Elizabeth looked exhausted and she knew it. Okay. So neither of them had found last night an easy experience, she silently admitted. She kept her plastic smile in place and wheeled Karl in the direction of her workshop.

"If you're interested in seeing some of my work, you're welcome to join us," she murmured.

Blake fell in behind her. "I thought Karl usually slept late."

"He does," Elizabeth said.

"But this morning, Miss Rossi thought it would be nice if her father came along and helped out," Cassie interjected eagerly. "And she came down to wake me up, too, so that I could see. Wasn't that nice of her?"

"It was a very thoughtful move," Blake agreed. "If I didn't know better, I'd think you were assembling a crowd, Elizabeth."

Elizabeth unlocked the workshop and opened the door. Cassie wheeled Karl into the room, and Elizabeth faced Blake for a moment as they stood together in the entryway.

"Were you afraid to be alone with me?" he asked, giving her a penetrating look. He spoke quietly; neither Karl nor Cassie appeared to have heard his question.

"Yes," she admitted with quiet dignity. "I was afraid." Her smile had disappeared, and now the look in her face was that of a woman eager to get through a difficult scene with as little damage as possible. She hesitated, as if still struggling to find the right words with which to persuade him. "I think it would be better for both of us if we weren't alone."

"What about your assignment from Dorian?" he asked sardonically.

Elizabeth's cheeks suffered another wave of color. "I told you last night that I wasn't going through with that." She nodded toward the work area. Karl and Cassie had now turned and were watching them. "I think we'd better get on with this. The sooner it's over, the better."

From the way she said it, though, it was clear that she wasn't just referring to showing him her work. She meant that the sooner the whole weekend visit came to a close, the better it would be for both of them.

Blake knew that he should wholeheartedly agree with that sentiment. Perversely, however, her stated desire to be done with it made him resist the idea.

Like a hound watching a fleeing rabbit, her running away made him want to pursue her. Realizing what was happening to him, unfortunately, didn't help him undo the feeling.

His hatred for her had eased into suspicion, and as the hatred had mellowed, it had made room for his passion for her to reappear. He still wanted her, physically, at least. He was still a little confused about the other feelings, but surely they could be sorted out after he met the most primal urge consuming him.

He watched her pick up a portfolio and show him photos of some of her work, and he knew that his plans for her had changed again in the last twenty-four hours. He wanted her, damn it, and this time he was going to have her. Not forever, of course. He wasn't so completely dominated by his sex drive that he'd ask her to marry him again! But he would have her until he was satiated with the taste of her, the feel of her, the warmth of her.

At least this time he wouldn't have to worry about her virginity. That particular issue had undoubtedly been resolved by some man years ago.

He watched her hands move across the page, remembering how they had felt on his body. The delicate scent of her perfume made him want to lean closer to her, and he leaned down, putting a hand on her back, as he looked over her shoulder at the photos. He felt her grow very still beneath his touch, felt her tense a little, and he smiled slowly.

Elizabeth was as physically aware of him as he was of her. That would make his seduction of her a little easier. With

Dorian urging her into his arms for business reasons, she would have difficulty avoiding going out with him. And once he had her alone, nature would be on his side in full force.

Blake smiled grimly. Nothing else had ever exorcised her. Perhaps making love with her would do the trick. Perhaps then he would be free of her at last.

Elizabeth turned her head and saw the expression in his eyes. The photo slipped from her fingers.

Their eyes met and held for a long moment.

"Is something wrong?" he asked softly, slowly gliding his hand down to the small of her back.

Elizabeth wasn't deceived by his casually voiced question. The seductive message she was receiving from his hand and the determined gleam in his eyes were impossible to misunderstand. Yes, something was wrong. She tore her gaze away from his and tried to find the photograph that had fallen from her nerveless fingers.

He bent down and retrieved it from the wooden floor before she could reach it. He was smiling as he returned it with a courtly flair.

"Thank you," Elizabeth murmured.

"You're welcome."

The warmth in his voice went beyond the customary platitude, making it sound more like an invitation than an acknowledgment. Elizabeth ignored it and quickly leafed through the next few pages of her portfolio.

A flash of brilliant greens and yellows caught Blake's eyes, and he stilled her hand by covering it with his.

"Wait a minute. I recognize that piece," he said, frowning. Surprised, he demanded, "Did you design that?"

Elizabeth pulled her hand from beneath his. "Yes. I also made it." She smiled slightly. "It took quite a bit longer than I had expected, but I think it was worth the effort. It turned out rather nicely, don't you think?"

He laughed. "Nicely?" he said incredulously. "Are you kidding? It's sensational, and you know it."

Elizabeth blushed in pleasure. She smiled, and there was a breathless quality she couldn't suppress as she said, "Thank you." Praise from a man with Blake's expertise was an honor, but in this instance, it was especially sweet for another reason, as well. She had rarely heard such words from the people who had bought her work over the years. Dorian had been the one speaking to them, not her. Their compliments had been lavished on his ears, not hers, and what little praise she had received had been filtered through his reluctant lips. He had been unwilling for her to discover how good she was.

Blake was still staring at the picture, wondering how in the devil he could have bought that necklace without having been informed that Elizabeth had designed it. Pieces of such originality and fine caliber were proudly attributed to their designers and craftsmen. Why not in Elizabeth's case? He delved into his memory, trying to recall what he had known about it. He clearly recalled being told it was the creation of one of Dorian's young but brilliant junior designers. He didn't know which feeling was worse, the fury of having been misled or the triumph of having now discovered the truth.

"I bought that necklace," he said, as if daring someone to deny it.

"Yes," Elizabeth agreed. "I know."

"How could you know that?" he demanded, thunderstruck. "I was dealing through a middleman in Paris, and I specifically told him to keep my name out of it."

Elizabeth smiled. "Jacques Martin is a friend of mine," she explained patiently. "He wanted me to know how much you had been taken with the piece," she admitted patiently. "He knew you wished to be incognito, so he didn't tell Dorian who you were, but he knew that I would not tell Dorian if he asked me not to."

"That sounds pretty bizarre," Blake pointed out, laughing in astonishment. "Why would he risk breaking faith with me to tell Dorian's designer that she had an admirer?"

"I think he wanted to keep my spirits up. You know, encourage me to design another one like it...." She sighed. "I hope you won't hold it against Jacques. He's a very kind man, and he was trying to help me. That was the first time he ever revealed your interest in my work, Blake." She paused and added quietly, "I never told Dorian what I knew. I gave Jacques my word that I wouldn't. So your secret is safe, from Dorian, anyway...." If that had ever mattered. She didn't know, but it was the best she could offer him.

Blake absorbed that in silence. It didn't make any sense to him. It sounded as if Elizabeth and Dorian were at war with one another, instead of being partners.

"All right," he conceded. "I won't mention it to Jacques." He smiled wryly. "That means that you owe me a favor for my silence," he murmured.

Elizabeth laughed, relieved that he was being so reasonable and forgiving. She knew he could have chosen to stop dealing with Jacques for such a fundamental breach of trust. She gave Blake a warm smile.

"Thank you," she said gratefully. "I know you won't regret it."

He lifted his brow in amusement. "You shouldn't thank me yet," he warned her. "You haven't heard what I want as a favor."

Her smile waffled.

Blake let her think about that. He was wondering why she would need to have her spirits supported by a Parisian diamond import-export specialist. Surely someone who had created such beautiful jewelry would have had more than enough encouragement over the years.

He glanced in frustration at Cassie, who was hanging raptly on their every word, and he silently cursed the crowd that Elizabeth had assembled as some sort of protection for herself. He didn't want to get into too much detail with an audience, especially when it involved not only personal matters but business ones, as well.

There will be another time, Elizabeth, he swore. You can count on it.

"Why isn't there some record of you in the transaction?" he asked on a more casual note. As he recalled, there had been only some sort of Rand insignia engraved on the piece.

Elizabeth hesitated. "I have kept in the background," she hedged.

"That is *painfully* obvious," Blake said dryly. "I want to know why."

"I don't think I'm under any obligation to tell you the answer to that," she objected testily.

"But you are, Elizabeth. After all, it appears that I may be one of your best customers," he said tightly. He flipped back through the portfolio, stabbing a photo when he recognized the piece. "I bought that sapphire dinner ring, and that set of diamond teardrop earrings, the yellow diamond and ruby necklace with earrings and matching bracelet, those matching marquise cut—"

"All right!" She grabbed his wrist, but the physical contact only made her feel worse, and she quickly let go of him. "All right," she said, trying for calm. "It's true. You've bought many pieces that I've created."

She had treasured each and every call that she'd had from Jacques, telling her about his customer in Washington. The first time, however, when she'd sold the necklace three years ago and Jacques had told her the truth, she had been in his store, and they had spoken in person, where Jacques had been certain no one else would hear what he was telling her. It had been the only time she'd heard the buyer's real name. Afterward, however, it had been easy to see a pattern. There had been several purchases a year, all through Jacques. Jacques had never admitted in so many words that the other pieces had gone to Malone's, but Elizabeth had thought that they probably had.

"Well, then?" Blake asked persuasively. "Why have you portrayed yourself to the outside world as one of a team of young, nameless designers in Dorian's employ?" His expression hardened. "Or was that impression just being given to me? Were others receiving more accurate information?"

"No!" Elizabeth exclaimed. "You weren't being singled out. All the retail buyers were being told the same thing."

Blake leaned closer to her, ignoring their audience. "Then why?"

"Because Dorian wanted it that way!"

Blake was stunned into silence. When he recovered his speech, he demanded in a growl, "Why in the hell did you let him get away with it? Why didn't you demand recognition? Or go somewhere else to work?''

Karl made a garbled noise, drawing Blake and Elizabeth's attention. He was pointing toward the two large steamer trunks occupying the one empty corner of Elizabeth's workshop and anxiously indicating that some action was needed right away.

Blake's frown became mystified. "What does he want?"

"I don't know," Elizabeth lied. She would never let Blake see the contents of those trunks.

"Can I help?" Cassie asked cheerfully. She hurried across the room, preparing to open them and fetch whatever was needed.

"No!" Elizabeth exclaimed. Seeing Blake's eyes narrow at her agitation, she forced herself to calm down. "There's nothing in there worth bothering with, Cassie. I think Father just wants me to show Blake the insignia that I use.'' She hadn't intended to show Blake that, but it was the only thing she could think of in a hurry to put him off Karl's real purpose.

Karl shook his head and growled, "No! Row! Row! Dre! Dre!" He was trying to say Rose! Rose! and Dress! Dress! but only Elizabeth understood him well enough to guess his meaning, and she chose to pretend that she didn't.

Elizabeth glared unhappily at her father and whispered fiercely, "You promised!"

He stuck out his lower lip stubbornly and glared right back at her.

Elizabeth gave her father a pleading look. "Darling, I don't want you to get upset. Please, please just let me handle this my way? I beg of you . . ."

Cassie, seeing her patient's agitation, had quickly returned to his side. Blake, trying to figure out what was going on between Karl and Elizabeth, turned to Karl himself.

"Do you want something in those trunks, Karl?" he asked softly.

Karl's eyes acquired an expression of confusion. He looked at Blake for a long time, then turned unhappily to Elizabeth. He was torn between two opposing avenues of action.

"Karl?" Blake repeated with soft insistence. "Can I help?"

Karl nodded vigorously, then closed his eyes and leaned his head against the back of his wheelchair. He seemed to have given up the herculean effort of trying to explain to Blake how he could help. He had done as much as he could for the present. He was going to sit on the sidelines a little while. He was too tired and confused to be certain of what to do.

"Father, are you all right?" Elizabeth asked urgently, leaning toward him. She placed a gentle hand on his withered knee, terribly afraid that having him "chaperone" had been an awful mistake. "Darling?"

He opened his tired gray eyes and stared at her in resignation. He waved his left hand toward the photos, indicating for her to go on with her show, that he would not interfere anymore. He looked like a man in defeat.

Elizabeth's heart squeezed in regret at what he was suffering. She knew, however, that if she didn't quickly refocus Blake's attention on her red herring, he would want to pursue Karl's concern about the steamer trunks.

"There is a way to identify my pieces of jewelry," she said.

"How?" he demanded, frowning both at the possibility he had missed her signature and at the fact that she was obviously redirecting the conversation.

Elizabeth picked up a small magnifying glass and handed it to Blake. Then she flipped through the photographic portfolio until she reached a picture displaying the reverse side of the necklace Blake had recognized. The piece had been stamped 18K for its gold content. A few inches away, she pointed to a small design engraved in the piece.

Blake examined it. A small rose had been stamped on the precious metal. As he looked more closely, he could see that it had been created by taking a small letter *r* and stamping it repeatedly in a circular rotation. The small *r*, placed like the spoke in a wheel, was difficult to discern, having been swallowed up by the larger pattern. Unless one looked closely, it simply looked like the lines to form the petal of the flower. He straightened.

"That is your signature?" he demanded.

Elizabeth nodded.

He frowned. "I remember examining that. It appears on a number of items. I was told it's a house stamp belonging to Rand, Limited, one that several of Dorian's designers use."

Elizabeth smiled. "Yes, but my rose is composed of an eight-*r* pattern. The others use nine."

"I see." He stared at it pensively.

"Maybe we should go down to breakfast," she suggested. "It's almost ten-fifteen...."

"In a minute." He searched through a few pages of the portfolio and relocated the photograph of the necklace. "I can't believe I bought this and never knew it was yours...." he murmured.

"Why should you have known?" she asked in surprise.

He glanced at her sharply. "Because I know you."

Their eyes locked. Elizabeth looked away first, her heart beating a little harder, as if she were already running from his pursuit.

Blake turned his attention back to the necklace. It was a stunning piece of yellow gold studded with emeralds and yellow diamonds. The yellow diamonds had been cut in ovals, then set in small beds of white diamonds. The emeralds, traditionally cut, had been delicately embellished with tiny yellow and white diamonds. The most intriguing aspect of the design, however, was the manner in which the large oval diamonds and rectangularly shaped emeralds had been settled into the liquid gold of the necklace. They appeared to have been dropped by a mighty hand as the molten gold had poured forth, smooth and flawless, like a river. The jewels were not evenly spaced, and yet the overall impression was one of balance. That was not an easy achievement. It had been one of the reasons that he had wanted to buy the piece when he had seen its picture in one of Dorian's quarterly catalogues. It was also one of the reasons that he had paid a very hefty price for it and received even more when he had sold it himself a few months later.

Blake looked at Karl. "She's done you proud," he said. He turned to Elizabeth, the admiration for her work unshielded in his eyes. "I have to admit, I'm surprised."

Elizabeth soaked up his praise with pleasure.

Dorian's voice at the door to her workshop destroyed the mood.

"There you are!" he exclaimed as he limped into the room. "Isn't Elizabeth magnificent?" he declared, having accurately assessed the mood.

"She certainly is," Blake agreed smoothly. "And I hope she'll agree to let me continue *renewing our acquaintance,*" he added. "It seems I have a great deal to learn."

Dorian cackled and nodded his head in approval. "There will be more than enough time for that, I am sure," he agreed.

Elizabeth's heart sank. Blake hadn't been listening to her, she thought in despair. She had told him last night that Dorian wanted her to spy on him, and what did he do? He was playing right into Dorian's hand, suggesting that he would like to see more of her! She slapped the portfolio shut and stood up abruptly.

"If we don't get downstairs to the buffet table, Mrs. Einer will be bringing the food upstairs to us," she said determinedly.

Cassie, ever hungry, took the hint and began to wheel Karl toward the hallway. "I'm starving! Aren't you Mr. Rossi? Mrs. Einer told me she was fixing blueberry pancakes this morning! I know you'll especially enjoy that ... After all, blueberries are kinda close to prunes, and remember how much you liked that prune compote?"

Karl made a disgusted sound as he was rolled down the hallway. Dorian laughed and followed along behind them.

Blake strolled beside Elizabeth as she fumbled with her keys and prepared to lock up. They were standing in the hall, but they could see Dorian, limping away from them at a snail's pace, glance slyly over his shoulder at them.

"Dorian is displaying his jewelry next Saturday, isn't he?" Blake asked. He already knew the answer, of course, but it was a convenient way to nail down Elizabeth's attendance, in case she was entertaining any ideas of not showing up. He didn't mind if Dorian heard what he was asking, either. It might prove to be useful in the long run.

"Yes," she admitted. She turned the key in the lock and started to walk down the hall after Dorian and the others. "I'll be there."

A smile spread across Blake's features. "I'm glad to hear that," he said.

"I can't imagine why," she muttered under her breath. She glanced at him sharply. "Weren't you listening to what I said?" she demanded in whisper. She didn't care if Dorian saw her aggressively attempting to drive Blake away. It was more important that Blake not be tempted to get involved.

Blake grinned. "I was listening to you," he whispered back. "And I was also doing a few other things to you, and you were doing them to me, and frankly, I liked it. I'd like to do it some more." He saw the rose color stain her cheeks, and he laughed softly. "You liked it that much? I'm flattered, Elizabeth."

"That's not why I'm blushing!" she whispered angrily, nearly stamping her foot in frustration. "I just can't believe you're letting yourself get pulled into this mess! Didn't you believe what I was saying?"

"I believed you." He lowered his voice and added, "And I'll bet that Dorian thinks we're whispering sweet nothings to each other, instead of fencing over whether I'm going to get to continue this conversation alone with you some other time."

She glanced at Dorian and saw his satisfied smirk as he stepped into the elevator. "You're probably right."

"Your boss must think you're doing a very good job of seduction," he pointed out dryly.

"I'm glad you find it all so amusing," she said in exasperation.

"Not exactly amusing," he admitted noncommittally. "Intriguing might be a more appropriate word."

He touched her back lightly with his hand as he stepped into the elevator with her.

"I'll look forward to seeing you next weekend at the display, then, Elizabeth," he said, speaking quietly, but no longer whispering. He glanced at Dorian. "You'll make sure that she doesn't try to run out on me, won't you, Dorian?"

Dorian chuckled. "Of course, my boy. It will be a pleasure. She'll be there." Dorian's eyes were beady, like a hawk's. "I can guarantee it."

"I thought you might," Blake murmured.

Elizabeth felt heartsick. Blake had trapped her. With Dorian knowing that Blake expected to see her there, she couldn't avoid going unless she had to be hospitalized. Apparently he was going to pretend to pursue her, she realized in dismay. She wasn't sure just how hot a pursuit he had in mind, but he was obviously going to continue seeing her for a while. Not knowing exactly what she was getting into was not a comforting feeling.

Blake looked down at her and teased, "You could look a little happier about it, Elizabeth. I swear on my honor as a gentleman, you'll have nothing to complain about."

She managed a doubtful smile. "I certainly hope you're right."

Blake laughed, and his relaxed attitude reassured the others, who had begun to wonder what to make of their strained conversation.

"It's been an interesting weekend, Dorian," Blake told his host as they walked into the dining room for the buffet brunch. "I hope I'll be able to return the favor someday."

Dorian chuckled slyly. "I am confident that you will, my boy. Absolutely confident."

Chapter 9

Blake was getting ready to leave Malone's to attend Dorian's pre-auction jewelry display the following Saturday evening when Alex and Grant walked into his office. They had been out of town on business for the previous week and were surprised to see him dressed up and on his way out.

"Not bad, Blake," Grant said admiringly as he looked over his partner's dark gray-striped suit and dress white shirt. He wiggled his eyebrows suggestively. "Who's the lucky girl?"

Blake laughed. "Give me a break, will you? I'm going to see what Dorian Rand's going to be offering at auction. Care to come with me?"

Grant held up his hand and shook his head. "Not if I can avoid it. Shelby's expecting me to pick her up in less than an hour."

Blake smiled. "Going someplace special?"

Grant looked in Alex's direction. "We've been invited to see how Alex and Sarah's place on the Chesapeake is coming along now that its sprucing-up is about done."

"The work's finished?" Blake asked in surprise, turning to Alex.

Alex nodded. "Yes. Thanks to a little help from my friend in the shadow side of government," he added in amusement.

Sarah's house had been badly damaged in a shootout involving Alex and a government intelligence operation that had gone sour. Two of her dogs had died in the hail of bullets. They had been irreplaceable. Her ramshackle house, however, had received an extensive facelift after she married Alex, and this weekend was its coming-out party.

"How is Sarah feeling?" Blake asked affectionately.

"Extremely pregnant," Alex said with a laugh. He shook his head. "I'll be glad when it's all safely over and behind her."

Grant and Blake both laughed sympathetically.

"Sarah wants you to drop in sometime, Blake," Alex told him. "She's got a new dog she's training, and she was hoping you could volunteer to test him . . . see if he'll follow her attack orders on a stranger."

"Terrific!" Blake groaned. "Why doesn't she use you or Grant? You're a couple of rough, tough types. I'm just a highly skilled craftsman!"

Grant snorted derisively. "You're not a wimp! Besides, the dog knows Alex and me. It wouldn't be a fair test."

Blake shook his head. "Why do you two always maneuver me into these corners?"

"Say, you've done your share of maneuvering!" Grant reminded him. "I have a very clear memory of being maneuvered into baby-sitting your old friend, Shelby. . . ."

Blake tried to look suitably shocked at his partner's analogy. "If it hadn't been for that, you'd still be a lonely, single man."

Grant laughed. "Yeah. Say, that reminds me. . . . You agreed to take off a month and enjoy the finer things in life this winter. So when in the hell are you going to do it?"

Blake fiddled with his tie and took his car keys out of his desk drawer. "Soon." Sooner than he had planned, certainly.

Alex looked a little dubious. "Could you narrow that definition a little? For example, will it be before or after Sarah goes into labor?"

Blake glanced at his wristwatch and gave his partners an apologetic smile. "That depends on when she goes into labor."

GOOD NEWS! You can get up to SIX GIFTS—FREE!

NO POSTAGE
NECESSARY
IF MAILED
IN THE
UNITED STATES

BUSINESS REPLY MAIL
FIRST CLASS MAIL   PERMIT NO. 717   BUFFALO, NY

POSTAGE WILL BE PAID BY ADDRESSEE

SILHOUETTE READER SERVICE
3010 WALDEN AVE
PO BOX 1867
BUFFALO NY 14240-9952

FIND OUT <u>INSTANTLY</u> IF YOU GET
UP TO 6 FREE GIFTS IN THE

Lucky Carnival Wheel

▼   **SCRATCH-OFF GAME!**   ▼

Scratch off ALL 4 gold areas

YES! I have scratched off the 4 Gold Areas above. Please send me all the gifts for which I qualify. I understand I am under no obligation to purchase any books, as explained on the opposite page.

240 CIS ACJD
(U-SIL-IM-05/91)

NAME

ADDRESS   APT.

CITY   STATE   ZIP

"Blake!" Grant and Alex chorused threateningly, standing shoulder to shoulder and staring at him intently.

Blake sighed. "Look...as a matter of fact, tonight is not just business. It's also pleasure. Does that help my case any?"

His partners looked unimpressed. They'd been hoodwinked before. Alex asked, "What's her name?"

Blake frowned. "It's a little early to be giving out names...."

"What's her name?" Alex repeated, laughing. "Hell, you know Grant and I will just start digging around and find out for ourselves if you won't tell us."

Grant seemed to think that was a good idea. "Sure. We'll just tail you, and when we see the woman, we'll walk up to her and ask her to identify herself, tell her that we have an interest in who our pal goes out with."

Blake groaned. "I'll bet you would, too."

Grant just laughed.

"Elizabeth Rossi," Blake said reluctantly.

Alex and Grant stopped smiling quite so broadly, and the teasing quality went out of their speech. They recognized the note in Blake's voice when he'd said her name. Elizabeth Rossi wasn't just a passing fancy. Something was going on here.

They followed him out into the showroom and helped lock up.

As he got into the elevator to go into the garage, Blake called out to them, "About that vacation . . . I'll take a rain check for the time being. Okay?"

"Sure thing," Grant drawled, shaking his head. "We'll make reservations for two, if you like."

Blake waved them off with a wry grin as the elevator doors slid shut.

"Won't Shelby love to hear about this!" Grant muttered with amusement. He turned to Alex and clapped him lightly on the back. "Come on, mon," he suggested, imitating the Caymanian patois of Alex's Caribbean roots. "Let's go get our wives and put up our feet for the weekend. Looking at Blake is making me remember how lonely life used to be."

Alex laughed. "I know what you mean."

The jewelry that would be going on the auction block was being stored in a bank vault. Since the more than forty pieces were expected to sell for close to four million dollars, the insurance company underwriting Dorian's theft/loss policy had insisted that the pre-auction display be conducted as close to the bank as feasible.

That turned out to be a fortuitous condition. One of Washington's poshest hotels was two doors down the street and fully accustomed to the intimidating stares of security guards. Political and business leaders from every corner of the globe stayed there, trailing their gray-suited bodyguards like a human cloak. The phalanx of guards and equipment that arrived with Dorian's jewelry was small in comparison to the brigades that checked in with some of the hotel's other guests.

Dorian had arranged to use a small ballroom on the second floor to show his precious wares. The jewelry was displayed behind special bulletproof glass, with armed guards posted at the exits and scattered around the room. Closed circuit television monitors were being watched continuously by a security employee in another room, with a telephone at his side in case it was necessary to call for assistance. The police had sent a plainclothes detective and a pair of uniformed officers to stroll through the proceedings, just in case anyone was foolish enough to try to steal any of the elegant baubles on display.

Dorian surveyed the elegantly dressed crowd flowing through the ballroom and chuckled.

"Do you think they're adding on another fifteen percent to their price estimates after seeing the expense the insurance company insisted we go to in order to protect these little beauties?" he asked of Elizabeth, who was standing at his side as she had been for the past hour, greeting newcomers and answering questions.

"At least fifteen percent," she murmured, smiling across the room at a potential buyer from Toronto who'd just flown in that afternoon. "Seeing all the armed guards makes *me* think they're worth a great deal more than I had thought," she admitted. She had to laugh. "And I already *knew* they were valuable."

Dorian motioned to the hotel employee coordinating the use of the room. When the man reached them, Dorian asked in a harsh, raspy whisper, "Are the musicians and hors d'oeuvres ready down the hall?"

"Yes, Mr. Rand." The man checked his watch. "Everything seems to be going very smoothly."

"Yes," Dorian conceded. Then his eyes narrowed. He'd seen a man enter the room, hesitate, and look around as if searching for someone specific. Dorian dismissed the hotel employee with a curt thank-you and growled under his breath at Elizabeth, "My sweet, I believe your assignment has arrived."

Elizabeth followed the direction of Dorian's gaze. It was Blake. Her assignment.

Dorian noted her hesitation with displeasure. "I am expecting you to provide me with the information I require, Elizabeth," he reminded her. "Have I made myself clear?"

She stiffened. "Perfectly." She gave him a cool look. "Just remember, Dorian, that Blake isn't a fool when it comes to business, and he isn't the type to be seduced."

Dorian laughed, and his face crinkled like worn leather at her description. "Malone isn't the type to be seduced?" he mocked her. "You have a great deal to learn about men, my dear." Amused, he added, "Perhaps your old flame will be the one to finally educate you." He chuckled again. "Not the type to be seduced, indeed!"

Elizabeth, who had been hoping for an excuse to separate herself from Dorian, decided that she had waited long enough.

"If you'll excuse me, I'll welcome our victim," she told Dorian with exaggerated sweetness.

"Remember, Elizabeth," he warned. "A practical woman makes the correct decisions. She does what is necessary."

Elizabeth's eyes flashed angrily. She turned on her heel, the skirt of her dress swishing as she quickly walked away.

She made her way across the room to Blake, but it was slow going. As people recognized her, she had to hesitate long enough to smile graciously or offer a brief response to their casual questions. She lost sight of him occasionally as people moved around, blocking her view, and she had to peruse the undulating sea of bodies to find him again.

Blake had spotted her, as well, and he was also working his way toward her. He had shouldered through several clusters of curiosity seekers when a plain-looking young woman in a mousy brown suit caught him lightly by the arm and engaged him in animated conversation. He was reluctantly answering a question she had asked when Elizabeth finally reached him.

"...so if you're still interested, Marian, why don't you come in next week ... say Thursday afternoon? We can talk about it then. Call Janet on Monday and have her pencil you in for an appointment. We'll have plenty of time then. All right?"

Mousy little Marian sighed rapturously. "Oh, thank you, Blake!" she cooed. "You don't know how much this means to me!"

Blake smiled. "My pleasure, Marian."

Then, as if alerted by some sixth sense, he turned to see Elizabeth standing behind him. The kindly smile that he had worn for shy, unassuming little Marian metamorphosed into a more mature, more calculating, more unsettling one.

"Elizabeth," he said in mock surprise. "What a pleasure to see you again." He made no effort to shield his admiration as he looked at her, taking in her appearance with interest.

She was wearing an electric-blue silk dress with loosely cut sleeves and a full skirt that gave it a frothy look. An intricately carved antique silver necklace and its matching, dangling earrings flashed brightly as they caught the light. Whenever she moved, ornately engraved silver bangles on her left wrist tinkled like Indian temple bells. Beneath his fascinated perusal, Elizabeth flushed with pleasure.

The young woman in the brown suit blinked owlishly at Blake and then at Elizabeth. They barely noticed as she murmured farewell and melted into the crowd flowing gently around them.

"I didn't mean to chase your friend away," Elizabeth murmured, struggling to feel genuinely apologetic. It was difficult. What she really felt was relief that the other woman had fled and guilty delight that she now had Blake all to herself.

Blake's smile became slightly amused. "My *friend?*" he asked, having heard the ambivalence that lay just beneath her lightly spoken words. "Do I detect a note of curiosity in your voice?" he teased.

Elizabeth, who could have shot herself for being so transparent, lifted her chin defensively. "Of course I'm curious. That's natural, don't you think? After all, I don't know anything about you anymore," she hurried to point out. She glanced into the throng of people who had closed ranks around the woman with whom Blake had been speaking. "For all I know she's a very important person in your life and I barged in at the wrong moment. I hope I didn't interrupt anything...." She trailed off lamely.

"You interrupted," he conceded, grinning at her discomfort. It was as close to jealous as he'd ever seen Elizabeth. "It doesn't matter. I'll see Marian later." He thought he'd let it dangle like that for a moment. He found he enjoyed the spark of green in Elizabeth's eyes.

"Marian?"

Blake looked at her curiously. "You really wonder about her?"

"I'm merely making conversation," she said testily. She frowned. The conversation was not going the way she had planned it. "Look, I really came over to welcome you and to see if you had any questions about the jewelry. I didn't mean to—" she glanced unhappily in the direction that Marian had vanished "—I didn't mean to interfere with your personal life."

He saw her stop dead in her conversational tracks and try to figure out why they were suddenly sparring like suspicious lovers. It came as something of a jolt to him, too. He had sensed Elizabeth's feminine curiosity about Marian and enjoyed using it to tease her. He had wanted to find some way to prick her emotions, to inflict some small pain on her, and that wasn't like him. He frowned. He had to put a stop to this, for his own sake as well as Elizabeth's. It would be better for both of them if they kept their fencing honest.

"Marian has been interested in becoming an apprentice to a watchmaker in Gaithersburg," Blake explained. "He happens to be an old friend of mine, and Marian wants me to give her a reference." He saw the trust, the relief, in Elizabeth's eyes and was glad he hadn't chosen to taunt her about the shy young woman.

"She looked at you as if you were standing on a pedestal," Elizabeth murmured, feeling a great deal of sympathy with Marian in that regard. She tended to think of Blake that way herself.

Blake shrugged philosophically. "I'm an older man. She's an impressionable young woman." He could see that Elizabeth wouldn't ask, didn't want to appear to pry, but was wondering how he came to know Marian. He paused for a moment, trying to decide if he should let her wonder. It seemed a churlish thing to do, especially since there were absolutely no grounds for jealousy when it came to his relationship with the woman. "Marian worked for Malone's for the past three summers. She was attending college and needed a job. She's the friend of a daughter of one of my other employees. I've known her for several years." He looked directly into Elizabeth's beautiful eyes and added, quite distinctly, "I make it a point not to seduce my employees, if that's what you're not asking." When Elizabeth's cheeks colored with embarrassment he added, very softly, "I also make it a rule to avoid seducing women who are still too young to know what they're getting into." Elizabeth, you of all people, ought to know that, he thought grimly.

"You didn't have to explain," she murmured, staring at him, wondering why he had.

There was a peculiar expression in his eyes as he said, "I disagree."

Elizabeth's heart turned over, and she smiled at him tremulously. "You're still a very kind man at heart, Blake," she murmured.

Someone jostled Elizabeth, pushing her a step closer to Blake. He caught her gently by the arm, steadying her. For a moment they stood together, absorbing the unexpected sense of closeness that was enveloping them. Neither of them wanted to break the spell by speaking or moving.

A jeweler from Amsterdam, oblivious to their silent communion, strode over to ask Elizabeth a question. She answered him, but her eyes barely left Blake's face. He, in turn, never released his light hold on her arm. The jeweler, a little mystified by the response he received from them, wandered into the crowd, mumbling under his breath.

"Now Jan will be spreading tales about us," Blake murmured, his eyes locked with hers.

Elizabeth blinked. "I suppose he will," she murmured uneasily, then smiled. "That will please Dorian, but I hope it doesn't cause you any problems."

"None that I can't handle," Blake murmured. He nodded toward the assembly of would-be buyers. "They remind me of bees hunting down the tastiest pollen." He put her hand through his arm and maneuvered them through the crowd. "Why don't you give me a personalized tour of the clover?"

"I told you last weekend that Dorian has put me completely at your disposal," she reminded him. Embarrassment sharpened her voice.

Blake's eyes narrowed. "Yes. So you did." He saw a dealer from Hong Kong bearing down on them. "Before Mr. Sen grabs you, why don't you take me through the display and give me your most persuasive sales pitch?" he suggested neutrally.

Elizabeth tried to ignore the traitorous warmth sliding over her at his nearness, the wonderful sensation of pleasure at listening to his voice.

"All right," she agreed, smiling into his enigmatic eyes. "Come with me. Dorian really has some spectacular pieces going on the block. I'm sure you'll find something worth bidding on."

"I'm sure you're right," he murmured.

It took them nearly two hours to examine the forty-odd pieces on display. Blake took his time, pausing to examine each one through his jeweler's loupe. The bulletproof glass distorted the examination a little, but he could still make a more critical assessment of the gems through the loupe than he could by simply relying on the naked eye.

Elizabeth had been correct, he decided. It was a spectacular selection of jewelry. Some pieces had been crafted two hundred years ago. The most recently made piece had been fashioned five years ago in Bulgaria by an eighty-year-old goldsmith whose name was enough to put a five figure price on any piece of jewelry, sight unseen.

There were pieces in 18k yellow gold, in platinum, and in combinations of the two precious metals. They were inlaid with rare blue sapphires from Kashmir, the finest early Colombian emeralds, pigeon's blood rubies fit for a queen, and flawless diamonds that literally took the viewer's breath away with their brilliantine fire.

Some of the most famous designers of the last two hundred years were represented among the items on display. Dorian had bought them over the course of his fifty years in the jewelry business, saving them until now to sell. They had been his life insurance policy, his old age pension, his gem-studded, golden nest egg.

There was a piece of jewelry presumed to have been smuggled out of Russia during the Bolshevik Revolution. It was reputed to have belonged to the czars. The Russian emeralds mounted on the 18k gold brooch hadn't been seen on the market for decades. Then there was the delicate gold necklace set with demantoid garnets from the Urals. Quite a crowd had gathered around the garnets; no one in forty years had seen any of these rare, fiery green, "Uralian emeralds" outside of the personal collections of a few wealthy families.

When they had finished examining the last diamond-encrusted bracelet, Blake put his loupe inside his suit pocket.

"That's quite a collection," he admitted. He frowned slightly.

"What is it?" she asked cautiously.

"I don't understand why Dorian is so eager to discover how much money I'm willing to spend. He'll have no trouble at all getting top prices for these. And if he doesn't get the prices he wants, all he'll have to do is wait a few years. Their value is only going to increase."

Elizabeth shrugged. "I have no idea why he wants to know," she admitted. "He hasn't confided in me." She smiled ruefully. "He doesn't trust me."

Blake laughed. "He's certainly astute." No one had ever accused Dorian of stupidity.

She began backing away. "Well, now that you've seen everything, I've done my duty." She glanced around, wondering where Dorian had gone. "I had better get back to Dorian and see what else he wants me to do today. The security people are going to want to close things up in the next hour. They've been going crazy having the display last this long...."

Blake's hand closed warmly around her wrist, and he pulled her gently toward him.

"You may have done your duty," he conceded dryly. "But you aren't finished quite yet."

"I'm not?" She had little choice but to follow along as he pulled her through the crowd. He was taking her toward one of the exits. "I can't leave...." she protested.

"Why not? Dorian won't object. You're with me."

"But . . ."

"I want to talk to you without wondering who's overhearing everything we say," he told her quietly, bending his head a little closer and pulling her next to his side as he spoke. He let his lips brush the hair at her temple. "I insist. . . ."

A light flashed, and they looked up in surprise to see a camera being pointed at them by someone wearing a press badge.

"It looks like we're candidates for the gossip columns," Blake observed.

Elizabeth groaned. "I'm sorry."

Blake laughed. "What for? You'll only make my other women friends jealous," he teased.

Elizabeth bristled. She didn't care for his observation at all. "Well, maybe I should charge for the help I'm giving you," she muttered.

He laughed again and hustled her through the metal detectors out into the hallway. Music was floating in the air, and the murmur of people strolling through the plushly carpeted halls replaced the sounds of the display they had left behind.

"Did you bring a purse?" Blake asked.

"No. I came with Dorian." They had hired a driver, so she hadn't needed car keys. Someone was always at the house to let her in, so she hadn't needed her house keys, either. It had seemed foolish to bring money, and she was going to need both hands free to shake hands with people and point out items of interest, so she'd left the purse at home.

He put his hand on the middle of her back and firmly steered her into the room where the small orchestra was playing. There was a dance floor in the middle and tables scattered around the edge, filled with people.

Elizabeth looked at Blake fatalistically. "You're playing into Dorian's hands again," she told him reluctantly.

"The hotel has a band, hors d'oeuvres and drinks every week," Blake told her. He looked at her in mild surprise. "Dorian coordinated his display so that there would be music and hors d'oeuvres close at hand?"

She nodded.

Blake laughed. "I have to hand it to the old fox. He certainly plans well. In this particular instance, I find myself quite indebted to him." He pulled her into his arms, pressing her resisting body close when she would have drawn away. "Don't hold back, Elizabeth. It's your duty to try to get as close to me as you can."

He began moving slowly to the music, and Elizabeth followed him automatically. She put her arm around his shoulders and accepted his firm grip on her hand, but she leaned a little away in order to see his face.

"Is this your idea of finding a place for quiet conversation?" she asked suspiciously.

His eyes were gleaming with amusement as he murmured, "No, Elizabeth. This is my idea of finding a good excuse to hold you in my arms again."

Her mouth dropped, then snapped shut. Maybe he was kidding, she thought.

He looked at her and shook his head. "No. I'm not kidding." He pulled her close and leaned his chin against the top of her head. "Relax," he murmured. "We're just old friends enjoying each other's company. What harm can come of that?"

She closed her eyes and leaned her cheek against his jaw. What harm? She didn't know. There was a niggling fear deep inside her heart that warned her not to relax in his arms, that great pain could come to her if she did. That small cry of warning faded away, however, as she became aware of the man in whose arms she was held.

Blake danced with an ease that was contagious. It took no effort to follow his lead. With her eyes closed, her body moving in synchrony with his, it was easy to let the feeling of oneness envelope her.

His arms felt strong, and his body was hard and warm through the many layers of clothes. The rustling of her dress against his trousers made her want to snuggle closer to him. Embarrassed at her own eagerness, she tried to pull a little away.

He pulled her tightly against his body, muttering, "Cut it out."

She heard the slight strain in his voice and realized that he was enjoying the closeness as much as she was. She sighed, wishing the years could somehow melt away and they could pick up where they had left off fifteen years ago. Even if it was just for a night.

She felt the skin of his cheek against her temple, rougher than hers and warmly intoxicating. She shyly slid her fingers back to his neck, letting them brush the soft hair above his collar. His jaw tightened; she felt the muscles tense against her cheek, and she smiled. At least they still had physical attraction in common. It was too bad they couldn't do anything about it, she thought wistfully.

She had always loved being in his arms. The years had just intensified that, apparently. His nearness was making her feel warm all over. A peculiar eagerness was filtering into her system, making her senses more acute. Everything about him was becoming an aphrodisiac, she realized hazily. The touch of his hand sliding warmly down her back, the hardness of his torso against her tightening breasts, the pressure of his knee against her thigh as he turned her smoothly in rhythm with the melancholy love songs.

She whispered, "We shouldn't be doing this."

"Shhh." His breath warmed her ear, and he tightened his hold on her, pulling her more intimately into his embrace. "We should have been doing this for years and you know it," he murmured huskily. He pressed a light kiss along her ear. "Forget about everything for a few hours, all right? I think we deserve that much."

It was so close to what she had been thinking herself that she sighed her acceptance and relaxed in his arms.

"'Til midnight, it's just the two of us," she agreed. "Like Cinderella," she added whimsically, smiling.

"Like Cinderella," he agreed, pressing his advantage with another light touch of his lips to her throat.

The evening passed like a dream to Elizabeth. It was everything she could have asked for, if anyone had solicited her opinion.

They danced, sampled the delicacies and drank the wine until eight o'clock. Mellowed by the physical closeness and the alcohol, Elizabeth was happy to accept Blake's invitation to dinner. It seemed natural to her that he would walk hand-in-hand with her to the dining room, get them an expensive table in the corner by quickly pressing money into the head waiter's palm.

"Dorian must have left already," Elizabeth murmured in surprise, glancing at Blake as they sat down.

"He saw us dancing."

"Why didn't you say something?"

"And spoil the mood?"

Elizabeth felt a moment of uneasiness at the dry amusement in his voice, but she shook it off. Anyway, Dorian had given his tacit approval to her staying, apparently. That was no surprise, of course.

"I guess I'll have to find my own ride home," she said good-naturedly. "How much are taxis around here, anyway?"

Blake's smile was a quick flash of white teeth. "I'd consider it a privilege to offer you my services, ma'am."

Elizabeth laughed, and this time the sparkle returned to her eyes. "Thank you. I accept."

The wine steward came by, and Blake asked Elizabeth for her preference and made a selection. Then he leaned back in his chair and smiled at her.

"We have fifteen years of stories to exchange," he said easily. "Where shall we begin?"

Elizabeth swallowed. Not at the beginning, she thought. Hastily, she suggested, "Why don't you tell me how you started up Malone's?"

His smile hardened ever so slightly, as if he had cynically expected her to avoid sharing her own history. "All right," he agreed. "Casper Anders owned the Anders Jewelry Stores in San Francisco and Washington. I went to work for him after I left Arkansas." He paused fractionally. "Casper was an old friend of my grandfather's, and had no children of his own. When he died a few years after I started working with him, he left everything to me."

Elizabeth was fascinated. She hadn't known any of the details of Blake's business beginnings. She laced her fingers and rested her chin on them. "Did you keep the San Francisco shop?" she asked.

"Not for long. It made for a stronger business to consolidate in Washington at the time. The capital was just beginning to boom. People with money were pouring into the area, real estate prices were skyrocketing, the world's wealthy were arriving in droves." He smiled wryly. "I wanted to make luxury jewelry purchases easy for them, so I sold out the San Francisco holdings and used the extra capital to build up the Washington store." He shrugged. "A decade of hard work later and here we are."

Elizabeth smiled and shook her head. "You've left out all the gory details," she pointed out. "I heard about a couple of the battles you had with diamond cutters in Brussels and jewelry designers in Paris...."

He lifted a brow in surprise. "Really?"

Elizabeth nodded her head. "You've been a very astute businessman."

"Thank you."

"And you've kept your sense of taste. The pieces I saw at Malone's were exquisite."

"I'm flattered that you found them attractive."

The steward came with the wine and poured it. Elizabeth took a sip as Blake stared at her with a curiously intent expression in his eyes. She wondered if she had been a little rash in spilling forth her praise for him. Then they ordered dinner, and the intent look vanished, replaced by the easygoing courtesy that she remembered so well.

He had always known how to make her feel important, and the intervening years had only improved his ability, she discovered. He kept his eyes on her when they talked, as if she were the only person in the room. He smiled and teased and joked with her on a wide variety of subjects, from mutual business acquaintances in Europe to the latest gossip in the news. He managed to draw her out, in spite of her reluctance to tell him too much about herself. Before she knew it she'd told him about the early days with Dorian and Karl in Switzerland, while Karl was going through rehabilitation and she was struggling to learn design at a professional level.

"Is that when you learned to ski?" he asked casually as their plates were being cleared away and their after-dinner coffee was being poured.

Elizabeth blinked. "How did you know that?"

He shrugged. "Lucky guess." His eyes narrowed slightly. "I hear the ski instructors in the Alps are very successful with the *frauleins,*" he teased softly.

"Is that a roundabout way of asking me if I got involved with any of them?" she asked, laughing, although a little nervously. He was smiling, but she noticed the intent look had returned to his eyes.

"As a matter of fact, it is."

Elizabeth felt a small whisper of concern. There was something about the way he admitted his interest that bothered her. Every feminine instinct cried out that his interest wasn't as casual as he wanted her to believe.

"I enjoyed the company of a few people," she stalled. She didn't really want to get onto the subject of her social life, not to mention her nonexistent sex life.

"Enjoyed the company?" he repeated thoughtfully. "Is that a euphemism for something?"

"No. It means just what it sounds like it means," she said, rather stiffly. She folded her napkin and placed it carefully on the table.

They sat in silence for a long moment. A subtle tension had invaded what had been a relaxed and easy familiarity. Elizabeth wondered what had happened.

"Thank you for the dinner and the conversation," she said quietly. "I've enjoyed it very much. More than I was expecting, to be honest."

She smiled shyly. It was easy to say it, glowing with the wine and the intimacy and the hours of talking and dancing. She sighed. It was getting close to ten-thirty. By the time he drove her home it would be eleven, or later. It was time to close the Pandora's box they had opened and return to the safety of their separate lives.

"It's getting rather late, for me, anyway. So would you mind driving me home now?" she asked quietly.

"Certainly," he agreed smoothly.

Elizabeth had the feeling that this was too easy. Some ancient instinct warned her the evening was not yet over.

"My car is in the garage," he said, touching her arm lightly as they left the dining room. "This way..."

Chapter 10

It was close to eleven when Blake pulled his car in front of the curving staircase, doused the headlights and killed the motor. It was dark, except for the faint light of a quarter moon and the distant floodlights illuminating the mansion's exterior.

The late March night air was chilly and damp, but inside the car, Elizabeth felt numb. Blake had played a tape as he drove her home, easing the silence that had stretched between them on the long drive. Now there was nothing to relieve the quiet.

Blake sat back in the seat and looked at her.

She reached for the door handle, murmuring, "Thanks again for dinner, and the ride home, and . . ." He pressed down the master control, locking all the doors in the car. As the locks clicked, Elizabeth twisted to look at him warily.

"We have until midnight," he reminded her softly, resting his arm along the back of the car seat. "This car won't turn into a pumpkin quite yet."

"Perhaps not, but I'll turn into a very tired-looking old crone if I don't get to sleep."

"I find that hard to believe." He touched the back of her neck lightly with his fingertips.

The feathery sensation made her shiver.

"Cold?" he asked softly.

"No."

He smiled slightly. "I don't believe you." He caressed her cheek with his knuckles. "Your skin is icy." His gaze dropped to her lips. "I had the heater on. The car is warm. Now why would you be cold? Surely you're not afraid of me?"

The delicate kiss of his knuckles across her cheek made her half close her eyes. The cadence of his voice was soothing, inviting her to lay her head on his shoulder, to slide her arm around him, to feel the touch of his lips on her throat again. Lightly. Gently. With a soft promise of heat. A hint of latent desire.

"You're not quite finished yet," he told her softly.

His eyes were hypnotic, she thought, as she found herself staring into them, drowning in his dark, intent gaze.

"I'm not?" she murmured. She should leave. But she was so tempted to stay. So very tempted. She licked her lips and saw his eyes drop to follow the sweep of her tongue over her mouth, saw his eyes darken and his face become still and serious. A rush of awareness coursed through her like the fabled March winds.

He pulled her across the seat to him, bringing her into his arms and half onto his lap.

"You're supposed to seduce me," he reminded her huskily, brushing his lips lightly across her cheek, making her shiver again.

She tried to pull away, but his arms tightened. She pleaded with her eyes and then her voice, "Let me go, Blake. Please..."

"I wish I could," he muttered. He ran his fingers through her hair, then anchored his hand in it with a twist of his wrist, cradling her head firmly. "Stay with me yet awhile," he murmured whimsically.

She wanted to resist the pull of his low, coaxing voice, his firmly insistent hands, his dark and compelling gaze. She wanted desperately to resist them all, but she knew as he slowly lowered his mouth to hers that she didn't have the will to do it.

His lips touched hers, gently. The petal soft kiss, the warmth of his breath, the sweet scent of his skin, were indescribably intoxicating to her. She moaned softly and slid her arms around him, closing her eyes as she slowly gave herself up to his embrace.

The sensation of her yielding had a devastating affect on him. As her arms went around him and her mouth softened beneath his, desire burst into flames within him. Heat raced through his veins and poured across his skin. He wanted to strip away her clothes and feel her naked skin against his. Her softening brought out the deeply buried ruthlessness within him. He wanted to make love to her in the most primitive, brutal way possible, branding her as his.

Hungrily, he slanted his mouth and pulled her roughly against his rapidly heating body. He smothered a sound of pleasure as she instinctively responded to him by parting her lips to receive his invading tongue. He caressed her lips and mouth with slow, sensuous strokes, moving in the rhythm that gave them both the most pleasure. He stroked her body with one hand in long, exciting caresses, following her curves, sliding around them, back up across them, arousing her surely and steadily with each skillful sweep of his hand.

Elizabeth ran her hands through his hair, down across his neck and shoulders, eager to touch him, frustrated at the thick layers of clothing that kept his body from her palms. Then he was pulling her hands roughly inside his jacket, freeing his shirt from his pants, sliding her hands beneath his T-shirt. He made a low sound of pleasure as she touched his bare, warm skin.

His mouth was still working its magic on hers, and her dress had somehow been loosened as she reveled in touching his chest with its light dusting of hair and firm muscle. She felt him pull the top of her dress down to her waist and threw back her head as he lowered his head to her breasts. His mouth was warm and enticing against the soft skin, then suddenly her bra was loose and his hands were on her breasts, caressing, teasing, rousing the flesh into rosy pouts.

He lifted her up in his arms a little, and his mouth closed over her nipple. As he slowly ran his tongue over the tightly knotted flesh, Elizabeth gasped and clutched his shoulders.

"Too light a touch?" he murmured against her breasts, running his hand across the delicate skin.

"No," she moaned softly, sinking her face against his dark hair. "It feels wonderful...."

He heard the unmistakable note of deep pleasure vibrating in her voice, and his own arousal deepened in response. He ran his tongue over the other nipple, flicking it gently, holding her tight every time she flinched in pleasurable reaction. He could almost feel the pleasure coursing down through her body in his own, fire from the tiny nipple spiraling downward deep into the heart of her desire, making her want more, and more, and more.

She caressed his chest convulsively, stroking in rhythm with the sweep of his tongue on her breasts, harmonizing with the downward motion of his hand on her hips and thighs. The pressure was building deep inside her, the heat enveloping her until there was nothing in the world but Blake touching her, arousing her, exciting her.

Loving her.

She choked back a cry. How she wished he did still love her. How desperately she wished that. She slid her hands down to his hips, remembering how wildly they had loved each other once. How abandoned they had been with each other. How eager to touch, to kiss, to laugh and please each other.

He was even better now, she thought hazily, as she felt his hand glide smoothly up the inside of her thigh, caressing her through the fine nylon of her pantyhose, applying light pressure at first, teasing her into readiness.

She tried to pull away from his questing hand, murmuring, "No . . . we can't . . . ."

But he lifted his head from her breasts and fastened his mouth on hers ruthlessly, holding her still with his iron strength, finding the damp swell of her secret body with the skillful, feathery light touch of his fingers.

"We can," he growled against her lips as he lifted his head to look into her glazed eyes.

He pressed the heel of his hand gently against her hidden apex, smiling grimly as her face contorted at the pleasure that pulsed through her lower body in response to his touch. Urgently, he kissed her lips, her cheek, her throat, her shoulders, sending wave after wave of sensation pouring across her, within her, through her. And always he applied just enough suction, just enough pressure, to keep her begging him silently for more.

He rotated his hand in a slow circle, and she lifted her hips helplessly in response.

"Elizabeth," he moaned against her mouth. "Touch me."

It was an order, but there was pain, and need, buried within it that twisted Elizabeth's heart. He shifted them so that he was half lying across the seat, holding her half over him, and he loosened his belt, pulling her hand to his crotch. He was hard and swollen, and he moved her hand slowly over his arousal, his eyes closing, his breath hissing in pleasure as she took over the rhythm for him, slid down the zipper, found his aching flesh.

It was as if the years suddenly fell away between them, and they were in the backseat of his second-hand car, pressed together so that they could imitate making love without actually going all the way. Elizabeth pushed him down on the front seat, straddling him as she had years ago, her dress bunched up around her waist, her breasts swaying against his naked chest, staring down into his glittering eyes as his face hardened in passion and he caressed her eager flesh.

He pulled her hips in a slow rocking motion against him, letting her slick, nylon-covered body flow across him.

She felt the tightening deep inside her begin, and she looked at him helplessly. He knew what was happening, and he smiled grimly.

"Not this way," he muttered harshly. He gripped her hips with his hands, holding her still, keeping her on the knife edge of release, not letting her climax.

She was shaking with need, helpless in his hands. "Please," she whispered brokenly. *I love you.* She had never been very forward with him when they were younger, letting him remove their clothes, letting him take the lead. But she wanted him more intensely than she had ever in her life wanted anything or anyone. He knew it, she realized. But the knowledge did nothing to ease her desperation. "Please," she whispered again, lowering her lips to his, kissing him with every ounce of pleading and persuasion she could.

"Please what?" he demanded softly, holding her a little away from his throbbing body, gritting his teeth against the nearly overwhelming urge to strip her and take her there in the car. God, how was he going to keep from doing it? he wondered desperately. He closed his eyes, trying to take a long, deep gulp of air to cling to.

Her mouth near his ear, she was sprawled across his chest, begging him, "Please love me...."

He smiled grimly. "I've wanted to hear you say that for a long time," he admitted. His voice was rough from the effort it was taking to rein in his rampaging need to consummate what they'd begun.

"You wanted to hear me beg you to make love to me?" she asked, her voice shaking.

He locked his arms around her back and buried his face in the sweet softness of her neck. "Yes, damn it. I wanted you to beg me for that," he growled. "I've wanted to hear you say it for fifteen years. Why in the hell does that surprise you, Elizabeth? What kind of man did you think I was? I never forgot."

Tears welled in her eyes, and she clung to him. She loved him so much, she shook with it. If having her beg for him would help him heal at long last, she was willing to beg, she realized. She loved him that much. It was incomprehensible to do such a thing for anyone else, but not for Blake. For him, anything.

He lifted her a little away, holding her by the shoulders, trying to discover where the wetness on his cheek was coming from. "You're crying," he muttered. Part of him was glad she was hurting. He still hurt, damn it. His heart hurt. And right now, his groin hurt like hell. But something within him broke when he saw the vulnerable expression in her eyes, fringed with tear-wet lashes. He pulled her down onto him and held her comfortingly. Sighing, he admitted, "I've never been a bastard to any woman until tonight. I'm sorry Elizabeth. I guess I never completely accepted being jilted." He hesitated, not wanting her to misunderstand. "It's not that I still...love you." It was hard to say the words. He was a little surprised at just how hard. He stumbled over the rest of it quickly. "But I still want you. Obviously."

She put her hands on his shoulders and pushed herself up to look at him. He was so handsome, even looking a little disgusted with himself and exhausted and sexually frustrated. She tenderly cupped his face with her hands.

"We aren't kids anymore," she said slowly.

His eyes were dark with arousal, his body still hot and hard with desire, but his voice was relatively controlled as he muttered, "True enough." A grin tugged at his mouth as he added, "Although you make me feel like a kid again. I can't remember the last time I resorted to seduction in a car. Probably not since we steamed up the windows together back in Arkansas."

Elizabeth giggled, partly in reaction to the nerve-racking situation they were in, partly in relief that his sense of humor had not yet deserted him, in spite of everything.

She kissed him lightly on the mouth, but when he would have deepened the kiss, she pulled away.

"What I meant," she said shyly, "was that, since we're not kids anymore, it's no one's business if we . . . want to do this."

He lay very still beneath her, his hands frozen at her waist. There was a wary expression in his eyes as he stared up at her.

"What exactly are you trying to say?" he asked.

Elizabeth blushed. She wasn't sure how you were supposed to phrase something like this. If she didn't say it in the next minute, she was going to lose her nerve, she thought. She remembered the look of deep pain on his face when he had confessed his need to hear her beg for him a few minutes ago. That was enough to spur her on.

"When we parted fifteen years ago, we had some unfinished business."

He stared at her. She couldn't be saying what he thought she was saying. It had to be his libido trying to hear what it wanted, he thought.

Elizabeth swallowed and forged ahead. "We were two people left on the brink of physical intimacy, with all our fantasies and desires tangled up together."

He lifted a brow and reminded her, cynically, "That may describe me a little better than you. You apparently shifted your fantasies elsewhere."

She lowered her eyes and turned her head away. "That's not quite true," she hedged. "But in any event, it's left us . . . frustrated."

He laughed, a trace of harshness in the sound due to his current condition. "I'm certainly in no position to argue with that at the moment," he agreed. He slid his hand up across her throat and slowly down across her bare breasts, watching in fascination as her skin puckered anew beneath his touch. "And you give a convincing performance as a woman whose body is willing. I'll grant you that."

She smiled at the grudging tone in his voice. He was having a hard time believing that she really wanted him, she realized. Any reservations she had melted away then. She could sacrifice her pride for his.

"I'm trying to make you a proposition," she told him, her voice trembling in spite of her best effort to sound blasé.

His hand stilled on her breast, and his eyes jerked upward to hers. "Are you serious?" he asked in surprise.

She nodded. She rubbed her breast gently against his hand and closed her eyes in pleasure, letting him see how much she enjoyed his touch. When she opened her eyes again, she saw that he was willing to listen. Not convinced. But willing to hear.

"Could we go away, Blake?" she asked tentatively. "Just for a weekend, say. Someplace where we could be alone? Finish what we started fifteen years ago?"

He stared at her for a solid minute. "You *are* serious," he said at last, a little amazed.

She sank against his chest and buried her face in his neck, cuddling against him. When his arms closed around her protectively, she sighed and kissed his throat. Her legs tangled with his. Her whole body spoke to him of affection, of trust, of surrender.

"All right," he agreed slowly. "That might be the best way to take care of this." He gently held her jaw, turning her mouth so he could kiss her deeply and satisfyingly, sealing their bargain. "When do you want to do it?"

She smiled against his jaw. "As soon as possible," she whispered unsteadily. She trapped his thigh between her legs and squeezed against him. She wanted him, and she wanted him to know it. At least she could give him that.

His arms tightened around her, and he kissed her again, only this time it was a rougher, more exciting kiss. When he broke away they were both breathing a little hard. His eyes glittered in the darkness as he pushed her up, straightening, so they could rearrange their clothing and get out of the car.

"I'll call you this week," he said abruptly. "We'll iron out the specifics then." He looked at her strangely. "Will that be all right with you?"

She pulled her clothing smooth and turned so that he could refasten her bra and dress. She felt his fingers touch her skin and smiled at the familiar sensation.

"That will be wonderful," she murmured. "I'll be waiting to hear from you."

Blake got out of the car and went around to open Elizabeth's door. As she stepped out, he took off his jacket and slipped it around her shoulders, then draped his arm around her to walk her to the front door. Her coat had been left in Dorin's car earlier in the day, and the damp, chilly air felt raw in the darkness of midnight. Their breath misted in soft plumes as they climbed the crumbling staircase, matching their steps, stride for stride.

Elizabeth turned the knob. She turned to look up at Blake one last time. He had withdrawn a little, as if trying to see her from a more objective distance. He wasn't certain what to make of her offer of a brief liaison with him. She stood on her toes and kissed him tenderly. It was the closest she could come to an honest explanation. Then she shrugged out of his jacket and returned it to him.

"Good night," she murmured as she stepped inside. She held the door open, waiting for him to leave.

He slung the jacket over his shoulder and hesitated on her doorstep. There was a slight frown on his face. "You're sure about this?" he asked seriously.

She smiled. "Yes. I'm sure."

He nodded. "All right." He stepped forward and kissed her lightly on the mouth. "I'll be in touch."

He turned, walked quickly down the staircase, got into his car and turned on the engine. He glanced up at her as he turned the car down the drive to leave, but his expression was hidden by the darkness.

Elizabeth watched until the red taillights disappeared from view. *I'll be waiting, my love.*

Blake spent Sunday working his way through sheaves of legal papers and technical correspondence, but he found time

Sunday night to call and suggest something that had occurred
to him halfway through the restless day. The phone rang. Mrs.
Einer answered. Then...

"Hello."

"Elizabeth?"

"Blake! Hi..." Her voice, excited at first, became soft and
distant, as if she were a little unsure of herself with him.

The words that had been on the tip of his tongue suddenly
vanished. He cleared his throat. What had he been going to
say? Oh, yes. First...

"Did Dorian grill you on how the seduction is progressing?" he asked dryly.

She laughed, relaxing a little. "Of course. I got a very shrewd
look from him over breakfast and a couple of oblique questions during dinner...related to your smooth dancing."

"I hope you haven't been removed from my case?"

Her laughter tinkled lightly across the wires. "No. You're
stuck with me."

"Good. Uh, before I start checking around for our hide-
away, I thought I'd better clear the dates with you...." He
shook his head. He didn't mean to sound as if he were making
a business appointment in his cluttered schedule. What had
happened to his finesse?

"Fine." No trace of reluctance in her voice. She could be
crisp, too. "What's good for you?"

He grinned. "I thought I'd take my time *showing* you the
answer to that one," he teased softly. "When we've finally got
some privacy."

Silence, then a slightly embarrassed laugh. "Okay. But that
wasn't exactly what I meant."

He chuckled. "Well, next weekend is a little complicated,"
he admitted. "The earliest I can leave is Sunday afternoon." He
paused significantly. "If you'd be interested, we could take the
whole week afterward, though, instead of squeezing the trip
into a two-day weekend." He began flipping the calendar pages
on his desk, saying in a completely neutral voice, "If a weekend is easier for you, however, I could do it the second weekend in April...the third weekend in April...the first weekend
in May..."

"Blake?"

"Yes?"

"Next week would be fine."

Pause.

"The whole week?" he repeated carefully.

He could hear the smile in her voice as she answered, softly, "Yes. The whole week."

"All right. I'll make the arrangements, then. Sunday night to Sunday afternoon. At a mountain retreat where people are least likely to track us down and make nuisances of themselves."

She laughed again, but there was a trace of sadness in the sound.

"Blake, this isn't going to cause any problems for you at work, is it? I mean...it must be difficult rearranging your schedule on such short notice."

"Don't worry about it."

"It isn't worry, exactly. I just don't want to be the cause of any dissension with your partners, or anything like that."

"Believe me, they've been trying to get me to take a vacation for a long time. They'd kiss your feet if they knew you'd managed to get me out of here."

"Oh. Well...that's good."

"Elizabeth?"

"What?"

"Are you going to tell Dorian, Karl and the others that you'll be with me?"

"I'll leave them a phone number in case of emergency, but that's all." She paused. "I think they'll guess the truth, though." Stubbornly, she added, "It's none of their business, especially not Dorian's. If I want to go away for a week, I can. I've done it before."

Of course she had, he thought tightly. Stupid of him to have temporarily taken leave of his senses and forgotten she was used to traveling in Europe on her own. Well, maybe not on her own. As she had just said, she'd done this before. He tried not to wonder who the man, or men, had been.

"Blake? Are you still there?"

"Yes. Just thinking."

"You sound...farther away...."

"You're very perceptive. I was envisioning you getting away for the weekend to a ski lodge in the Alps."

"It wasn't quite the same thing."

Probably not, he thought. No one could have been as obsessed with her as he was.

"I'll call you when I've got the details worked out. Probably about Wednesday," he said briskly.

"All right."

Pause.

"Elizabeth?"

"Yes?"

"This is going to be a very long week."

"For me, too," she assured him in a soft, husky voice. "But the wait will be worth it."

"I hope you feel that way afterward," he said wryly.

"I will."

He was a little surprised at the strength of her conviction. Her certainty erased some of his jealousy about the other liaisons he assumed she had enjoyed over the years.

"Goodbye," he said. He had to clear his damn throat again. Just talking to her was arousing, he realized in amazement.

"Good night," she replied.

Click.

On Monday morning Blake was staring at a brochure he had picked up from a travel agent on his way to work when he heard someone walk into his office unannounced. He looked up and slid the brochure half under a folder at the same time.

"Shelby!" he exclaimed, rising to his feet to greet her. "What a pleasant surprise! I wasn't expecting you today." He frowned and leaned over to doublecheck his calendar. "I wasn't, was I?"

She laughed and gave him a quick, light hug. "No. You weren't. I've been assigned to snoop around."

He laughed. "Really?"

She glanced over his desk, her eyes stopping at the blue-and-green splash of glossy advertising poking out from beneath the white business papers. "Is that a travel guide to somewhere?" she asked curiously.

He sat down as she pulled it free. "Did Grant and Alex put you up to this?" he demanded in amusement.

She smiled and sat in the plush chair nearest to him. "How did you guess?" she teased. She tapped the brochure. "Are you actually going away?"

"Yes. But not there."

"I don't believe it!" she exclaimed, her delicate features alive with affection for him. "You're going to take a woman with you, aren't you?" she guessed, amazed.

He actually blushed a little. Grumpily, he objected, "I don't recall grilling you on your personal affairs, Shelby."

"No. But you gave me plenty of unsolicited opinions about my inappropriate taste in wimpy male friends," she reminded him.

"Well, that first fiancé you picked was a real loser!" he defended himself sarcastically. He'd never understood why she'd bothered with that slippery charmer.

She smiled contentedly. "'All's well that ends well,'" she pointed out. "And I couldn't have ended up any better than I have by marrying Grant," she added softly, glowing with love and happiness.

He sighed. "That's true." He glanced toward the door. "And speaking of your husband, where is he?"

"I'm supposed to meet him for lunch. He's flying back from New York this morning. He should be at National Airport now." She assumed a more businesslike attitude. "I really was sent here to find out what was going on. First, how did Saturday with 'Elizabeth' go?"

He laughed. "You aren't going to let me keep this private, are you?" She'd obviously been speaking with Grant and Alex.

"No," she said blithely. "We love you. We want to meddle."

He shook his head. "I suppose, if I refuse to answer, you'll just make a pest of yourself."

She grinned. "Yes. And if my methods are unsuccessful, Sarah volunteered to bring in her attack-dog-in-training and keep you in a corner until you confess."

He rolled his eyes heavenward. "Terrific!" he groaned. "My office has become a prison camp and torture chamber."

"Stop stalling," she warned him affectionately. "Who's this Elizabeth, and is she going with you...wherever you're going?"

He spread his hands in defeat and sighed. "Elizabeth Rossi is the daughter of the man I was apprenticed to in Arkansas."

Shelby stared at him. "She's the one..." she breathed.

He lifted a brow sardonically. "Yes. She's the one."

Shelby bit her lip. "I thought you'd gotten over that years ago."

He shrugged. "Sure."

She looked unconvinced. "Then why...?"

He grinned. "Why not? She's a very attractive woman. I need a vacation. We're both adults. Any more questions?"

Shelby considered him for a moment. "Are you sure you're being honest with yourself about this, Blake? I mean...we were all excited thinking that you might be having a little fun again, and heaven knows we all want you to get away and relax, have a real vacation. You're welcome to use Alex's place on Cayman Brac. Grant can fix you up at a terrific inn in Japan. But..." She hesitated.

"But?" he prompted her, becoming stone-faced. He wasn't about to slit his heart open and bare his wounded memories or lustful obsessions to Shelby, even if she was the closest thing to a sister that he had. "But what, Shelby?"

She reached out and covered his hand with hers. "This doesn't quite sound like you. There was something about the way you said her name that made Grant and Alex think that she was special...."

His jaw tightened. "She was. Once."

"What about now?" she asked, her delicate features showing her worry.

"Now?" He frowned. What could he say? "She's sort of like an ex, I guess."

"An ex?"

"You know...an ex-wife."

"So you're going to bed with each other out of familiarity?" Shelby asked in amazement.

Blake glowered at her. "That's a little direct, even for you and me, Shelby!"

She stared at him, agape. "You're either completely out of your mind, or you're not being honest with yourself," she told him seriously. "This isn't like you, Blake."

"It's the new me," he declared cynically. "Hell, Shelby, you've all been hounding me to go have a good time. Why are you complaining now that I've decided what that is?"

"We just don't want you to get hurt while you're having fun," she pointed out.

"Yeah. Well, I'm a big boy, Shelby. I roll with the punches."

"Among other things," she teased him.

He tried to look shocked. "Grant is having a bad affect on your mind," he declared puritanically. "I'm going to have to talk to him about that."

Shelby laughed. Seeing the time, she jumped to her feet. "I'm sorry to dash through here like this, but Grant's going to meet me halfway, in Arlington, in half an hour.... I've really got to run."

He kissed her cheek as they walked to his office door. "He's made you very happy," he told her, pleased for them both.

She stopped at the door, recalling the difficult period just before Grant had proposed to her. "We had a little help from our friends," she pointed out. "When no one would talk to him about me, he came looking for me."

Blake nodded. "Yeah. He was really going nuts."

She gave him an affectionate smile. "Keep us friends informed, Blake. We're ready and willing to help you, too."

"Get outta here!" he ordered her, laughing as he held a threatening arm out, pointing the way to the door.

"I'm going!"

Chapter 11

"Elizabeth?"

She held the telephone a little tighter. "Blake?"

Something had gone wrong, she thought, her heart sinking with disappointment. It was Saturday afternoon. He wasn't supposed to be calling her. He was supposed to be arranging a publicity photo shoot. She braced herself to hear him tell her that their week together was being cancelled because something unexpected had come up at work.

"Are you busy this evening?"

She blinked. "Am I busy?" He didn't sound like a man trying to cancel an affair. He sounded exasperated, and not with her. "No. I'm not busy."

He sighed audibly. "Could you do me a favor?"

"Sure."

"Don't you even want to hear what it is first?" he asked in surprise.

"No. You're not the type to ask me to do something illegal, immoral or dangerous."

"I wouldn't be so sure," he muttered.

"What favor?" she prompted him gently.

"I was supposed to take a Washington socialite to the Kennedy Center tonight for a special performance of *Rigoletto*. She's ill and just called to tell me she can't go."

She glanced at her wristwatch. It was getting a little late to make it to the Opera House by eight. Besides, she was reluctant to be a last-minute replacement for another date. "Perhaps you should just go alone," she suggested, trying to keep the hurt and disappointment out of her voice.

"I made this arrangement three months ago," he explained, sensing her unwillingness to be a last-minute substitute for another woman. His voice lowered a little more as he added, "This wasn't as much a date as it was a mutually beneficial publicity effort."

She twisted the telephone cord around her finger. "I see."

He sighed. "No. You don't. I don't blame you. Look...let me explain. My date is the daughter of a European diplomat. A necklace I'm going to be selling was designed by a craftsman from her country, using diamonds that came through one of their diamond importers. Both her embassy and my publicist recommended having us go to this gala charity event with her wearing the necklace. We'd be photographed, get some free mileage from the papers." He hesitated. "Elizabeth? Are you still with me?"

"Yes." It sounded very plausible, and she could detect nothing in his voice that hinted of deception. But the green-eyed monster gnawed at her as she envisioned his going out with this other woman draped over his arm. Jealousy's sharp bite made it difficult for her to accept his explanation.

"Elizabeth?" he asked softly. "Would you come with me?" She could hear the half smile on his face as he added, "Please?"

The small strand of stubborn resistance weakened at the warmth and sincerity in his voice. "Of course. But I don't have anything terribly elegant. And I can't get to a hair dresser...."

"You're beautiful in rags, Elizabeth."

And from the way he said it, she thought he really believed it.

It was quite a change from their last encounter, she decided, as she walked with him into the Kennedy Center Opera House almost two hours later. He was as diffident and courteous as a military attaché assigned to a visiting dignitary. His hand was light and guiding at her elbow, his eyes warm yet slightly impersonal.

He was impersonal, however, only until the opera was over. Their car arrived at the huge doors to pick them up, and the guard assigned to protect the expensive necklace discreetly stepped forward to open the car door for them. As the elegant crowds and red-carpeted halls of the Kennedy Center faded into the glittering distance, Blake loosened his tie and stared at Elizabeth thoughtfully.

"Take us around to the Tidal Basin," he instructed the driver of the limousine he was using for the evening.

He sat back, his face impassive in the dark shadows.

"Isn't it a little late at night for a paddleboat ride?" she teased.

He grinned. "If you want to take one, I'll wake up the park police and see if we can find an attendant to take our money."

The limousine glided smoothly down the highway that paralleled the Potomac. Twenty-five minutes later they were pulling into the empty parking lot behind the Jefferson Memorial's pillared dome, one of the many stately white monuments for which the nation's capital was famous.

Blake came around and opened Elizabeth's door, taking her hand in his as she stepped into the night air.

"The cherry blossoms!" she murmured in surprise. She glanced into his face. "You brought us here to see the cherry blossoms?"

He grinned more broadly. "It's the end of March, and I hear we're due for a storm tomorrow. We get them every year. They were lucky to have the Cherry Blossom Festival before the storm carpets the city with flowers. If you don't see them tonight, you'll have to wait 'til next year for them."

"They're a very fleeting pleasure," she reflected somberly.

Blake frowned. "Yes. That's why they're treasured. Their beauty can only be enjoyed for a few days ... a week or two, if you're very fortunate."

"I've never been in Washington when they were in bloom," she admitted, smiling at him.

"Then I'm glad we've come. I thought it would be a small gesture of thanks, after you saved my publicity at the eleventh

our.'' He began walking, still holding her hand. ''This is a first
f sorts for me, too.''

''Really?''

''I've never seen them by moonlight,'' he said with a grin.

Elizabeth laughed softly. How romantic, she thought.

They strolled along the walk decorated by gnarled dark trees
eavily frosted with delicate white-pink blossoms. A light
reeze lifted a branch, loosening a few petals and sending them
howering to the ground.

Blake halted and looked down into Elizabeth's face.

''You look very beautiful in the moonlight, Elizabeth,'' he
murmured. His eyes fell to the exquisite jewels adorning her
eck. ''They look like they were made for you.''

She touched the richly decorated necklace around her bare
eck. Its gold, rubies and diamonds made her feel like a wealthy
oman, but the look in Blake's eyes made her feel like a queen.

He bent his head to kiss her lips, and she felt the sweet warm
leasure swirl through her like the windswept blossoms.

''Tomorrow we leave for our vacation,'' he reminded her,
ressing her close, wrapping his arms around her to ward off
e chilly night air.

''I'm ready,'' she murmured. ''Everything's packed and
aiting.''

He looked into her face. He hadn't wanted to ask her over the
hone, and he hadn't had a chance to see her in person until
onight.

''There's something we need to talk about before we leave
omorrow,'' he said huskily, sliding his hand over her arm.

Her eyes were wide and trusting, but she hadn't a clue what
e was talking about. ''What?'' she asked.

He brushed a light kiss across her lips and whispered in her
ar. ''How do you want to handle the birth control issue?''

She'd been wondering about that. And the more she had
ondered, the more she had found herself aching to let nature
ake its course. She had the most irrational urge to feel his child
nside her, to hold his child lovingly in her arms. She looked at
e white moonlight glistening on the india-ink waters of the
'idal Basin, hoping he couldn't see the wistful desire in her
yes.

''Do you want me to take care of it?'' he asked unevenly.

She certainly had withdrawn, he thought uneasily. Was th
prospect of an unwanted pregnancy with his child such a turr
off? He felt the old anger surge up inside him. He would gladl
have made her the mother of his children fifteen years ago, h
thought. He fought off the bitterness. There had been a warr
closeness between them until he'd mentioned the words *birt
control*. He gritted his teeth. Surely she had gotten used t
planning for protection before going off with other men. Thei
"vacation" was supposed to purge him of his obsession wit
her, he reminded himself sharply, intentionally overstating th
case in an effort to toughen his own attitude. They shouldn
complicate the situation by making a baby. The image of Eli
abeth pregnant with his child made him feel strange. There ha
been a time . . . But that was then, and this was now.

"Look . . . we're adults," he pointed out. "We don't fall int
bed as though we're controlled by forces greater than ou
selves. And we're both a little old to claim that we 'didn't thin
it could happen to us.'

She looked at him then and searched his face. "Fifteen year
ago, did you ever think about the possibility of my gettin
pregnant if we went any further than we did?"

"Yes." He laughed humorlessly. "It was the *only* thing tha
kept me off you." His laughter faded as he saw the seriou
expression she was wearing and its attendant hint of yearning
He cupped her jaw with his hand and murmured, "Fiftee
years ago I would have been the proudest father in the countr
if you'd conceived my child, Elizabeth. I was in love with you."

She closed her eyes and put her arms around him, holdin
him tight. "Thank you," she whispered. It was bittersweet t
hear the admission, but she treasured it deeply. He had love
her as much as she had thought, perhaps even more. Nothin
could ever take that from her now, and she hugged it fiercel
to her lonely heart.

He didn't know what was going on. She was trembling, an
she felt fragile all of a sudden. He caressed her and held her an
kissed her temple, trying to comfort her. "Elizabeth? What i
it?"

She got a grip on herself and pulled a little away. Smiling, sh
told him, "You don't have to worry about birth control
Everything will be taken care of." *If I conceive your child, I wil*

love him or her with all my heart, and I won't ask a thing of you in return. I'll go away. You'll never need to know.

He kissed her softly on the mouth, wondering why her lips trembled beneath his. "All right," he murmured. He nuzzled her neck and swung her up in his arms. His eyes were burning as he asked her in a low, serious voice, "Something's worrying you, isn't it? For the past few minutes you've acted like a ghost walked over your grave." He kissed her lightly on the lips, letting their mouths cling for a moment before he reluctantly broke the contact. "Tell me what you're worried about. Maybe I can help."

She rested her forehead against his, smiling as they stared at each other at point-blank range. "You've already helped me," she told him softly. "Everything's going to be fine."

He was about to argue the point, but the guard who had accompanied them at a distance to protect the necklace was waving for them to return to the car. He was pointing at his watch in agitation.

"We'll continue this conversation later," Blake muttered, exasperated that they never seemed to be able to work all the way through an issue before it was time to part. He let her slide down his body until her feet were firmly on the ground, staring into her eyes like a man intent on having his question answered. "We'll have plenty of time in the next week."

Elizabeth smiled and slid her arm through his. She was sure they would find other, much more pleasant, activities to occupy them. It seemed more diplomatic at the moment, however, to simply agree. "You're right," she murmured.

"We'll take you home. Then I've got to get this necklace into the vault," he said. He hugged her shoulder to him apologetically as they walked. "I'm sorry I can't stick around and have an after-the-performance coffee with you."

"I'll take a rain check," she teased. "We'll have the next seven days to drink coffee together."

His eyes darkened and glittered in the moonlight. "Very true," he breathed. They got into the limousine and held hands on the long drive to Dorian's. Elizabeth had fallen asleep on Blake's shoulder by the time they arrived.

"I'll walk you to the door," he told her softly.

As she unlocked it, he stayed her hand and pushed her against the wood, pressing his body against hers from chest to thigh and kissing her so thoroughly that her knees began to weaken.

"Thank God I don't have to wait any longer," he muttered as he lifted his head to look at her one last time before leaving. From the expression in her eyes, he thought she agreed. "I thought this week would never end."

"Me too," she whispered.

Reluctantly, he stepped away. "What time shall I pick you up?" he asked softly.

Elizabeth swallowed. She'd been avoiding this, but now she had to tell him. "I'd rather meet you downtown somewhere, Blake."

He looked surprised. With a slightly disbelieving laugh, he asked, "What's the matter, Elizabeth? Ashamed to be seen going off with me for the week?"

She grasped his arms and shook her head vehemently. "Of course not. But . . ." She let go of him and bit her lip. He was staring at her in a very peculiar way. It made her heart ache with guilt. "I'm not ashamed," she promised softly. "I'm looking forward to it." She sighed. "But I don't want Dorian or the others to know," she said, lowering her voice to a whisper so soft he had to lean close to catch her words. "I'll tell my father something, but . . ."

He reached out and slid his fingers through her hair until he had a gentle hold on the back of her head and neck. "I'm not particularly sure I like the sound of this," he admitted quietly.

She pleaded with him with her eyes and with her voice. "I'm sorry, Blake. Please, believe me. It has nothing to do with you. But it will be much easier for me." *And safer for you, my love,* she added silently.

He looked unconvinced, and withdrew his hand, moving away again. "All right," he agreed at length. He suggested a time and smiled slightly as Elizabeth eagerly agreed. "Would you like to meet at Malone's?" he asked.

Elizabeth nodded her head and smiled at him gratefully. "Yes. Thank you, Blake."

He nodded. "You're welcome," he said with a crooked grin. "All right, then. That's it." As if putting her unexpected request behind him, his smile warmed and became more personal. "Sleep well, Elizabeth. I can't guarantee how much of that you'll be getting for the next seven days," he warned her softly.

She was laughing as she watched him run down the steps. She wrapped her arms around her waist and twirled into the house. She was so happy, so excited, she felt as if she could fly.

Dorian was reading the paper when she came down to Sunday brunch. When she sat down with her coffee and omelet, he shook the section he'd been reading, folded it in half and handed it to her.

"Good morning, *ma belle,*" he greeted her, giving her a gleaming smile and a grand wave of his hand.

"Good morning, Dorian." She drank her coffee and looked at the newspaper. "What am I supposed to see?" she asked.

"Look at the first column on the left. The article about the Saturday night activities of Washington's rich and famous."

There were the usual listings of who had dinner with whom and where, which wealthy developer was courting which powerful government leader, which cultural event brought out the largest number of big-name movers and shakers.

"The picture, my sweet," Dorian hinted. "At the bottom of the column . . ."

"Good heavens," she murmured. There was a montage of photos of people attending *Rigoletto* at the Kennedy Center. In back of a more famous couple in one photo, she could clearly see Blake and herself. She rapidly scanned the column, looking for the names in bold black print. Then she saw it.

Jeweler Blake Malone escorted lovely Elizabeth Rossi, recently arrived in the nation's capital from the alpine reaches of Switzerland. How many men can adorn their date with such a spectacular necklace? While it didn't seem to be uppermost in their minds all evening, a number of others present are undoubtedly planning on dropping in at Malone's to try it on for a longer-term engagement.

"That was very shrewd of you," Dorian said admiringly.

Elizabeth ignored him. Further on, the article mentioned the woman he had originally planned on taking. Her fingers tightened on the paper.

Katrin Louwens, often seen with Mr. Malone in recent months at similar events, was laid low by the spring virus that has kept the federal capital in its collective bed for the past two weeks.

The woman had a name. Elizabeth put down the paper and tried to finish her coffee. Somehow she'd been able to ignore her a little bit better when she was nameless, faceless. She was still faceless. But her name was Katrin.

"Is something amiss, my dear?" Dorian asked, his eyes narrowing shrewdly.

"No. I think I'll go up to the workshop, if you'll excuse me. I was in the middle of something yesterday before I went out. I'd like to finish it before I leave."

"Of course." He smiled. "Mrs. Einer says you have given the staff a telephone number where you can be reached this week."

"Yes," she said stiffly, rising to go.

"Will you be going with Blake?"

"That is none of your business, Dorian," she said coolly. "I'm going on a vacation. That's all that I intend to say about it."

His eyes narrowed. "I'm not so easily fooled, my dear," he pointed out. "I'd be quite surprised if Mr. Malone isn't in your company, for part of the time, at least, no matter how the official arrangements may read."

She walked toward the doorway, not bothering to argue with him.

"Do not forget," he told her sharply. "The auction will be held next month. I want to know how much he'll spend, Elizabeth. Don't fail me."

She hesitated. "I've told you, Dorian. Blake Malone isn't a fool. You can force me to be nice to him and to listen to what he might say. However, you're being wildly optimistic if you truly believe that he's going to whisper that kind of information in my ear."

"Perhaps. Perhaps not." A cruel smile played across his thin lips. "Nevertheless, I have the utmost faith in you, my sweet. I wish you a most productive and satisfying 'vacation'!"

In the end, Elizabeth decided to tell Karl that she was going to the country for a week, that she was going to be with Blake, and that she hadn't told anyone else that Blake was going to be with her. She felt she owed her father the truth. It was the only way she could stand leaving him with Dorian.

When the taxi came to pick her up, a little after noon, she was surprised to see her father waiting by the front door in his wheelchair.

"Are you here to tell me goodbye?" she asked in surprise.

He nodded.

She put down her luggage and bent over to give him a hug and a kiss. Smiling, she told him, "I wouldn't have left without saying goodbye."

"I . . . know." It sounded a little warped, like a record changing speeds as it was being played.

"I'll call."

"O . . . kay."

"If you need me, I'll come back. You know that, don't you, darling?"

He nodded and patted her arm with his good left hand. He was smiling, that awkward, aching smile that was all he could manage now that the muscles on the right side of his face were weakened from the stroke. It was a contented smile, a smile of satisfaction. He placed his hand on her bowed head in the ageless gesture of paternal blessing.

"You're happy that I'm going with him, aren't you?" she asked softly.

"Yes." The word quavered from the effort Karl had to make to pronounce it.

Some of the unhappiness that had burdened her as a result of wondering about Katrin and ruminating over Dorian's persistent pressuring eased. She had been worried that her father would be upset at her extended absence; she rarely left him for more than a couple of days at a time, if that. Instead, he was giving her his permission, urging her to go.

The lighthearted feeling she had experienced when Blake had left her at the front door the previous night came back. With a smile on her face, she gathered up her luggage and ran down the steps.

A little after one, just as they had agreed, she got out of the taxi at the garage next to Malone's. Blake was already there, waiting for her. He paid the driver before she could get the money from her purse.

"The car's over there," he said, bending to give her a light kiss and take her bags. "Let's go."

A little less than three hours later, Blake pulled into the secluded driveway of an old stone cottage nestled high in the mountains west of Washington.

"How did you find this place?" Elizabeth asked, every syllable filled with admiration for his discovery.

"With a lot of hard work." He grinned at her apologetic expression. "Not mine. The rental agent's. She worked her tail off finding something that met my requirements."

Elizabeth looked at the flowering dogwoods nestled among the forest greens and the two-story building that looked like it had watched John Brown's men march on their way to Harper's Ferry well over a hundred years ago. A bird was singing a complicated, melodic song, and somewhere in the background she thought she heard the sound of water falling over rocks.

He unloaded the trunk, and they took their things to the front door. The key, as the agent had arranged, was taped under the mailbox. He opened the door, bent at the waist and made a flourishing gesture with his hand.

"After you." There was a gleam in his dark eyes and a lilt in his voice that made his invitation sound deliciously sinful.

With a slight shiver of anticipation, Elizabeth took her bags and went inside. "Oh, Blake!" she exclaimed as she saw the interior.

"It's not bad, is it?"

"Not bad? It's wonderful!" She left her things by the wooden staircase that curved up to the second floor and wandered from the large sunken living room, which held all the music and entertainment equipment anyone could want, to the dining room set for a candlelight dinner for two, then into the kitchen with its state-of-the-art appliances and onto a glass-enclosed porch that ran the length of the back of the house. From the porch, with its lounge chairs and lamps, she could see the gorge and the small waterfall that had made the sounds she had heard earlier.

"There should be a heated swimming pool around to the right back there somewhere," Blake said.

He was standing a little behind her, and his voice, at such close quarters, felt as if it vibrated through her.

Elizabeth turned. She hardly knew what to say. "This looks like someone's home."

"It was. It's for sale, has been for a little while. They're showing it furnished. I told them I wanted to rent it for a week, and they were delighted."

"Do you know the owners?"

"No." He came closer and rested his arms on her shoulders, lacing his fingers together behind her back. "Why all the questions?"

She stared at him.

"Why, Elizabeth?" He lightly brushed a kiss across her lips and pulled her closer, resting his chin on her head.

She swallowed hard. "I wasn't expecting so much...."

He frowned a little. "What did you think I was going to do?"

"I don't know. Register at a motel, perhaps. Take a week at a resort...."

He laughed. "I considered it, but I decided we might find solitude a little more relaxing. All those crowds at the cashier's desk and the restaurant and the parking lot would have been a pain in the neck."

She leaned back and looked into his eyes. "You're a very sensitive and perceptive man," she said honestly.

"Thank you," he murmured. He slid his hands down over her shoulder blades, then let them slowly travel down her back to her hips.

"Are you hungry?" she asked softly.

He buried his face in her hair, nuzzled her, growling low in his throat. "I've been hungry for a very long time."

She slid her fingers into his soft, dark hair and giggled. "Yes. But do you want to eat some food first?"

He was working his way down across her ear, her jaw and her throat, kissing her and sending tendrils of desire curling across her skin. She was feeling breathless when he lifted his head and looked into her eyes. "What I want is to respect myself when this is behind us," he explained evenly. He ran his fingers through her hair and took a moment to enjoy a leisurely study of her face. "You're a very beautiful woman," he told her slowly. "I want to savor you in bed, but I also want to enjoy you out of bed." A slight, rueful grin slid across his features. "So while my animal nature may be straining to throw you on your back and strip your clothes off and take you before we've gone another step, I will restrain it."

Elizabeth laughed at his teasing, but listening to him say what he would like to do made her want him to do it. She was a little shocked at herself, too. If he'd wanted to fall on her right then, she would have thought it wildly exciting. She'd been thinking about him doing it for years, and her thinking had been extremely graphic for the past endlessly frustrating week.

He saw the color in her cheeks and grinned. "Don't tell me you want to skip dinner and try out the living-room rug?"

She laughed and buried her face in his neck, hugging him as he tightly hugged her back.

He kissed her ear, sliding his tongue around the sensitive whorls, making her squirm and moan softly in pleasure. He kissed her soundly on the mouth and looked down at her, feeling himself falling into a bottomless pool of desire.

"Is it getting hot in here?" he asked huskily.

"I don't think so. I think it's us."

He grinned slightly. "Yeah." He let the grin slide away and said, on a more serious note. "Let's enjoy this...take it one step at a time. Naturally."

Elizabeth nodded. She would have agreed to anything, though, staring at his burning eyes, listening to his hypnotic voice, protected by his strong arms.

"Let's unpack a few things...get some dinner... drinks...take it easy...."

He made it sound like they were living together, she thought. Embarking on a life together, instead of a mere week. She knew

he didn't mean to sound that way. He'd made no commitments beyond a week of satisfying their need to become lust-
fully disentangled from each other. But the way he had put it
made it easier for her.

She smiled at him and kissed him lightly on the lips. "All
right," she agreed. "What's for dinner?"

He draped his arm casually over her shoulders as they walked
back to get their luggage. "I gave the agent a shopping list for
the week. If she stocked it the way I asked, we should have
French onion soup, marinated flank steaks, salad vinaigrette
and some blush wine."

The agent had done as she had been requested.

Everything was waiting for them in the refrigerator. All they
had to do was turn on the indoor grill, microwave the soup, toss
the salad, uncork the wine and serve the meal.

The candlelight was a very romantic touch, Elizabeth
thought as she watched Blake lift his wine in a toast. The flickering, pale lemon-yellow light glinted on the glass.

"To pleasures too long delayed," he said quietly.

She touched her glass to his and drank.

The meal was delicious. Its charm was enhanced not only by
the flickering candles, but by the soft and romantic music and
Blake's relaxed repartee.

They discovered that the more they talked, the more they
found to talk about. By the time they had put the dishes in the
dishwasher and snuffed out the dining-room candles, they were
both in a very mellow mood.

Blake snagged a bottle and two liqueur glasses, and carried
them into the sunken living room.

"Take off your shoes," he suggested as he poured their
drinks.

She pushed a toe against the opposite heel and a shoe
plopped off. Again. The other shoe joined the first.

She sat on the plush, king-sized, wraparound sofa, curling
her feet up under her. She could see out the huge picture window and watch the stars.

Blake sat down next to her and handed her the liqueur.

"What is it?" she asked. She took a sip and looked at him in surprise. "This is delicious!" The sweet, light flavor of the pear liqueur tantalized her palate and warmed her blood.

"It's Pear William." He stretched his arm behind her and drank some of his. He watched her thoughtfully, his eyes dark and unreadable. He flicked off the lamp, leaving them in darkness alleviated only by a few faint nightlights, and the moon and stars outside.

The last song on the CD player ended, and the stereo system automatically clicked off. Blake put his empty liqueur glass on a nearby table, took Elizabeth's and did the same with it. He pulled her onto his lap, cradling her in his arms. There were dark flames in the backs of his eyes as he stared into her half-lidded gaze.

"There are two bathrooms upstairs," he reminded her softly, pausing to brush a feathery kiss persuasively across her parted lips. "Why don't you take one, and I'll take the other." He rubbed his open mouth lightly across her jaw, smiling darkly as she arched and moaned softly in pleasure.

"Fine," she managed to say. His closeness, his warmth and sensuous touch, the languid relaxation brought about by the food, liquor and their conversation, combined to make her feel like warm honey. She was more than ready for the feast to come. She slid off his lap, loving the reluctance with which he let her go and the dark embers coming to life in his eyes as he watched her take her leave.

"I'll meet you at the bed," he told her softly.

Chapter 12

It was a big bed. King-sized. Covered with lemon sheets and a soft, cinnamon-brown comforter. The carpeting was soft beneath Elizabeth's bare feet as she neatly folded back the covers. She heard the shower in the other bathroom cut off. Blake would be stepping into the room very soon, she realized. She tried not to pace.

In spite of the knowledge that she wanted him, and that she had just spent a very subtly seductive evening with him, the cold fact that he would soon walk in, take her in his arms and thrust his body into hers brought on a virginal attack of nerves. She knew he'd never believe it, either. How could she be the way he expected her to be? she wondered.

She was wearing a white lacy nightgown, knee length and slit up one thigh to her hip. It was brand new, bought specifically with tonight in mind, but she hadn't realized how cold she would be feeling at this moment when she'd made the purchase. She wrapped her arms around her middle and stared through the veiled windows into the night. The trickling waterfall sounded louder, now that it was so very quiet, she thought, rubbing her goose-bumped arms in a failing attempt to get warm. Most women got through this, she told herself reasonably. And Blake would make it easy, she thought, feeling a renewed rush of anticipation, thinking about him.

She heard the bathroom door open, and swallowed hard. When he came into the bedroom, she heard his approach in spite of the carpet. His warmth preceded him as he stopped at her back, wrapping his arms around her and pressing a slow, meaningful kiss on her shoulder.

"You look very beautiful," he murmured huskily, nuzzling the nape of her neck and sliding his warm hands beneath her arms and around her waist.

She leaned back against him, closing her eyes and telling herself, *This is Blake. This is what should have happened between us years ago.* Still, she trembled. She had a case of stage fright, she thought, barely controlling a desperate urge to giggle. She could tell that he realized she was tense. He grew very still, and he made no immediate move to proceed. Instead he talked to her in that soothing voice that she loved.

"I used to dream about you," he whispered, gently laying his cheek against the back of her head.

His admission made her smile and relax a little. "Did you? That's funny. I used to dream about you, too," she murmured shyly.

His arms tightened slightly, and he swayed a little, bringing her with him, as if they were swaying in time to some unheard love song. The slight friction produced by their bodies warmed her, and she barely noticed when he slowly began to glide one hand over her stomach, waist and hips.

"Your dreams must have been similar to mine," he murmured teasingly. "Because you've picked out one of the nightgowns I used to envision removing from your delectable body." He pulled lightly at the fabric at her breast, then ran his hand over it provocatively.

Elizabeth shivered again, but this time it was from a small lancet of desire piercing her from her nipples to her groin as his thumb delicately rubbed each turgid peak. Her back was warming from the heat of his body, and so were her shoulders, encircled by his strong arms. His breath was hot and sweet on her neck as he whispered to her. The sensations combined to make her feel weak and yielding and incredibly alive. She let her head roll back against his muscular shoulder and raised one hand to caress his hard cheek.

He turned his mouth into her palm and kissed it. At the same time he slid both of his own hands up under her breasts, cupping them firmly, caressing them, gently sliding over the nipples that were poking against the frothy lace.

He slid his hands down to her hips and gently but firmly turned her to face him. Then his mouth found hers, and he pulled her close, sliding his tongue between her lips, deepening the kiss as she yielded against him.

He had been planning on going slowly, on savoring this first time with her. He had intentionally lingered earlier in the evening, enjoying prolonging the pleasure of finally seducing her into his bed. As she opened her mouth to receive him, closed her arms around his shoulders and moaned softly with delight, he felt tongues of fire leap high in his loins. It was going to be very difficult to force himself to go slowly tonight, he realized grimly.

The sight of her naked flesh peeking from beneath the fragile white lace had made his groin tighten as he'd walked into the room. He had tied a terry cloth towel around his waist, partly to keep from feeling her naked skin against his before he was prepared to control his reaction, and partly to let her have time to accustom herself to his nakedness. But when she had leaned back against him, touching his face and arching with pleasure while he caressed her breasts, he'd felt himself thicken with desire. He might just as well have been bare, for all the good the damned towel had done to slow his reaction to her. Now, holding her body frontally, the process was rocketing along.

He slid his fingers through her hair, making a supreme effort to calm himself down. He wanted this to last, damn it. This first time would be his only once. He wanted to savor every flicker of her eyes, every moan, every sigh, every sweet ounce of it. As he stared into her eyes, he realized in surprise that they were wide with what looked like apprehension. She looked as if it were the first time she'd gone to bed with a man. He supposed it was, in a way. It would certainly be the first time she'd gone to bed with *him*. They had never been fully intimate. This would be the first time that he would enter her body.

Thinking about penetrating her was not a calming experi-ence, he quickly discovered, as he felt himself tighten and jerk against her.

Elizabeth could feel his desire, and his obvious arousal made her feel terribly proud that he wanted her. She kissed his lips, sliding her tongue delicately across them, smiling when he moaned softly and tightened his hold in response. Then she worked her way slowly down his hard jaw and the beating pulse along his throat, kissing, licking, nuzzling, relishing his plea-sure at her touch, swelling with pride that he enjoyed her. Smiling like the cat that got the cream, she rubbed her body sensuously against him, caressing his hard ribs and sleekly muscled back with eager hands. His harsh intake of breath at every pleasurable sensation sent fresh rivers of desire curling through her body, pooling in a dull ache between her legs. She instinctively pressed against him, wanting to ease the building pressure, frustrated that she wasn't able to in their present po-sition.

Blake jerked the towel free from his waist, letting it fall to the floor. More carefully, he lifted the lace nightie from her body and slipped it over her head. He tossed it uncaringly across the foot of the bed. Hungrily, he feasted his eyes on the sight of her.

The night stars gleamed white on their naked bodies, and they stood, barely touching each other, savoring the first mo-ments of visual discovery.

His voice sounded thick and peculiar as he told her, "You're more beautiful than I've been dreaming all these years." He ran his hand across her throat, across her breast, and down across her hip. He stopped at her thigh, pulling her against him, cup-ping her buttocks with both hands. Then he lifted her a little, groaning softly as he found the position he wanted and slid himself between her damp, warm thighs to nestle against her soft, slippery folds.

The feel of his aroused manhood thrust strongly against her wet and aching flesh sent pleasure shooting through her. She put her arms around his neck and resisted the urge to wrap her legs around his hips, but, oh, did she ache to do it. The heat from their bodies was making her feel as if they were turning into a small furnace. Mysteriously, the heat they were gener-ating seemed to augment the rich, radiant pleasure that was spreading throughout them with every beat of their hearts. She could feel her own heart pounding in her chest, and she felt his, too, slamming against his heavily ribbed chest wall.

"Do you think we should continue this in the bed?" she asked tremulously. "I seem to be getting rather weak in the knees...."

He laughed, but she noticed that his voice shook, too. They were both trembling slightly, she realized in surprise, but before she could say or do anything about it, she felt him lift her thighs around his hips.

"I almost did that," she admitted, amazed that she could talk and that he could stand while they were both getting so hot and slippery, literally shaking with desire. She buried her face in his neck, savoring the scent of his skin, relishing his strength.

"Why didn't you?" His voice was beginning to sound definitely strained. He positioned her wet body against him and slid a little into her, just enough to make them both groan. He swore softly at the resulting onrush of pleasure.

"I wasn't sure I should," she admitted, gasping with delight as he moved against her again, sliding a little deeper into her, sending pleasure like molten lava through her aching flesh.

He swore and took the two steps necessary to get to the bed, laying her down and keeping himself between her thighs as they rolled onto the soft, cool sheets.

She felt so soft and delicate beneath him, he thought, running his hands over her again, enjoying the puckering of her flesh as he touched her. He silently ordered himself to remember not to crush her when he was in the throes of completion, which, at the rate he was going, would be pretty damned soon.

He nuzzled her neck and arched to find her nipples with his mouth, savoring her cries of encouragement and the helpless way she lifted up to him in her eagerness for his caress. In spite of her responsiveness, though, she was shyly pliant, he realized, her thighs open and relaxed as he lay between them, her hands hesitant as they touched his back. She projected a virginal timidity that was incredibly arousing to him. It was exactly the way he had always imagined her being on their wedding night fifteen years ago.

The yearning for her that had never died rushed through him like a violent desert wind. Seeing her skin flushed with desire, her eyes hungrily watching him, and feeling her hands gently caressing his bare skin, had the effect of oil being thrown on a hot fire. Her open thighs and yielding warmth made him urgently want to thrust into her.

His body ached so much that he clenched his hands, literally trying to grip his raging desire and choke it off for at least a little while longer. Quickly he eased himself away from her, separating their bodies enough for him to slide his fingers down across her flat belly to the soft damp curls between her thighs. He gently caressed that part of her body which would soon receive him and at long last ease his years of obsessive wanting. When he did, he wanted her to crave it, too. He wanted her to hunger for his body the way he had hungered for hers. He smiled with grim satisfaction as she moaned at his touch. She wanted him, all right.

She arched as he found her delicate pleasure points and that tiny but especially sensitive swell of eager feminine flesh. There was a look of surprise in her eyes as he lowered his mouth to kiss her, while his fingers engaged in a rhythmic massage that had her clamping her thighs and writhing beneath him within moments. As she twisted wildly beneath him, his kiss became ravenous. Years of wanting made his mouth hard and demanding, his tongue stroking with the same brutal mastery that his fingers were using on her yielding femininity.

He shifted suddenly, putting his hands beside her shoulders, thrusting the tip of his rigid member against her quivering flesh, skillfully teased into full readiness by his caressing fingertips. His mouth moved on hers and, as her arms closed tightly around his shoulders, he pushed fully into her body. The sensation of her tight, slick warmth gloving his hard and pulsing manhood wrenched a groan of extreme pleasure and satisfaction from him and a soft moan of equal appreciation from her. The sounds of her delight drove him to the edge of madness. He thrust into her as slowly as he could, his hips and back rigid and shaking with the effort required to restrain himself. Each slick stroke shot waves of red-hot sweetness up through his shaft into his loins and across his entire body. He felt hot-wired and ready to go off like a firecracker.

"Sweet Elizabeth," he murmured hotly against her soft mouth. His kisses became hard and urgent, and he felt himself going into a tailspin, his control disappearing, unable to hold himself back any longer. He slanted his mouth, sealing the wetly intimate kiss, and closed his arms tightly around her.

Their mouths made love, their bodies made love, and with every stroke and slide, their emotions poured out like sweet fire to each other.

She had never dreamed that it would be like this between them. The groans, the sighs, the heat, the eager demanding, the pleading touches that burned her to ash and sent her rising, reborn, like the phoenix, once again.

She felt the pleasure pool and tighten into an unbearable coil deep inside her abdomen, and she moaned as he slid his hands down, holding her hips, sliding her thighs up to embrace his. Instinctively, she arched and found the point of contact that was needed.

"There?" he asked, his voice a taut shred of its usual self.

"Yes," she gasped.

And he thrust up against her one last time, filling her, sending her into the diamond fires, melting her in the heat of his passion. She cried out, and he covered her mouth desperately with his again, thrusting into her in hard, rapid strokes gone wild and out of control. His total loss of control made her feel a renewed surge of desire and, as he arched against her, convulsing in his own violent climax, she shattered again.

He was still kissing her, and he kissed her all the way down from the incredible pinnacle they had climbed together, all the way down to the calm, peaceful waters that awaited them at the end.

He buried his face in the pillow next to her, brokenly whispering incoherent love words against her ear.

Elizabeth held him tightly, letting her damp thighs slide down to softly cradle him. She pretended that his unintelligible murmurings were the words that she wanted to hear, the words he would have given her years ago, on their wedding night. *I love you, Elizabeth. God, how I love you. You'll never know how much.*

Her eyes closed as she turned her head and blindly found his mouth with hers. Their lingering kiss was indescribably sweet. His full length covered her like a heavy blanket, and gradually he began to ease away from her.

"No," she murmured anxiously, tightening her arms around his warm, naked back. She snuggled up against him, burrowing like an animal.

"I'll squash you flat," he protested huskily, sounding both surprised and amused that she seemed to like it. He braced some of his weight on his forearms and rubbed his cheek tenderly against hers. "We can roll over together," he told her softly, plying her willing lips with another slow, sweet kiss. He slid his arms beneath her, captured her legs with a scissoring movement of his own and rolled onto his back, taking her with him, so that she was now sprawled intimately atop him.

Elizabeth clung to him, sighing. "I wouldn't mind being squashed," she said. "It would have been worth it."

He laughed and caressed her bare back and bottom. "You idiot," he teased her affectionately.

She giggled, lifted her head to look down at him and smiled shyly.

"Are you feeling better now?" she asked, remembering that night in his car when she had told him she was willing to satisfy his lust.

He looked a little surprised at first. Then the surprise changed into amusement. "Yes and no."

She laughed and placed a light, playful punch on his bare shoulder. "What am I supposed to make of an answer like that?"

He caught her striking hand and held it behind her back. His eyes were gleaming with possibilities.

"Yes, I am feeling one hell of a lot better, you temptress," he told her, grinning. "And no, I haven't had enough to make it last."

Her whole face softened with the tender love she felt for him, and she gently slid her free hand through his hair.

"I'm so glad to hear that," she whispered. She closed her eyes and snuggled against him, smiling as he released her hand and wrapped her warmly in his arms.

For a long time they lay together, hearing each other's breathing, feeling the pulsebeat of their hearts, savoring the wonderful sensation of their intimately entangled bodies, while the soft rushing of cool water cascading down through the rocks outside played nature's ancient lullaby.

Elizabeth felt his occasional kiss, the slow and undemanding caress that assured her he had not yet completely fallen asleep. It was wonderful. Beautiful. Everything she had wanted, or ever would want, she thought.

She felt cherished, and even though she knew it wasn't really true, she treasured his tender and passionate care for her.

"Thank you," she whispered unsteadily, half hoping he might be dozing off and not hear her faintly uttered words.

He moved a little, trying to see her face, but she buried it deeper against his neck

"Thank you?" he repeated slowly.

He couldn't miss the sincerity and the awed tone in her voice. He was uncertain how to respond to it. If she had been inexperienced, he might have understood, but he hadn't torn her apart when he'd entered her, so he assumed he was right, and she had been with at least one other man at some time. A flame of anger heated him, thinking about it, and he quickly clamped down on what he recognized was jealousy. He had no business indulging in any jealousy with her, he told himself. He was trying to get over her, not re-engaged to her.

And yet... He sighed and pressed a kiss against the pulse beating slowly in her soft neck. She had no reason to thank him, he thought. He was the one who should be doing the thanking. He had never felt so completely...transported. Lust deeper than he had ever felt had wrung ecstasy from cells he had never known he had. And he had felt what surely must have been bliss at the end, when he had seen her joy in her face, felt it in her loving response to him. Every emotion in him had been fully engaged in the act. She had satisfied not only his physical craving for her, but somehow, she had satisfied some of his emotional longing, as well. Longing, he still kept telling himself, was just a lingering memory from their past.

"Elizabeth," he whispered huskily.

"Yes?"

"If it were fifteen years ago, this is where I would have told you how much I loved you."

"I know." There was a wealth of sad regret hidden beneath her soft words.

He felt an unexpected twinge of guilt. Was he taking advantage of her, sleeping with her like this? Making love with the express intent of being able to walk away from her forever when they were done?

She sensed the change in him and raised her head to look at him. "You aren't feeling guilty, are you?" she asked in surprise, seeing the answer to her question in his eyes. "I volunteered," she reminded him with a rather embarrassed smile.

He grinned slightly. "I know you did." He frowned. "Still, now that I have what I want, I guess my conscience is making a service call."

"Tell it to go back to sleep until next week. Tell it to mind its own business," she suggested, trying to sound lighthearted. When she saw his ambivalence she drew up her courage and admitted rosily, "You aren't the only one who got what he wanted."

His eyes darkened, and he pulled her head down to kiss her with slow, thorough intimacy. "I'm glad to hear that," he whispered huskily.

He couldn't seem to keep from searching her face. It was as if he were discovering her again for the first time. Her delicate bones, the creamy softness of her skin, the sea-green eyes that reminded him of misty nights and foghorns warning sailors away, the champagne-gold glimmering in her auburn hair falling damply about them now like a veil.

"You're a mystery to me," he murmured. "A beautiful, seductive, unforgettable mystery."

The husky desire in his voice made her tingle. She smiled at him. "Those are nice words to hear, my love," she murmured, grateful for the ones he could honestly give her. She lightly kissed his lips in homage.

My love. Her words reverberated in his heart and singed his mind, burned his loins. They lanced open the rage he had buried, letting it rise in him like bile. He had loved her so totally, so completely, without restraint. How could she have walked off after all they had been to each other? He closed his eyes and tried to swallow it back.

"Blake?" She was a little worried. "Are you all right? You look . . . strange."

He swallowed. His eyes opened.

"Would you tell me now who he was?" he asked, his voice low and absolutely without inflection. "The older man, the rich one you left me for.'' He saw her swallow, knew she was going to say no, and he grasped her arms firmly in his hands, holding her hostage with his steady gaze. ''You didn't want to answer that question when I asked you at Dorian's. Frankly, I don't particularly enjoy hearing myself ask it. Put it down to wounded male vanity wanting to learn from its mistakes, if you like, but I'd like an answer. Who was he?''

She closed her eyes. Pain washed over her heart. ''I can't tell you what you want to know,'' she said in a broken whisper. ''Please, please, don't let it spoil what we can have together now.'' She opened her eyes, begging him silently. ''I know you'll never forgive what I did. It was unforgivable.'' She hoped her willingness to take full responsibility would ease his anger and frustration at not knowing.

''You can still twist me around your little finger,'' he said, sighing and grimacing wryly. ''Hell, I can't even stay indignantly outraged at your stubbornness when you use that soft, pleading voice on me.'' He pulled her fiercely into his arms and buried his face in her neck. ''I loved you, damn it, Elizabeth. We could have had this fifteen years ago. We could have been happy together.'' He sighed and let her go. He searched for his sense of humor to restore the peaceful affection that had filled them after making love. Grinning, he amended, ''Well, maybe not. I probably would have been in a much bigger hurry fifteen years ago, and you wouldn't have had enough experience to have an orgasm for years.''

Elizabeth choked on her laughter. ''I doubt that,'' she murmured.

He laced his hands behind his head as she slid to his side, draping her arm and leg over him affectionately.

Frowning slightly, he asked her, ''I didn't hurt you, did I?''

''Hurt me? No.'' She blushed and muttered, ''You gave me pleasure.'' That had to be one of the biggest understatements in the history of the world, she thought.

''I'm glad,'' he murmured, smiling briefly. The slight frown returned, however. She had been so tight. It must have been a long time for her, he decided, finding the thought quite appealing. He rolled onto his side and tucked her into his body. He cupped her breast tenderly with one hand and pressed his thighs warmly against the backs of hers.

Sighing with contentment, she placed her hand over his and let her leaden eyes close. She hadn't realized how tired she was until now. Treasuring the feeling of being held protectively in his arms, she sank slowly beneath the dark waves of unconsciousness.

She murmured something as she was falling asleep, but he couldn't figure out what it was. His brain was fogged and his body relaxed, and he had been in the process of falling into a contented sleep. Her mumblings sounded good, though, warm and tender and affectionate. It sounded like they came straight from her heart.

He pulled her more snugly against him and pressed a sleepy kiss on the nape of her neck. Whatever else happened, for now she was thoroughly, irrevocably and quite willingly his. In spite of everything that still lay unresolved and unexplained between them, that thought made him feel like a king.

A faint ribbon of fire-opal colors was streaking morning across the sky when Elizabeth gradually became aware of several pleasurable sensations stealing across her skin. A warm, open-mouthed kiss on her neck, a hand sliding across her thigh in a lazily seductive movement, and a hard, male body sliding on top of her, easing her thighs apart with his.

She opened her arms and her body to him with a sleepy but very welcoming smile on her face. His mouth met hers in a slow, sweet kiss.

"Don't you think you should open your eyes?" he teased her in a hoarse whisper.

"I don't need them to know who you are," she murmured. "I can see you with my body. Like this . . ." She ran her hands slowly over his back and shoulder blades, rubbed her face cat-like against his with a purr. Then she arched her hips, accommodating the slight pressure of his thrusting manhood, inviting his penetration. She made a sound that was half sigh and half moan when he immediately accommodated her desire, filling her with his fully aroused member.

"You are so hard," she murmured in surprise and awe. She felt him swell in response to her admiration, and she laughed with pleasure. He seemed to grow harder and bigger still, and she couldn't imagine how; he'd been more than ready when he'd entered her.

He sank his teeth playfully into her soft shoulder, raking her flesh with gentle love bites as he slowly withdrew a little from her.

She moaned, "No. Don't leave me."

"I wouldn't think of it," he growled hoarsely, demonstrating good faith by sliding fully into her body and holding her hips hard against him with his hands. "Your body is like heaven to me," he whispered. "Smooth, sweet, hot, yielding." He fastened his mouth on hers, thrusting his tongue inside to sweep the tender nerve endings with an arousing caress. His face tensed in concentration as he broke off the kiss; his breathing became harsh.

She slid her thighs up alongside his flanks and locked her heels behind his buttocks, as he'd showed her the previous night. The sensation of him full and hard and throbbing with need inside her was beginning to drive her to distraction. She held him tight and ran her lips seductively over his grimly tight mouth, his clenched jaw, his neck with its throbbing artery.

He was trying to hold her still, but she felt the most unbearable urge to move, and she wriggled against him, making little pleading noises deep in her throat, raking his naked back with her fingers.

He swore and began to move.

"Love me," she begged him, caught between the hazy remnants of sleep and the fiercely building fires of passion.

"Yes," he gasped, burying his hot face against her neck as she found the rhythm with him, and they began moving in perfect, exquisite harmony.

His mouth found hers, and he caught her head with both hands, smiling as he felt her tighten her legs and arms and go rigid in ecstasy beneath him. He thrust into her, and the world cleaved around them.

Yes! Yes! Yes! he cried out in the silent reaches of his mind as the splendor tore through him with a savagery he had never expected to feel again in his life. His seed spilled violently into her as he moaned his satisfaction against her mouth. When the delicious spasms eventually eased their stranglehold on his loins, he lay heavily on her, breathing hard.

"I thought nothing could be as good as it was with you last night," he told her in a stunned, husky whisper. He nuzzled her damp throat and slid his arms around her hips and waist, holding her with great tenderness. "But this was even better."

He sounded incredulous, she thought, smiling. She slid her hands over his back, tightened her legs around his hips lovingly and playfully ruffled his sweat-dampened hair.

"If this was a real affair, instead of a week of two people working off their lust," she said softly, "this is where I would tell you how much I love you."

He grew very still in her arms.

She kissed his face. "I do still love you, you know," she murmured. "I wouldn't be here if I didn't." She knew she shouldn't be admitting this to him, but she had loved him very much for a very long time. Surrendering to the physical intimacy of making love with him had strained her silence beyond the breaking point.

He lifted his head and looked into her eyes. It was obvious that he very much wanted to believe her, and that he very much wanted to keep from being burned a second time by a lie.

She smiled sadly and ran her fingers through his hair, letting it spill softly against her knuckles. She massaged his temples with great gentleness and delicacy. Her eyes were clear and honest when she repeated what she had said, looking him straight in the eyes. "I love you."

His eyes darkened, and his body hardened within her. "Your effect on me is obvious," he muttered, lowering his mouth to hers for another slow, drugging kiss. "I want you again," he groaned incredulously, beginning to thrust slowly again. "I thought having you would ease the need. But it's making it grow more intense." He choked back a laugh, and it became a moan of pleasure as she writhed and panted beneath him.

"I love you," she murmured, not realizing how much pain and regret and desperation came out with the words this time. She only realized that he became incredibly attentive, raising her slowly to a fever pitch, murmuring sweet words against her damp skin, caressing her and loving her with his body until they burst into the burning fires of sunrise together.

Chapter 13

The glow of their first night and morning together grew stronger as the days rolled by. Love was not mentioned again. Nor did Blake demand the name of the man she'd left him for. It didn't matter for a while. It was enough to be together.

There was breakfast to have, and a walk through the woods to see the waterfall. It was a little cold. There had been a frost overnight, and Blake bundled her up in one of his heavy sweaters, laughing at the way it swallowed her.

She walked stride for stride with him, complaining that his long legs made it hard for her. He laughed, but he agreeably shortened his stride to accommodate her. She had forgotten how good it was to have her arm around a man's waist, feel his across her shoulders, his hand relaxed and dangling. Each simple joy was a precious jewel.

He would catch her face between his hands while their breaths made warm cloudy mists, and he'd bend to kiss her. There was a lot of that . . . spontaneous kisses, a gentle hug, a touch that lingered.

Neither of them was particularly hungry, but the rental agent had painstakingly supplied the feasts that Blake had wanted, and they tried to go through the motions of meals. It was difficult. Blake would lift his head from concentrating on carving a steak and see the rapt look in her eyes before she could hide it.

"Come here for a minute," he would say in that low voice that she found so utterly irresistible. Then they'd be kissing again, touching, making love again, and it was just the way he'd told her he wanted it to be: natural. As natural as breathing.

By the end of the week she was used to waking up to the enticing view of his magnificent, naked body sprawled comfortably across the bed. He'd stretch and yawn and open his eyes, immediately seeking her out. The blush and the grin on her face would make him laugh, and he'd pull her onto him for another long, arousing kiss.

They made love in the sunken living room and in the showers...his and hers. They made love in the bed and once, to her surprise, in the kitchen.

"This is our last dinner here," he told her softly on Saturday night. He was bare chested, wearing jeans, holding the pasta to put in the boiling water. A silent tension passed between them, and when she looped her arms around his neck and kissed him, something happened that hadn't before. An urgency, a desperation, rose up in him, in the way he kissed her, the way he handled her body. It was as if he had to get enough for the rest of his life.

She felt it, too, and the catch in her breathing was really an effort not to sob. She was wearing one of his shirts and her underpants, having just showered after swimming in the heated pool with him, and he pulled the panties down with one harsh yank. He fumbled with his pants, freed himself and pulled her down on his arousal. The rough urgency she felt in him was wildly exciting, and she responded immediately. Their mouths fused as he rolled his hips. The spaghetti fell in a shower of spindles to the floor. The chair rattled beneath them. As she splintered into a thousand brilliantine points of ecstasy, he shuddered and filled her with his seed.

They were both too shaken by the experience to move for a long time. She sat draped over him, her bare thighs and legs dangling over his, her head on his shoulder, their bodies intimately joined.

There was a different quality in their union this time. She didn't know what to call it, but she thought that he was aware of it, too. It was as if he had surrendered a small part of himself that he had been withholding earlier. Not all of himself, but a very personal piece that he could no longer keep back.

She remembered the strangely haunted look in his eyes as he finally drew her chin up and examined her face. Then he closed his eyes and sealed their mouths with another long, sweet, deeply intimate kiss. When he opened his eyes, the haunted look was wiped away. He hadn't wanted her to see it.

"Spaghetti dinners are going to make me hard," he teased her mournfully. "Every time I think of boiling the pasta I'm going to remember pulling you down onto me in this damned kitchen chair."

She giggled, and then she laughed, and then they both laughed until the tears rolled down her cheeks, and he was nearly doubled over, forcing her to dismount.

Sunday morning, as they lay in bed, the sheet over their legs, still damp from making slow, leisurely love, Blake turned onto his back and stared at the ceiling.

"How long did you stay in Arkansas after I left?" he asked casually.

Elizabeth lay on her side and feasted her eyes on him. Their time was almost over, and she wanted to enjoy every last second of it. Looking at him was one of the greatest of those pleasures, and she looked to her heart's content as she replied.

"Not long. About two months, I guess."

"Where did you go?"

"To Zurich."

"To Dorian?"

"Yes." She trailed her fingers lightly across his chest, across the light dusting of hair, the flat tight male nipples, the warm muscle and hard ribs.

"That feels good," he said with an appreciative grin.

She smiled and pressed a kiss to his chest.

He kept asking questions, however. He wasn't going to be sidetracked this time. Not if he could help it, anyway. "Did Karl go with you? At the same time?"

"Yes." Blake had the most marvelous body, she thought. Was it a sin to be so captivated? She sighed. She really didn't care whether it was or not. Anything this rich and deep and beautiful had to be goodness. She rested her head on his chest and slid her hand across his flat, hard stomach.

"Elizabeth?" He chuckled, and his chest vibrated with the sound of his laughter. "I'm glad you crave my body. God knows I crave yours. But I'd like to communicate with your mind for a few minutes. Could you raise your hand a few inches and help me out?"

She giggled and slid her hand down instead across the bush of hair and the swelling male flesh rising from it.

He grabbed her hand and said in a rather strained voice, "I want a rain check on that."

She curled against his body and nestled her head comfortably in the hollow of his shoulder. "Why do they call it a rain check? Does it mean I can't do it again until it rains?"

"Not in my dictionary," he promised her, grinning and lacing their fingers together tenderly. "Now, where was I? Oh yes. So Karl and you went to Switzerland to join Dorian a couple of months after I left for San Francisco."

"Yes." She was beginning to get a little concerned. He had a single-mindedness in his questioning that could only bode trouble for her in the end. "Why don't we go fix lunch and get the rest of the things packed . . . ?"

"We've got plenty of time," he said smoothly. "Did you start working for Rand, Limited then?"

"Yes."

"And Karl . . . did he work for Dorian, too?"

"Yes."

"How long after he started work did he have the stroke?"

She swallowed, remembering the terrible scene that had triggered it. She knew Blake could feel her tension. They were naked and intimately entwined. She felt him shift his gaze from the ceiling to her face, half buried against his chest.

"How long, Elizabeth?" he asked softly, as if there could be no harm in her telling him something as simple as that.

"About six months."

"Had he been ill before?"

"Not that we knew. He never would go to a doctor, though. You know how he was. After they got him to the hospital, they said he'd been at risk for several years and just didn't know it."

"What brought it on, then?" he asked, his curiosity mingling with empathy for Elizabeth and Karl.

She swallowed and tried to pull away from him, but he tightened his fingers on her hand and caught her leg with his. "The doctor said stress...."

"Stress? What kind of stress?"

"Working for Dorian..."

"Why did he work for Rand? I never understood that. I thought Karl loathed him."

"He...did."

"Then why did he go to work for him?" he demanded softly.

"Dorian...offered him what he wanted," she said, struggling to be honest without telling the complete truth.

She struggled a little harder to free herself and was surprised to feel his hands grip her waist and turn her over on her back. He covered her with his body, holding her hands on either side of her head. His eyes glittered with determination. Elizabeth felt a frisson of fear dance down her spine.

"What hold does Dorian have over you and Karl?" he asked, his voice hardening. "I want to know the truth, Elizabeth." His eyes fell to her parted lips, and desire darkened his face. "I'm not your enemy." A dark flush of embarrassment colored his cheeks, and he reluctantly admitted, "I had planned to be your enemy, but I've found that it isn't so simple to hate someone that I once loved." He raised his eyes to hers. "I wanted to feel indifferent to you. I wanted revenge. And then I realized what I truly wanted was *you*." He saw the slight alarm in her eyes and frowned. "You said you loved me. Why should my admission of wanting you make you afraid?" He laughed harshly. "I'm not such an inexperienced fool that I think you mean you love me as in 'forever after,' Elizabeth. Don't worry about that."

She swallowed hard to keep from telling him that was exactly what she meant; she knew she mustn't do that. She had to let him go free. "This isn't the way the week should end," she whispered. "I mean...you're supposed to have me out of your system and I..."

"And you?" He stared at her intently. "What has this meant to you, Elizabeth? I'd like to know that."

She closed her eyes as the pain ached in her throat and spread to her heart and threatened dangerously behind her eyes. "It has been the fantasy I've always wanted," she said, searching painfully for the words. She licked her lips and squeezed her eyes tight, fighting the liquid pressure. "I know you think we're despicable for having thrown in our lot with Dorian, but that's the way we've chosen to live. It's done. I have nothing more to say on that subject."

"Open your eyes," he ordered her, nuzzling each lid with a kiss, softening the demand.

She opened them, blinking hard to flutter away the telltale moisture. She saw his frown at the tears shining in her eyes, but she stared right back at him, determined to draw the line on her revelations.

"Was there a man waiting for you in Switzerland?"

She didn't want to answer that.

"Answer me."

She wouldn't.

His eyes narrowed. "If you won't, I'll hire a private detective to find out."

She was shocked. "You wouldn't!"

"Watch me."

Maybe pleading would help. It couldn't hurt, she thought. "You don't want to dig into this, Blake. Please, believe me. It will only rake up old tragedies." She struggled to free her hands from his, and she was a little surprised when he let her go. She put her arms around his neck and hugged him with her entire body, begging him to do as she wished. "Leave it alone, my love. I beg of you."

He nuzzled her throat and murmured harshly. "Either there was a man and he vanished from your life, or there never was a man and you invented him as an excuse to get rid of me. Which am I to believe?"

"It was fifteen years ago! It doesn't matter now."

He tightened his arms around her. "It does matter. It matters to me. I want the truth, Elizabeth." He captured her head and kissed her with ruthless thoroughness. He tore his mouth from hers, panting lightly at the renewed surge of desire flowing through him. "Shall I hire a detective, or are you going to answer me?"

She rolled her head helplessly from side to side, the tears welling tragically in her eyes. "There was a man. I loved him very dearly. He was older. He was wealthier than you. He needed me." With every word she uttered she saw him steel himself against a redoubled lash of pain and despair. For a second disbelief flickered in his eyes. He scowled fiercely, as if he would see the lie in her face if he could but scour it thoroughly enough. Then, having seen nothing but truth in her sea-green eyes, he closed his eyes and rolled off her onto his back.

"What happened to the son of a bitch?" he muttered tonelessly. "Was he already married? Did he die on the way to the altar?"

"He was a widower. He didn't die." That was true. She could see from Blake's stiffening that he didn't like the idea that the man was still alive on the planet somewhere.

"Why didn't you marry him?"

"It ... wasn't possible. There were ... legal impediments." Such as the fact that he was her father, and she was his daughter, and it wasn't the marrying kind of love at all. It was the love of parent and child. Seeing Blake's grim expression, she ached to comfort him, and she wrapped herself close to his side, sliding her arms around his unresponding body. "I wish you hadn't asked," she whispered brokenly.

He laughed harshly. "Yeah. So do I." He glanced down at her and, as if he couldn't help himself, he gently stroked her hair. "You know, I was wondering for a while this week if there had never been another man in your life. Sex seemed a little awkward for you at first, as if you weren't quite sure how to go about it once you got past the petting stage." He sank his fingers into her shining hair, letting it play across his knuckles like fine strands of red gold. "I hope he gave you something in exchange for all you gave up for him."

Elizabeth began to cry. She couldn't help it. She couldn't bear thinking that their intimacy had revived his wanting, the ashes of his love, and now she would be hurting him all over again. She flung her arms around his neck and kissed him on the mouth.

He was surprised by her outburst but reluctant to respond. He was hurting. Damn it. It wasn't supposed to have ended like this. He was supposed to have healed during this week with her.

Instead he had begun to feel knitted into her life again, and she had become welded into his body, soldered into his heart. He was falling in love with her all over again.

Her eyes were wet as she hovered over him, looking like a threatening angel.

"You are the only man I have ever slept with," she whispered unsteadily. She prayed that this would not prove to be her worst mistake yet. Seeing the dubious look in his eyes, she grabbed his shoulders and insisted, "It's true. I was a virgin when I came here with you. You are the only one...."

He laughed bitterly. "Why in the hell are you telling me something like this? You were tight, I grant you. I figured that meant it had been quite a while since you'd gone to bed with anyone."

"A very long while. My entire life!"

"But I didn't tear you when we made love the first time."

"By the time a woman hits thirty-three, she's been to the gynecologist, Blake." She nearly laughed at the slightly startled look in his eyes. That hadn't occurred to him, obviously. "You didn't hurt me the first time thanks to a doctor in Paris who gave me a pelvic exam ten years ago." She slumped across him, burrowing close to him, seeking the comfort of his warm strength.

Stunned, he held her in his arms. "Are you telling me the truth?"

"Yes."

How in the hell was he supposed to know for sure? Did it really matter now, anyway? He held her in his arms and rocked her gently. "Trust is a fragile thing," he reflected fatalistically.

"Like the cherry blossoms," she whispered, remembering their moonlit stroll by the Tidal Basin.

"Yes. Once they've been destroyed by a storm, there's no going back." He buried his face in her hair, inhaling the now familiar sweet scent. "I always thought of you as mine," he told her softly. "When you told me there was someone else, it was like having my heart ripped out without anesthesia. I was as enraged as a bull elephant for years after you walked out on me."

Elizabeth hugged him with her entire body, aching to comfort him as tears welled up into her eyes. "Oh, Blake..." She sobbed, tightening her arms around his shoulders, her legs around his thigh. It had hurt her, too. She told him that silently, though. She had already bared a dangerous amount of her heart to him. She didn't dare show him any more, not while Dorian held the trump card in his hand.

Blake sighed, and it was the sound of years of suffering-turned-to-hatred finally being released from his soul. "I got used to the idea that you had taken another man as a lover." He grimaced wryly. "Well, maybe not exactly *used to it,* but, hell, that's life. There was nothing to do about it but accept it. You were living on another continent, and the distance separating us helped make it more tolerable. Seeing you again brought back the old outrage and jealousy at first. Most of that was my 'rejected male' roar. I was furious...not because you had made yourself sexually available to another man, but because you'd turned me down first. I hurt for myself, and I envied him. It was infuriating that he had gotten what I had been denied. Wounded pride smarts almost as much as a bruised heart," he philosophized wryly.

She kissed his jaw and sniffled, trying surreptitiously to brush away the tears before they fell onto his face. He was intent on finishing what he had to say, though, and he didn't notice what she was doing.

"The reason I'm telling you all this is simple," he concluded, frowning. "The one thing I cannot stomach is being lied to. I can deal with just about anything else, if I have to. I want you to tell me the truth, Elizabeth, not something you think I might be flattered to hear, something I might enjoy hearing." He made a slight sound of exasperation. "After all, it isn't as if we're getting engaged or married, remember. We're ... Hell, I don't know what we are anymore, but at least we should be able to be honest with one another."

"Yes," she said, stumbling over the word and blinking back a renewed trickle of tears.

"Don't tell me that I'm the only man who ever had you unless it is the literal truth. If you think that telling me a pleasant lie will somehow soothe my old scars where you are concerned, forget it. I'd rather have brutal honesty." He turned on his side and looked into her face. He was completely sober and deadly serious. "I mean every word I've just said, Elizabeth."

She blinked rapidly and brushed away another renegade trickle. She saw him frown as he finally realized she was crying. He reached out to touch the tears with his fingertips, and she caught his hand, brought it swiftly to her lips and kissed it like a loyal vassal swearing fealty to her liege.

"I have *always* told you the truth," she swore. "I have not told you everything, and sometimes that has meant I have misled you. For that, I am and always will be sorry. It's a lie of a different sort . . . a lie of omission, I guess. But what I've told you is true."

Their eyes locked, hers open and loving . . . his dark and searching.

He uttered a painful growl, pulled her tenderly into his arms and closed his eyes. He wanted to believe her. That was the worst part of it. She was offering him a gift that he had hungered for, and he wanted to take it. She'd ferreted out another tightly locked corner of his heart and stolen it away from him. He wanted her to have it, and yet he was afraid to let her.

He was falling in love with her again and, like the last time, he couldn't seem to do a damned thing to stop it. He found her mouth and kissed her very slowly, moving with the warmth and sweetness born of the aching tenderness he felt for her. He felt her tears of pain change to tears of joy, and he felt a swift rush of pride that he could have that deep an effect on her. Although he still wasn't completely convinced she was telling him the truth, he was having an uphill battle reminding himself not to care one way or the other, in spite of his carefully outlined statement to her to the contrary.

If she told him that night was day, at the moment he might have agreed to accept it.

They reluctantly broke off the kiss and lay locked in each other's arms for close to an hour in silence, lost in their separate troubled thoughts and mutually soothed by their physical closeness.

Elizabeth finally spoke, but she had to clear her rusty throat twice before the words would come out. "We'd better start packing," she said huskily. "It's getting late."

"Yeah." He let her crawl out of his arms, and then he slowly rolled off the bed. He sounded tired as he quietly said, "I'll take you home."

It was already dark that night when Blake pulled into his parking space in the garage and took Elizabeth upstairs to his apartment. He unlocked the door and ushered her inside with a frown forming on his face.

"Are you sure I can't drive you home?" he asked.

Elizabeth smiled and shook her head. "I'd rather take a cab."

He stared at her pensively as she strolled about his living room, curiously examining his possessions. He didn't like the idea of her coming and going in a taxi, as if she were hiding their relationship. He knew it was ridiculous of him to take umbrage at that. With Dorian still pressuring her, the more privacy they had, the easier it would be for them to relax and enjoy each other, even if it was for a brief period of time. That was what he assumed she was willing to engage in, of course. A short affair. His frown became darker as he watched her wander around, looking over his things. He didn't want a short affair. He was beginning to think in terms of a long one, instead. It wasn't fair to her, of course. He wasn't offering her a future. On the other hand, she didn't seem to be worried about that, so why was he? Because he just didn't feel right about it, damn it.

"This is really nice, Blake," she said admiringly.

"Thanks. You'll have to come back."

"I'd like that." She trailed her fingers over a black glass vase filled with dried eucalyptus, pussy willows, delicate *monnaie-de pape*. "Very tasteful," she murmured.

He had sculptured wall-to-wall carpeting in a soft shade of desert-pink clay, a huge curving sofa, styled in Milan she thought, seeing its clean, modern lines. There was a large oil painting hanging on one wall. Its bold colors and geometric shapes brightened the otherwise smooth, soothing tones that dominated everything else she could see.

He had a Nakashima coffee table near the sofa, and it was spread with papers, pens, a calculator and a multibutton business phone. She looked up at him and was startled to discover that he was watching her with the intensity of a panther stalking its prey. She swallowed. It gave her the strangest pleasure to be on the receiving end of that predatory gaze.

He blinked and cleared his throat uncomfortably. He couldn't drag her down on his sofa, damn it. What was the matter with him? It wasn't as if he hadn't had any sex recently! He should have been drained dry for the rest of the year, ready to sack out alone in a hammock for the foreseeable future after the active love life they'd so vigorously pursued for the past seven days. His body apparently hadn't been counting. It was perfectly willing to rise to the occasion. He dragged his eyes away from her and tried to remember why they'd come up here. To phone a cab. That was it.

He walked over to the telephone and passed through air that had been kissed by her body. Her scent assailed him, and he felt an ache coil in his belly. He clenched his jaw and reached down to phone the taxi company.

"I'd like a cab in fifteen minutes," he told the dispatcher briskly. He gave them the address and hung up the phone. "Care for a cup of coffee while we wait?" he asked tightly. "I think I could use one." Or maybe a quart of hard liquor. That ought to render his libido non-functional for a while.

"No, thank you." She looked around. She knew she shouldn't feel shy about asking, especially after living with him for the past week on their "vacation," but she couldn't help it. A little awkwardly, she murmured, "Could I use your bathroom?"

He pointed down the hall. "Help yourself."

He seemed relieved that she was heading in the opposite direction, she thought. When she rejoined him, he was pouring boiling water in a mug of instant coffee in his kitchen. He looked up at her.

"Did you find what you need?" he deadpanned.

She laughed. "Yes. You're very tidy. Everything is neat and clean."

"I pay someone to come in and pick up a couple times a week," he said with a shrug.

She shook her head. "I think you're pretty good about picking up after yourself."

He laughed. "Not all bachelors are slobs," he pointed out.

She ran her fingertip over the faint shell pattern in the countertop. "Blake?"

"Yes?"

"Who is the girl in the picture with you?"

He was taking a swallow of his coffee, and it nearly went down the wrong way. He managed to clear his throat, then asked, "What girl? What picture?"

Elizabeth nodded toward the large, silver-framed photograph hung on the dining alcove wall. He followed the direction of her gaze, and his expression softened in affection.

"That's Shelby Mar...Macklin." He laughed. "I keep using her old name," he explained.

Elizabeth studied their smiling faces. "She's very pretty. You look very relaxed and happy together."

He put the mug down and leaned his hip against the counter. He heard the feminine curiosity in Elizabeth's voice, the slight hint of jealousy that she was obviously trying not to feel but couldn't entirely hide. He smiled. "She is very pretty. We've been very close friends for a very long time. Since San Francisco."

"Oh." Elizabeth went over to the window and looked down. No cab. She had to stand there and wonder about the beautiful Shelby while he watched her suffer, she thought miserably.

He came over and stood behind her.

"She's a friend, Elizabeth," he said softly.

"A *friend* friend? Or a *girlfriend* friend?" she asked, holding her breath.

He bent close to her ear. "A *friend* friend. If you're wondering if she's my lover, the answer is no."

"I wasn't wondering..." she protested faintly.

He turned her around to face him. "The hell you weren't."

She rested her head against his chest. "Well, maybe I was just the slightest bit curious."

He laughed softly and wrapped his arms around her. "I'm glad you're interested. I'll be happy to satisfy your curiosity on any subject."

Elizabeth remembered the article in the Sunday paper and bit her lip. She wasn't sure she should ask about Katrin Louwens. Sometimes it was wiser not to inquire, especially if you might not like the answer.

"Blake?" she asked instead.

"Hmm?"

"Were you ever engaged or married...after we broke up."

"No."

She looked up at him. She didn't want to ask him if he'd ever fallen in love, ever made love to another woman. She didn't want to hear him say yes to that, and she thought he probably would. He had handled her with a knowledge that had to have come from experience. He had been sensitive to her, of course, aware of her needs and responding to her particular expressions of pleasure. All the same, he must have done it before, and she knew she didn't want to hear about *that*.

There was something else she could ask him, though.

"Have you ever wanted to have a family someday?" she asked lightheartedly. She pulled a little away from him and, anticipating how he might take her question, amended, "Hypothetically speaking, of course." Not with her. Not with anyone in particular.

He was surprised. "Someday, I guess. If I find the right woman." She had once been that woman, of course. Angry that he was falling under her spell again, he responded more coldly than he would have otherwise. "If I find a woman who will stick with me through thick and thin, who'll love me as much as I love her, yes, I'd like kids." He shrugged and turned away from her, pacing back into the living room. "Kids deserve a stable, loving family. They're not for fly-by-night operations."

She flinched as if he'd slapped her. Was he referring to their past week as a "fly-by-night operation"? She put her hands to her abdomen, remembering how honeyed she had felt thinking that if she became pregnant, she would at least have his child to love for the rest of her life, even if she couldn't have him. But listening to him, she felt a terrible wave of guilt sweep over her. Blake deserved to know his own child. He would make a wonderful father, too, she thought. It would be tragic to keep his child from knowing him.

He stuffed his hands into his trouser pockets, thinking about Elizabeth bearing a child of his, hating the helplessness he felt knowing that would never happen. They were two people destined to want each other and not be able to make a life together, he thought. And yet, if she got pregnant, maybe... No. That was crazy thinking. Pregnancy didn't solve problems. It added to them.

"Speaking of children," he muttered. "You said you were going to take care of birth control. What did you use?" He laughed cheerlessly. "It's a little late for me to be expressing much interest, of course, but I don't remember seeing anything lying around. Pills require some time to take effect, don't they?"

Lies of omission, she had told him. She felt sick. Thinking of her own yearning for his child had been an act of incredible selfishness, she realized. It was a little late for that, though. She wouldn't know if she was pregnant for several weeks. She wanted to cry. She wanted to ask his forgiveness for this, too.

He turned to see why she wasn't answering him. "Elizabeth?"

She looked down at the street and saw her salvation. "The taxi is here!" she exclaimed joyfully.

She didn't have to be so damned happy about it, he thought furiously. Here he was wondering how in the hell he was going to get through the next two weeks without rolling over and finding her in his bed, and she was ready to run downstairs as if the cab were the Queen Mary about to take her on a luxury, all-expenses-paid trip around the world.

"Let's go, then," he growled, striding to the door. "By the way, I'll be out of town for a while. In the middle of next week I'm going to Paris. I'll be there next weekend."

"Oh," she murmured, faltering a step as she joined him in the elevator. Her heart was in her eyes as she said, "I'll miss you."

He pulled her into his arms and kissed her, grinding his mouth against hers; then, as the anger drained out of him, he gentled the kiss, taking them both to the heart of pleasure with it.

"I'll call you when I get back," he whispered against her mouth. The elevator doors opened, and he held her head still, gazing down into her face as if he would memorize it for all time. "Tell Dorian I'm willing to spend at least a quarter of a million dollars at his auction."

Her eyes grew round. Horrified, she protested, "No! Don't tell me that. I don't want to know!"

His hard lips softened into a tender smile. "I don't know what in the hell is going on between you and Karl and Dorian, but if you need the information I just gave you, use it. It's my gift to you."

Tears filled her eyes, and she wrapped her arms around him. "I don't know what to say, Blake," she cried brokenly.

He hugged her hard, then gently set her away. "Come on. Let's get your bags. You've got to get home before it gets any later."

Trailing behind his long stride, her hand held in his, she silently told him she loved him. She knew he couldn't hear, but their hands were warm and his grip hard, and the feeling was there between them, even without the words.

He put her into the cab and peeled off some money for the driver. "Make sure she gets in safely. Okay, buddy?" he said. Then, turning to Elizabeth, he murmured, "Good night."

"Have a safe trip," she told him, smiling tremulously.

"I'll do my best."

Chapter 14

Dorian wasted no time in finding her when she didn't come down to breakfast on Monday morning. He walked into her workshop immediately after he'd finished eating. As usual, he got right to the point.

"Welcome back, my dear. I hope you had a stimulating trip. Sorry I had already retired by the time you returned."

Elizabeth was bending over a metal gauge, trying to determine the precise thickness of silver wire that would be needed for a piece of jewelry she'd been constructing. She stopped focusing on the round, flat gauge with its circle of holes in progressively larger diameters and stared at a point in the air about a foot in front of her.

"Hello, Dorian," she said calmly.

"About that question I wanted answered..." He left the sentence hanging delicately incomplete.

Elizabeth reached for the soldering iron and began piecing the raw elements of the necklace together. Concentrating on the task helped her remain calm. She hoped Dorian took her mild disinterest to mean that she wasn't going to be affected by his efforts to push her into Blake's confidences.

"How much will he be bringing to spend at the auction?" Dorian demanded in an autocratic tone, losing patience.

"You're asking the wrong person," she said. The silver melted beneath the hot iron, and the two pieces of wire became welded into one.

Dorian paused. "You force me to do something... unpleasant, in that case."

Elizabeth gave him a mildly incredulous look and said with cool sarcasm, "You? Do something unpleasant?" She laughed. "It won't be much of a stretch for you, Dorian. You needn't play the nobleman with me, either. Remember? I've been your bonded servant for fifteen years. I know you."

His eyes glittered, and he clutched the cane in his hand until his twisted knuckles turned white. "Do you? I think not. Did you know that I am quite in debt?" He saw the flicker of surprise in her face and laughed harshly. "No. You didn't know. You guessed, of course, that I lived too flamboyant a life, but you didn't realize just how much I've overextended myself."

"Why didn't you stay in Zurich?" she asked in surprise. "You had bankers and creditors there. Surely..."

"My financial arrangements are none of your affair," he said coldly. "Suffice it to say that I require a substantial infusion of cash in order to pay off a particular creditor who no longer wishes to extend my payments."

Her blood chilled. "Who is the creditor?" she asked.

"He arranged for me to receive some emeralds from Colombia last year, and I was to have paid him by now. Alas, I cannot. He does not comprehend the functions of collection agencies or refinancing plans. If I do not pay, he will simply send someone to cut my throat." He laughed at the pallor in her face. "He may also cut yours. He has even fewer scruples than I do."

"That is a rare accomplishment," she whispered in horror. "What is he? A South American drug runner? A terrorist?"

Dorian shrugged. "He's a very determined man to whom I owe a substantial amount of money." He paused. "I will be able to raise enough from the sale of my prize collection to cover most of my needs for the next fifteen years. At my age, that may be more than enough. However, I will need additional funds to pay him off. So... I will be adding one more item to the auction.''

There was something in his tone that made Elizabeth suddenly alert. ''What piece?'' she asked.

He looked like a snake about to strike. ''The one piece of gold jewelry that someone might be willing to pay a significant price for...''

''Oh, no...'' Her eyes widened in horror. ''You promised...''

''It cannot be helped. The circumstances have changed. I must sell the gold-and-sapphire necklace that Karl made during your late mother's fatal illness.''

She dropped the silver and jumped to her feet. ''You *can't* Dorian. You *promised* that I could earn it from you. I've already given you a year's worth of work for it. I'll work for the next five, however long it takes to buy it from you....''

''I *cannot wait*,'' he said furiously. ''Do you think I would willingly abandon you if I could avoid it?'' He made a rude sound and glared at her as if she were a cretin. His eyes narrowed, and he said angrily, ''Fifteen years ago I had the good fortune to stumble across the information that would indenture Karl and you to me for as long as I wished. Unfortunately, Karl fell ill before I could fully realize my benefits from him. Nevertheless, it's worked out very well, I think. *You* became even better than I had expected, and I had expected much to begin with. I saw your potential even when you were slaving away with your father and Blake in Arkansas,'' he boasted.

''Then, why not continue?'' she interrupted desperately.

Dorian shot her a venomous look. ''Because I no longer need someone who will slave for years for me making money! I need to pay off a debt *immediately*. If I don't produce the money, my life will be very short, my dear,'' he snarled. ''In which case, I would not require your devoted service.''

Desperately, Elizabeth tried to think of some alternative. ''Perhaps someone could...'' Her voice trailed off. Someone could what? Buy the necklace and discover the fraud? That was it! Triumphantly, she turned on Dorian. ''You *can't* sell it! The buyer will discover you've defrauded him. You'd go to jail!''

Dorian laughed unpleasantly, rolling back his head and limping a few steps away. He shook his head and speared her with an implacable look. "No. Karl is so well respected, his name has been literally as good as gold for years, my dear Elizabeth. The pieces which I generously took the time to locate and purchase had happy owners who wouldn't have believed the gold was of lower value than Karl had stamped it," he pointed out. Then, shrugging, he added, "In my present situation, I am forced to take the chance of discovery, anyway. If I am fortunate, the purchaser will not test it. Or he will do only a surface test of the metal, rather than checking the content of the metal beneath."

"But what if the buyer *does* test the entire piece?" Elizabeth pressed him intently. "Then what, Dorian? Are you prepared to spend your declining years in jail?" She leaned toward him. "I can't imagine that, Dorian." He was much too arrogant to tolerate that.

Dorian inclined his head. "You are quite right, my dear. And I assure you I would not be the one to go to jail. Karl would go, if anyone must."

Elizabeth paled. "No!"

He shrugged philosophically. "Yes. You see, I would say that I had no knowledge of the misrepresentation of the gold content." He smiled silkily. "I have merely been kind enough to help my old friend, Karl, and you during difficult years of your lives. I've been generous enough to help collect some favorite pieces that Karl had expressed a desire to repurchase."

"No one would believe you," Elizabeth said heatedly. "I would tell them the truth. There would be no reason then for me to keep silent. Not if you were going to throw my father to the wolves."

Dorian appeared unimpressed by her threat. "My dear," he said condescendingly, leaning on his cane, "it would be your word against mine. You have absolutely no proof. The worst thing that could happen to me is that some people might doubt me. Doubt, Elizabeth, is not enough to put me behind bars. Karl, on the other hand, clearly lied. He created the pieces. He marked them incorrectly. An artist of his ability would never have done such a thing accidentally. And especially not more than once!''

Elizabeth stared at Dorian and felt a sudden sense of hopelessness. ''But I've worked to pay for some of it already, Dorian. If I could somehow get the balance, would you let me buy it?'' She swallowed the remnants of her pride and begged, softly. ''Please, Dorian?''

He stared at her through eagle eyes, obviously pondering how much it cost her pride to be reduced to pleading with him. ''I am sorry you did not marry my son, Elizabeth,'' he mused. ''You are indeed a magnificent woman.'' He frowned, and added briskly. ''However, this is business and a matter of life or death. Not that I wish to sound melodramatic,'' he added dryly. ''If I could keep the necklace, I would. The fact is that I cannot. Regrettably, the price has risen since you began working to purchase it. I don't think I will be able to credit your earnings toward the necklace now. The situation has changed, my dear.''

Elizabeth, stunned and bitter, stared at him in silence.

His lips twisted into a cynical smile. ''It may be difficult for you to believe, Elizabeth, but after the necklace has been sold, and you are no longer forced to submit to my employment, I am going to miss you. Ours has been a most stimulating battle of wills.'' He limped to the door. Then, as if having an afterthought, he tossed back at her, ''Of course, if by some miraculous intervention you *are* able to come up with the full price, by all means, come to the auction and put in a bid.'' He smiled coolly. ''Of course, I couldn't let it go for less than its full value. So unless you are prepared to offer more than anyone else could be expected to pay at the auction, I would not be inclined to engage in a private sale to you.''

''With what should I pay you, Dorian?'' she practically shouted at him. ''All my money has gone into your pockets, buying the other pieces over the years. I've already given a year's worth of work to you for this one. How much do you owe me for that?'' she demanded desperately.

He laughed. ''My dear, I fear that I am cash poor at the moment. It is embarrassing, but a fact. You will have to move to the back of the queue if you wish to submit a bill to me.''

She stared at him, torn between the urge to scream and the desire to destroy him.

He gave her a considering look. "Perhaps you *should* consider procuring financing and attempting to purchase the necklace at the auction," he conceded, apparently giving the idea serious thought for the first time. He smiled meaningfully. "You might consider expressing your interest in the item to your old friend, Blake Malone," he suggested.

Elizabeth paled. She tightened her hands into small fists at her side. "Leave Blake out of your plotting, Dorian," she warned him icily.

"What other alternatives are there?" he asked. With a last, shrewd look, he left, leaving her to consider the worrisome seeds he had planted.

Elizabeth paced back and forth across her workshop, lacing and unlacing her fingers, as she tried to think of a way out. If only she had the money to buy the necklace herself. How on earth could she get it? And what if someone wished to examine the gold content before taking possession? Her blood ran cold at the thought. It was a cruel twist of fate that she found herself so near and yet so far from her goal.

Should she confide in Blake? she wondered. She smiled, but the curve of her lips was bittersweet. He might be willing to help her, but she was not willing to let him become involved. She wanted him kept clear of her father's crime and her own fifteen-year effort to recover his fraudulently stamped creations.

There *had* to be another way, but who on the face of the earth might be willing and able to finance such a costly purchase for her? And what could she offer in exchange?

She bit her lip and frowned, pacing back and forth across the workshop. Then all of a sudden it hit her. She stopped dead in the middle of the floor and snapped her fingers. "Jacques Martin!" she exclaimed triumphantly. "I *know* he'd do it."

Jacques had enough working capital to buy the necklace ten times over without bothering to talk to anyone. Jacques loved her like a daughter, and he had often teased her that she should come to Paris and work with him.

Elizabeth sat down at her work bench and buried her face in her hands. Jacques would do it for her; he would buy the necklace, and he would not even insist on examining it first. He trusted her. God, he trusted her, she thought hysterically. Like Blake. Their faith was a terrible cross to bear, she thought despairingly. Forgive me . . .

There was one unfortunate aspect of having Jacques Martin purchase the necklace in exchange for her working for him. She would have to join him in Paris. She would have to leave Washington . . . and Blake. Again.

"My love," she whispered as she fought off the tears that suddenly threatened. "My love, my love . . ."

It was ironic that she should be so distraught at leaving him, she realized. When she had arrived here, she had been desperate to avoid seeing him again. She had always known what would happen to her, and, of course, it had. She was more deeply in love with him than ever before.

Could her heart break twice and still survive? She smiled wistfully at the trunk that contained her memories of happiness. Yes. She could survive. It wouldn't be easy, but she had their brief time together to comfort her.

And there was the faint possibility that she would have a living, breathing comforter, as well, if she had conceived his child after their week of loving. That was a bittersweet possibility. If she was pregnant, she knew that she would eventually have to tell Blake. She owed him that, at least. But if she was living in Paris, working with Jacques, she wouldn't have to be a burden to Blake. The French health-care system was marvelous for a woman in her situation. She would have medical care for herself and the child. And the French were very philosophical and realistic when it came to accepting pregnancy outside of marriage, fortunately.

She was getting way ahead of herself, she thought. She might not even be pregnant. She wouldn't know for a few weeks yet. First she had to take care of the most immediate crisis: preventing the sale of Karl's last remaining fraud to someone who might expose his crime before she could destroy the evidence.

She got a firm grip on her emotions and briskly wiped the tears off her cheeks. Crying wasn't going to save her or Karl. She had to write to Jacques, a personal letter, delivered through the international overnight express mail. He would keep her communication in complete confidence, she knew. She would have to give him a rather lengthy explanation, and a letter seemed the best way to do that without alerting Dorian to her plan.

She didn't want to call Jacques from the house. Dorian wasn't beneath listening in on the conversation, if he became aware of it. If she used the Rand, Limited telephone credit-card number and called from some other location, Dorian would see the record of it when he got the bill, ruling that possibility out, as well.

She was determined to keep Dorian in the dark about her efforts. Years of bitter experience with the man had taught her that the less he knew about her plans, the better her chances of success would be. In this case, she wasn't sure what he might do if he knew she had someone to turn to for help. He might raise the minimum bid for the necklace at the auction. Or he might withdraw the piece altogether and try to squeeze an outrageously high price from her benefactor. Then again, she thought unhappily, he might come up with some even wilder extortion that she couldn't even imagine. Where Dorian was concerned, anything was possible.

So let him think that she was at his mercy this time. Perhaps that way she could at last find a means to escape from him. And take her father, too. A free man at last.

Elizabeth scrounged through her desk drawer and located stationery and pen. She paused, wondering how to explain. Where should she begin? She touched pen to paper and wrote:

Dear Jacques

It has been many months since I have had the pleasure of seeing you, and I regret that, as I write to you now, I will be asking the greatest favor of you that I have ever asked of anyone in my life. Please do not tell anyone of this communication, even if you must decline my request. And if you do decline, I will understand. Believe me, it is very hard to have to ask.

You have no doubt heard about the auction that Dorian is having in three weeks. He has added another piece to the sale items. It is one which is more dear to me, and to my father, than anything else in the world. If I could afford to buy it myself, I would. As you probably can guess, I couldn't come near the price that Dorian will want for it. It is an exquisite necklace of gold set with brilliant, clear sapphires, made by my father thirty years ago, when he was living in New York and my mother lay dying of tuberculosis.

The favor I wish to ask of you is this: Would you consider purchasing the necklace at the auction and allowing me to work for you as a designer until I have been able to earn the money and pay you back?

Dorian and I have never had a contract, and now that he is liquidating everything, I am free to stay with him or leave, as I choose. I would be a free agent, Jacques, and I would be honored to design or work in any related capacity in your business that you might wish.

It is imperative that Dorian not know that I am asking this of you. If he was to discover my effort, he would raise the minimum bid until all of us were bled dry. You know how he is when he scents an open wallet!

If you participate in the auction, I will undoubtedly see you, or your agent, there. You can let me know at that time whether or not you are in a position to purchase the necklace. If you wish to agree to my plan, I will be happy to sign a written contract with you, with terms of your choosing. You know I trust you, Jacques.

No matter what you decide, I will of course be indebted to you for your many kindnesses to me over the years. You know how many times you have boosted my spirits when they were dragging so low that I thought I might never smile again.

Affectionately, your friend,

Elizabeth Rossi

She took a deep breath, folded the carefully penned message and put it into an international overnight-express envelope. She slipped the large red-white-black-and-blue envelope into a plastic bag bearing the logo of a local retail store. If

Dorian happened to be lurking about as she left the house, he wouldn't see what she was about to put in the mail.

Her purse was slung casually over the back of a chair, and she retrieved it as she phoned for a cab to take her to the nearest post office. Jacques would have her letter tomorrow, if he was in Paris. In three weeks, she would know his answer.

It would have been good to feel Blake's arms around her as she endured the wait, she thought, feeling very lonely again. She tried to remember the comforting sensation of being wrapped in his strength, and she found that even the memory of it helped.

"Thank you, my love," she murmured as she watched for the cab from the steps in front of the house. "You're here when I need you, even though you don't realize it."

She smiled. She hoped that he would have been flattered to know that she took strength from him even when he wasn't with her.

Blake had finished his business in Paris earlier than he had expected. He had twelve hours before he needed to begin checking in at Orly for the return flight to Washington. He'd been gone for six days and was more than ready to get back.

He could have spent the time at a sidewalk café, watching garrulous Parisians as they strolled by, arguing with their particularly Gallic brand of world-weary animation. For once, however, observing the sidewalk society held no appeal.

He was preoccupied, thinking about Elizabeth. He needed to solve the riddle of her, and he needed to decide how to approach her again when he got back to Washington. He knew he wasn't going to let her walk away, now that their week of lust-slaking was behind them. He laughed. It certainly had failed in so far as the slaking was concerned.

If he could only pry her loose from Dorian's grasp, perhaps they could find each other again. What in the devil could that old schemer have that exerted such control over her? He'd almost asked his partners, both of whom were well-connected with the intelligence community, to undertake a private investigation of Elizabeth, Karl and Dorian. He hated to do that, though, for Elizabeth's sake. So he'd put off asking and was still trying to find a way to break the mystery's shackles himself. Alone.

He was standing by the metro entrance nearest his hotel when he suddenly realized that he might be able to peel away a few layers of that mystery while he was in France. He didn't know why it had taken him so long to think of it, once the idea occurred to him.

Jacques Martin had a tender spot in his heart for Elizabeth. Perhaps *he* could fill in a few of the blanks in Karl and Elizabeth's life. Hell, he had nothing to lose.

Blake smiled grimly and hailed a taxi. "Jacques . . . you owe me for your breach of faith. If necessary, I'll stoop to pointing that out to you, old friend." He got into the cab, feeling more optimistic than he had for several days. He doubted that he would have to use more than friendly persuasion to get Jacques to tell him what he knew about the Rossis. His association with Jacques Martin went back quite a few years. But if he had to apply a little pressure, he was more than willing to do it.

The look of shock and joy on the French jewel trader's face was almost comical. After the customary hugs and an amusing exchange of anecdotes and gossip, Jacques settled comfortably across a coffee table from Blake and asked, "Eh, *bien!* What wonderful event has brought you to my door?"

"We have a mutual friend. . . ."

"C'est sûr," Jacques agreed with a robust laugh. "Many." He lifted his silvery brows with great expressiveness. "Which one did you come to discuss?"

"Elizabeth Rossi . . ."

Jacques' face became comically surprised. He glanced toward his desk and reached out to pick up an envelope. "What a bizarre coincidence!" he exclaimed. "I myself have just flown back from Algiers this morning, and my secretary told me that this arrived a few days ago. I was just going to open it when you arrived."

Blake saw Elizabeth's name and address clearly printed on the mailing label. He watched as Jacques opened the envelope and pulled out her letter.

Jacques had been beaming to begin with, but as he quickly read through the letter, his smile faded away. When he was finished, he carefully refolded it and put it away, giving Blake an embarrassed look. "It was, uh, personal. I, uh, shouldn't have interrupted you." He laughed awkwardly. "Forgive me... You were saying?"

Blake's eyes narrowed. "Personal?" he said softly.

"Oui." Jacques smiled and waved it off as of no consequence. However, his eyes had an unusually shrewd light in them as he looked at Blake. "You said you wanted to talk about Elizabeth? From the look in your face, my friend, I assume that the talk will not be, er, completely business?"

"No, it will be ... personal." Blake frowned slightly. "Did you know that Elizabeth and I were once engaged?"

Jacques looked astonished. *"Mais, non.* I did not."

Blake nodded. "Yes. Fifteen years ago. On the night we were to have eloped, she told me she was leaving me because she loved another man, older and wealthier than I."

Jacques was the picture of male empathy for Blake's plight. "That can be very difficult," he sympathized. He frowned and shook his head. "But I don't remember her ever being involved with an older man ... wealthy or poor. And I've known her since she was just a little girl. I think I would have heard about it. She..." Jacques hesitated.

"She what?" Blake asked.

"I am not sure she would like me to share her confidences...."

Blake smiled, but there was no joy in his face. "I spent the last week with her, Jacques," he told his old friend. "I want to spend many more with her. Something happened fifteen years ago that interfered with our lives, and Dorian had something to do with it. I'm sure. He has some sort of control over her. I came here today because I hoped you might know some of the pieces to this puzzle, and that you might love Elizabeth, and me, well enough to tell me what they are. I'd like to see her free of him."

Jacques nodded thoughtfully and pursed his plump lips as he thought. He glanced at Elizabeth's letter. "I wish I could tell you what she said there."

Blake glanced sharply at the missive. "Why?"

Jacques sighed. "I think that the situation will be coming to point of climax in the next few weeks." He spread his hands ologetically. "I cannot tell you what she wrote. She asked me keep everything in confidence. But . . ."

"But?" Blake pushed him, leaning forward in his chair. "But hat, Jacques?"

"I suppose I could tell you what I know about her and Karl d Dorian. Everything that is not in that letter."

"I'm listening."

"*Bien* . . . Let's see. . . ." Jacques stroked his double chin nsively. "Thirty years ago, Karl's wife became very ill. She d been worn out for years, because Karl earned very little and ey had gone without food and medical care on many occasions during their marriage. Giving birth to Elizabeth was very rd on her in such a weakened condition, but she was happy have the baby. The three of them loved one another very uch." Jacques cleared his throat, as if having a small attack emotion. "She came down with tuberculosis. Karl was living in New York, working for next to nothing in the diamond strict. He was cutting diamonds to keep clothes on their cks. The man he was working for in those days was even ore of a scrooge than Dorian."

"That's hard to imagine," Blake said in disgust.

"*Oui.* But it is true. Then Karl began having success with his signs. He had created six or seven especially fine pieces of welry over the previous several years. Gradually his reputation began to grow. Wealthy people wanted his work. They re eager to pay. There was a lot of money around at the time, d somehow he managed to scrape together enough gold and ne gems to keep creating magnificent pieces to sell. It was a od thing, of course, because he needed every penny to keep ilk in Elizabeth's stomach and to provide nursing care for his ring wife."

"I had no idea it was so tough for them," Blake muttered. e could imagine now, more easily than he could have at enty, what Karl must have felt like, desperate to save the oman he loved and to provide for a totally dependent child.

Jacques steepled his chubby fingers and stared at Blake. "After his wife died, Elizabeth was the only thing that kep Karl from going insane with grief. Many of us tried to help him We offered him jobs, and finally he took one down in Arkan sas. He wanted to raise Elizabeth someplace quiet, away fror the sweatshops and street crime of the big cities. By the time h moved down there, Elizabeth was in high school."

"That's where I met them," Blake said.

Jacques nodded. "Hmm. I see."

"You said there wasn't an older man in her life?" Blak asked, frowning. "Could there have been a young man?"

Jacques smiled. "Men have always approached Elizabeth When she and Karl were living with Dorian in Switzerland, sh had a steady stream of males dancing attendance on her. Bu she was unimpressed. And . . ." He grew somber.

"And?"

"She was working herself to the bone."

Blake frowned. "That's another part of the mystery Jacques. I've seen some of the things she's made. Damn it, I'v even bought them. You know that yourself. Why in the hell i she living a life worthy of someone who's sworn a vow of pov erty? Hasn't Dorian paid her?" He was furious at the idea o such ruthless exploitation, and he didn't bother to try to hid it.

Jacques chuckled, and his eyes gleamed. "You sound mor like an outraged lover than a concerned former fiancé," h pointed out.

Blake sighed. "It's pretty obvious, isn't it?"

Jacques clapped him on the shoulder sympathetically. "Sh always seemed very interested in what you were doing," he tol Blake encouragingly. "There were times when I wondere about that, but then she would back away, and I could onl guess at why she found your particular business so fascinat ing."

Blake ran his hands through his hair in frustration. "Wha hold could Dorian have over them, Jacques? There's *som thing,* but I'm damned if I can figure out what it could be."

Jacques frowned and his eyes drifted to the letter. "Are yo going to Dorian's auction?"

Blake stared at him. "Yes."

"I, too, will be attending." Jacques seemed to be turning over the possibilities in his mind. "Perhaps you and I should meet and continue this discussion there."

Blake had the impression that Jacques was doing his best to tell him something important, something he was constrained from saying directly. "All right."

Jacques frowned. "You asked why Elizabeth seems to have so little money, and I am not sure I have an answer for that. I do remember one strange incident that happened five years ago, and I will share it with you. It may be nothing, but . . . I was at Dorian's house in Zurich, and I went to see Elizabeth. She was melting a piece of gold in her crucible. I caught her at it, thinking to surprise her, but she leaped as if I had caught her breaking into a secret Swiss bank account!"

Blake frowned. That didn't sound like Elizabeth. "Maybe she was just nervous," he suggested. "What are you getting at, Jacques?"

The Frenchman shrugged. "Perhaps it is nothing. I could, of course, be very wrong. But there was a piece of the metal yet unmelted. It looked to me like one of the necklaces that Karl had sold to a woman in Paris years ago. She had died five years earlier, and her estate had gone to the auction block. I myself had bid on that necklace. It was one of Karl's finest pieces. But someone else bought it."

"Who?"

"Dorian Rand."

Blake grimaced. "Why would Elizabeth melt it down?"

Jacques laughed. "That, my friend, is a very interesting question. When I looked in the crucible, she told me it was her income for the past five years that was melting there. At the time, I thought she was teasing me. She laughed and took me by the arm and led me out into the garden. I let it go. And yet, today, when you ask where her money is, I think of that day in Zurich, and what she said. Perhaps it was the literal truth. Perhaps in return for her work, Dorian gave her back her father's necklace."

Blake shook his head. "I'm not sure this is clearing anything up for me," he muttered. "I feel like I'm walking deeper into the brambles in the woods."

Jacques nodded sympathetically. "*Oui*. It is a difficult problem to resolve. Still . . . I think it would be wise for us to meet again in Washington. Perhaps just before the auction?"

Blake glanced at his watch and rose to his feet. He had to leave, if he wanted to make his plane. "You have my numbers, Jacques. Call me when you get into town." He smiled. "Thank you, old friend, for your candor and your advice."

Jacques laughed robustly and walked him to the door. "Anything for *l'amour,* my friend! I am, after all, a Frenchman!" he exclaimed.

The day after Blake returned from Europe, he called Elizabeth. When she came to the phone, he felt years of tension roll off him.

"Hello, yourself," he teased her, replying to her breathless greeting. "Did you just run downstairs?"

She laughed. "As a matter of fact, I did."

"I'm flattered."

She smiled. "Did you have a good trip?"

"On balance, I guess you'd have to call it a success." He hesitated. "Do you have any free time in your schedule this week? Say for dinner?"

"Yes. When did you have in mind?" She tried to sound nonchalant, but it was very tough. She was dying to spend as much time as she could with him in the couple of weeks remaining before the auction.

He cleared his throat. "Well, how about tonight?"

She heard a note of insecurity in his otherwise suave delivery and was utterly charmed by him all over again. Softly, she said, "Tonight would be wonderful."

"Can I pick you up this time?" he asked dryly.

She laughed, feeling as free as a bird in spring. "Oh, yes. When do you want me?"

"All the time," he said starkly.

She ached with longing. "Me too," she whispered.

"I missed you," he told her softly. "If I didn't have so many damned things to take care of here at the office, I'd be having this conversation with you in person."

She didn't know what to say. If he was there, she would have hugged him. Instead she asked, "When should I expect you?"

"Give me a couple of hours. All right?"

"Of course."

"Elizabeth?"

"Yes?"

"Plan to stay late. At my place."

"All right," she agreed, smiling as she hung up the phone.

He kissed her lightly on the mouth the minute she sat down in the front seat of his car, then he walked around to slide into the driver's seat. He kept the conversation away from the high risk topics: Dorian's hold over her; her letter to Jacques; and what had happened to the older man she'd claimed to care for fifteen years ago. Instead, when they'd run through the usual light topics of conversation, he focused on the upcoming auction.

"Ready for the fire sale?" he asked wryly.

"Everything's set. Dorian's beating the auctioneers daily to increase participation. We're having additional catalogues printed for people who somehow missed the first batch."

"How about you?" He slid a glance in her direction as they stopped at a stop light. "Did he ask you how much I was going to be paying?"

She nodded. "He asked. I told him it was none of my business, and I wasn't interested in being a corporate spy."

"Did he give you any idea why he's trying to get the information?"

She hated to think about that. "Not exactly, but apparently one of his creditors is a rather . . . violent man."

He didn't like the sound of that. Grimly he demanded, "What's the man's name?"

"Dorian wouldn't say."

They pulled into his garage and went upstairs. The minute he shut the door behind them, he pulled her into his arms and kissed her until her arms curled around his neck and her toes lifted off the floor.

"God, I needed that," he said, grinning down at her. He lifted her in his arms, feeling a rush of potent desire course through every inch of his body. "How would you feel about waiting a little for dinner?"

She began unbuttoning his shirt. She laughed with pleasure as he took that as a yes and carried her straight to his bedroom. Three delightful hours later, they called the closest Chinese restaurant for dinner to be delivered. When they finally got around to eating, it was cold. Neither of them paid the slightest attention.

Chapter 15

Two weeks later, Blake still didn't know any of the answers, but he knew he was thoroughly addicted to making love to Elizabeth. She still eluded him when he brought the conversation around to the taboo topics that haunted him. That made it difficult for him to hand her his trust on a platter, so he held back a little, in the interest of self-protection. He knew that she probably interpreted that as a coolness on his part, a lack of complete emotional surrender to her, and he made no effort to disabuse her of that impression. He wasn't above using a shield.

He was musing about the painful dilemma of being passionately attached to a woman who refused to be completely honest with him when his secretary buzzed him on the office intercom.

"Yes, Janet?"

"Mr. Sutter is on line three for you."

"Thanks." He punched the button that would connect him to Alex's incoming call and said, "Hi, Alex. How's everything going?"

Alex had called several hours earlier announcing that he was taking Sarah to the hospital. She had gone into labor.

"Mother and daughter are doing fine," Alex announced. "I am the proud father of a beautiful little dark-haired, blue-eyed girl. Seven pounds. Eighteen inches long. A real beauty. Wait 'til you see her!"

Blake laughed. "Congratulations! Give Sarah a kiss from me."

"My pleasure."

"Did you give Grant the good news yet?"

"On his answering machine. He and Shelby must not be back yet from San Francisco."

"They're probably home by now."

"Say... meet me for a drink at The Gallery to celebrate?"

Blake laughed again. "Sure thing. Congratulations, Alex."

"Thanks. It's one hell of an experience, Blake. That little girl, mine and Sarah's..." His voice trailed off huskily. He cleared his throat. "See you in an hour or so."

"Right, Alex." Blake hung up the phone, surprised at the obvious awe and pride and love that had filled Alex's normally dry voice.

He could imagine what his partner had just gone through, and Alex certainly had his sympathy. It was a big responsibility, taking on a woman and the children you brought into the world together. Love like Alex and Sarah's would make it a pleasurable obligation, with rich and unique rewards, he thought.

He punched the intercom and told Janet the good news, adding that he'd be leaving in half an hour to drink the new father under the table.

Janet laughed. "It's the last chance he'll have for a while," she predicted. "Babies have a way of keeping everybody awake for the first year or two. He's going to need to be stone-cold sober."

The Gallery was a high-class Washington bar. It attracted a clientele of mid-level government employees, museum experts, Capitol Hill staffers, and political movers and shakers who preferred quiet to notoriety. No one ever snapped photos of people at The Gallery. You could go there and safely have a drink and let your hair down without worrying whether you'd be reading what you said in the next edition of *The Washington Post*.

Grant was already sitting on a stool when Blake arrived and sat down next to him.

"I guess you heard?" Grant said with a grin.

"Yes."

"Shelby went into the hospital to admire the baby and congratulate Sarah. Want to go in on a big bouquet of roses for her?"

"Sure." Blake's smile faded at the mention of the roses. It brought back the old memory of roses spilling from Elizabeth's hands. He ordered Scotch and nursed his drink.

"Still seeing Elizabeth?" Grant asked casually.

Blake nodded.

Grant laughed. "You don't look very happy about it. What's the matter? Tell Uncle Grant."

Blake gave a short laugh and took another drink of his Scotch. "Actually, I've been debating whether I should talk to you and Alex about her."

Grant seemed amused. "Sure. We can loan you some books. Anything to help nature along," he teased. "Want to ask a question? Just shoot. I'll try not to blush."

Blake briefly closed his eyes, as if struggling for patience. "I don't need any help in that area," he said dryly. Then, more seriously, he said, "I think Dorian Rand must have uncovered some sort of crime involving Elizabeth or her father, and he's been using it to force her to do what he wants."

"Hell!" Grant exclaimed under his breath. "I'm sorry to hear it. We'll be happy to look into it for you."

Blake frowned. "The problem is . . . I don't really want you to dig into her life, Grant. I don't want her to feel that I'm trampling all over her . . . the way Dorian apparently has for years."

"I see your point. What did you have in mind?" Grant asked.

"She said something about a violent creditor pressuring Dorian for cash. . . . He may hang around at the auction, waiting to get his hands on some of the money. I thought perhaps you two could cruise the crowd, see if you recognized any faces, take some photos and show them around to some of your friends in intelligence.'' He rolled the glass between his palms angrily. ''I don't want her getting caught in that kind of cross-fire.''

Grant nodded grimly. ''Nobody knows that feeling better than Alex or I,'' he said softly. Both of their wives had been in that position. Sarah still bore a scar on her back because of it. He saw the haunted look that had come into Blake's eyes and asked gently, ''There's something else, isn't there?''

Blake finished his drink and pushed his glass out for the bartender to refill. ''Yes. We've been seeing each other almost every day, as much as I can, but recently I've been getting the feeling that she's saying goodbye.''

Grant frowned. ''Why do you think that?''

He felt like a fool trying to explain it. It wasn't something he could put his finger on, exactly. ''It's hard to say. It's the way she looks at me, the way she acts.'' The way she'd seized on him when they made love last night, he thought, as if it were almost the end of their time together, and she wanted him imprinted in her soul. Softly, he said, ''She had tears in her eyes when I kissed her goodbye last night. And she came up with some lame excuse why we couldn't get together before the auction. Busy with reams of paperwork, or something like that.'' His frown became fierce. ''I feel it in my bones, Grant. She's getting ready to do the same thing she did fifteen years ago—walk out on me.''

Grant had heard about the broken engagement from Shelby after her visit to Blake weeks ago. As tactfully as possible, he pointed out, ''There is a difference this time.''

Blake looked at him blankly.

''You aren't engaged. You haven't asked her to marry you. Have you?''

''No.'' That was very true. There was another difference, too, he thought. This time, they were lovers, in every intimate sense of the word.

Alex walked into the bar, grinning ear to ear, and joined them. As he swung his leg over the stool, he handed them each a cigar and flashed a small photograph of his wife and baby.

"Aren't they beautiful? Okay, men," he declared magnanimously. "The drinks are on me."

Blake and Grant pushed their empty glasses forward and said in unison, "Hear! Hear!"

By the morning of the auction, Blake had been unable to reach Elizabeth for two days. He had his secretary check with Jacques Martin's office and found that Jacques had been unexpectedly delayed. There had been an engine problem on the airplane he'd been ticketed on. He was cooling his heels in Montreal, trying to get a connecting flight to New York, and from there an air shuttle to National Airport in Washington. He would make the auction, but he wouldn't arrive much ahead of time.

Blake had never enjoyed sitting around, waiting for events to unfold. Since he had the distinct impression that he was not going to enjoy these particular events if he did nothing to change them, he paced the floor of his office, silently debating with himself what actions to take . . . and which to avoid.

He came to a halt in the middle of the floor and stared at the vivid golds, reds and browns of the Caucasian rug beneath his feet. They had always reminded him of the vibrant colors of gemstones, sparkling beneath a jeweler's loupe.

That in turn brought to mind jewelers. And a particular jeweler. He was named Karl Rossi.

Blake frowned intently. He had never really been able to talk with Karl. There had always been someone else around. Frequently Elizabeth, trying to maneuver the conversation away from topics that upset her father. Or had it been Elizabeth they had upset, not Karl?

He recalled the morning he'd gone to her workshop and Karl had been trying desperately to tell him something. At the time he'd thought Karl was just frustrated because it was difficult for him to communicate. But what if that hadn't been the case? What if Karl had been trying to tell him something of great importance?

Blake swore. Karl *must* know something that could shed light on the miserable mystery. Even if he didn't know what Dorian's control over Elizabeth was, Karl could tell him what

Dorian's influence had been over *him*. Karl could explain why he had gone to Switzerland with Dorian fifteen years ago, for instance. That would certainly fill in a few big blanks in the puzzle as far as Blake was concerned.

Because of the effects of the stroke, Blake knew, Karl might not be able to remember everything. He certainly might have great difficulty conveying what he did recall. But Blake vividly remembered the lucid expression in Karl's eyes that weekend when he had stayed at Dorian's. Karl's mind might be damaged, but it was far from gone.

"If *you* won't talk to me, Elizabeth," Blake muttered, "perhaps Karl will."

The maid answered the front door, and Blake gave her a charming smile. She lit up prettily and stammered, "Mr. Malone! Come in, sir. I'm afraid Miss Rossi isn't here. Neither is Mr. Rand...."

"I haven't come to see Elizabeth or Dorian," he said smoothly as he walked inside. "I was hoping to visit Karl."

The maid blinked rapidly. "Oh. No one ever comes to see Mr. Rossi." She chewed her lip, as if trying to decide how to handle his request. "I don't know... His nurse is out taking a walk. She won't be back for half an hour or so. Maybe you should wait for her. He doesn't like her too much, but, well, I don't know whether Mr. Rossi is supposed to have any visitors."

"I'm sure it will be all right," Blake said. "Karl and I are old friends. If he's too tired to see me, I'm sure he'll tell us. Why don't we go upstairs and ask him? Hmm?"

The maid, accustomed to doing as she was told, dutifully led the way. She nodded her head and rolled her eyes in agreement. "I suppose it's all right. You're right about one thing. Mr. Rossi will tell us if he doesn't want any company. He sure does yell and shake his fist when he's put out about something!"

Blake stifled the urge to laugh. Karl clearly had the maid intimidated. She was approaching his room as if she were walking on eggshells. When they looked inside and saw no one, she warily suggested they look in Elizabeth's workshop.

"Sometimes he likes to sit in there and handle the pretty jewelry she's making, or the tools, that sort of thing," the maid explained. "Ah, there you are Mr. Rossi. I've brought you a visitor! Isn't that a nice surprise?"

Karl was sitting in his wheelchair, holding a palmful of polished white opals cut in cabochons. When he saw Blake in the doorway, they fell in a streamlet of milky fire from his hand, spilling onto the floor. He croaked a sound. It was unintelligible, but the expectant expression in his face and the outstretched welcome in his hand made it clear that he was happy to have Blake there.

"Why don't you go back to your duties?" Blake suggested to the young woman standing awkwardly in the hall.

"Thank you, sir. Ring if you need anything. I'll tell the nurse you're here when she comes back."

"Don't bother," Blake muttered under his breath as she disappeared down the hall. He walked across to Karl, shook the old man's trembling hand and grinned. "What are you doing in here? Working?"

Karl chuckled and nodded his head. He made a sound of disgust and gestured at the pale opals scattered across the floor.

"Elizabeth will scalp you if she sees this," Blake teased him, bending to collect the gemstones and put them back on the countertop. "She's got everything out of the boxes, I see," Blake observed, looking over her small shop.

Karl made a two-tone sound of agreement and wheeled his chair slowly along the edge of the room, motioning for Blake to come along for a tour.

Elizabeth had unpacked her books and set them up in racks along one wall. Next to them was her design area, with a drafting table, and a counter fitted with saws, clamps and a large number of small tools. Her swivel chair still had a forest-green sweater hung over the back of it. Blake brushed the thick ribbing with his fingers. He could imagine her wearing it as she bent over a setting, the expensive flash of fine gems burning beneath her slender fingers.

Karl was wheeling past the section that contained buffing and polishing equipment, and another that held three soldering irons, and containers of silver, gold, copper and platinum wire.

"You don't worry about theft, I see," Blake said, indicating the precious metals casually placed in the open room.

Karl smiled and lifted a fine chain that hung around his neck. At the end, a key was suspended.

"You and Elizabeth have keys to the workshop?" Blake surmised.

Karl nodded and resumed pushing his wheelchair past vats, a sink and several storage areas. He braked in front of a trunk and scowled, as if trying to recall how to get into it.

"I wanted to ask you some questions, Karl," Blake said, squatting down next to his old teacher.

Karl raised his brows and looked on expectantly. *Ask me,* he seemed to be saying.

"Do you know that I've been seeing Elizabeth again?"

Karl nodded. He smiled, obviously pleased at the news.

"I'm seeing her quite a lot, Karl," Blake said seriously.

Karl nodded again. Yes. He was aware of it.

Blake sighed. "Good. I've been trying to find out what happened fifteen years ago in Arkansas. I hoped you could tell me."

The old jeweler reached out with his good left hand and squeezed Blake's shoulder.

"You're pleased that I want to know?" Blake guessed.

Karl's pewter-gray eyes smiled back at him.

Blake was relieved. Karl, at least, was willing to be an ally. "Karl . . . why did you decide to work for Dorian?"

Karl's eyes flashed with anger. He made a fist with his hand and shook it in the air. "Made . . . me," he croaked.

Blake nodded. "Dorian made you." Seeing Karl's nod, he went on. "Is he blackmailing you?" he asked softly, keeping his eyes on Karl's. It had to be that. There was no other explanation at this point.

The man in the wheelchair nodded, and his face filled with sorrow and regret. He turned away and awkwardly pulled open a drawer, searching it with painful slowness.

Blake frowned. "Do you need some help?"

Karl shook his head and redoubled his concentration on the contents of the drawer.

"What is he blackmailing you with, Karl?"

Karl tried to say, but the words didn't make any sense. He became upset, and his incoherence became more pronounced. In his agitation, he flung pencils on the floor and tossed a sheaf of papers from the desk drawer onto the countertop.

"Hey, Karl, don't do that. Elizabeth might not like to have her things redistributed quite so haphazardly!" Blake tried to pick up the mess and put things away.

Karl ran his hand along the top of the interior of the desk drawer and fumbled with something. He cursed, and this time the Anglo-Saxon word came out with startling clarity.

Blake nearly laughed aloud, but then Karl grabbed his hand, dragged it into the drawer and shoved it against the top. There was a small key taped there. Karl hadn't been able to remove it. His dexterity was too limited now. Blake, however, had no trouble stripping it free.

He held the key up and looked at Karl questioningly. "What's this?"

Karl indicated one of the large steamer trunks.

"You were trying to get into those the last time I was here," Blake said, frowning as he recalled Elizabeth's quick intervention at the time. He looked at Karl. "I don't particularly want to invade Elizabeth's privacy," he pointed out, uncomfortable at physically riffling her things.

Karl made a rude sound.

Blake grinned. "You think she deserves to have her privacy invaded?"

Karl laughed; then, with a shrewd gleam in his eye, he pointed his finger at Blake's chest.

"You think she should have it invaded by *me?*" Blake guessed again.

Karl nodded and gestured impatiently for Blake to open the trunk.

It was simple enough. The trunk unlocked with a quick turn of the key. Blake glanced over at Karl. "I want to know what control Dorian has over you and Elizabeth. And I want to know what happened to make her leave me fifteen years ago, Karl. But I don't want to dig into areas of her life that she would prefer to keep private."

Karl nodded his head and rolled his eyes heavenward. It was clear he thought Blake would be doing the right thing if he opened the trunk and saw what was inside.

"Okay," Blake muttered. He opened it up.

At first it seemed like the kind of collection any young woman might keep in an old trunk in an attic. There was a photo album. Some books of poetry. A neatly stacked pile of old clothes. There was a book thick with pressed flowers. Boxes that had their contents neatly written in pencil across their sides: Jewelry; Hats; Mother's Things.

Blake touched them guiltily, feeling an ache of pity for Elizabeth. These were personal treasures one would keep hidden from uncaring eyes. They were heirlooms that contained loving memories, things that meant a lot to her, but which would have been meaningless to a stranger.

Karl had maneuvered the wheelchair next to Blake's side, and he leaned forward, pointing a bony finger at the book filled with pressed flowers.

Blake lifted it and began leafing carefully through the pages. He frowned and turned to look at Karl. "What am I supposed to see?"

The crippled man stared at him intently, then looked at the book in Blake's hands and pointed at it again.

Blake stared at the flowers. "They're dried flowers. The colors have faded. They've obviously been here for years. A couple of them are still attached to their branches." He saw the thorn, and then he examined the flower itself. "They're roses."

He looked at Karl as he realized what he must be seeing. "These are the roses that I picked for Elizabeth the night we were going to get married?" he said incredulously.

The older man nodded his head with sad deliberation.

"She kept them all these years?" he asked in surprise.

"Loved you," Karl said in a mangled voice.

Blake let out a strained breath. "If she loved me, then why the hell didn't she marry me?" He looked straight at Karl. "Who was the other man, Karl?" he demanded in a hard voice. He was sick and tired of not knowing the answer to that particular question. "Who was he?"

With greet sorrow, Karl swung his left hand toward his chest, pointing at himself.

For a minute Blake didn't understand. He thought Karl was just tired and was hugging his chest out of some sort of strange muscle reflex. But as Karl stared at him, clearly willing him to get the message, Blake realized what he was trying to say. '*You* were the man? She went to Switzerland with you and Dorian because she loved *you?*''

Karl nodded. This time, he made a fist with his left hand and lightly tapped his chest three times.

Blake recognized the gesture. *"Mea culpa. Mea culpa. Mea maxima culpa."* He stared at Karl. "What was your fault? What did you do?''

Karl wheeled over to the containers of precious metal wire. He pointed to the gold.

Blake, still holding the book of pressed roses in one hand, followed him. "Gold wire? What the hell am I supposed to conclude from that?''

Karl pointed to the small collection of acids neatly lined up near the sink. They were used by jewelers for various purposes, but the first one that came to Blake's mind was that of testing the karat value of gold. His suspicion was confirmed as Karl touched the bottle marked nitric acid and pointed to Elizabeth's ceramic touchstone. Smear a streak of an allegedly gold metal on the touchstone. Place a streak of known gold content beside it. Put a drop of nitric acid on the two streaks. If the one you're testing is gold, it will fade at a rate similar to the known gold streak placed next to it. The slower it faded, the higher its gold content. Gold was unaffected by the nitric acid, but the cheaper metals alloyed to it were quickly eaten up by the acid and faded into oblivion.

Karl kept jabbing at the touchstone, the nitric acid and the gold wire. "Lied," he gargled. "Lied!''

Blake stared at him, not wanting to believe the implication. The man was confused. It wasn't fair to be thinking what he was thinking now about Karl. Misrepresenting the gold content of an item was a very serious crime. No reputable jeweler or goldsmith would risk his freedom and professional reputation by lying about it. And yet, that was what Karl seemed to be saying.

Karl, seeing that Blake was resisting the idea that he could have been a crook, struck his heart three times with his fist again, then hung his head. It was the unmistakable gesture of a man admitting guilt.

Blake took a deep breath and slowly put the pieces of the puzzle together. Karl's admission of guilt. The gold that wouldn't pass a nitric acid test of its content. Jacques seeing Elizabeth melting down one of Karl's expensive necklaces. Karl's need for money when he was desperate to save his dying wife. Blake closed his eyes and swore.

"Why didn't she just tell me, damn it?" he muttered. Then, directing himself to Karl, he said, very gently, "You misrepresented the value of those necklaces you made when your wife was sick. Didn't you?"

Karl nodded. He reached out his good left hand, pleading with Blake. He motioned toward the roses, toward the trunk and then toward the door. "Please . . ." he croaked, the words barely distinguishable. "Elizabeth."

Blake looked at the book and the roses lovingly placed between the pages. He felt sick. "I'll take care of Elizabeth," he promised tightly. "I'd better get over to the auction."

Karl nodded and pursed his lips. He waved his hand like a commanding officer sending off his troops to do battle.

Blake didn't object. It seemed appropriate to him, under the circumstances.

Chapter 16

Elizabeth was standing at the back of the auction room, watching people filter in. They moved in sinuous riverlets, flowing through rows of folding chairs until they located their reserved seats by the numbered cards lying atop them.

Dorian was beside her, sporting his serpentine smile, his gnarled hand gripping the hard wood cane upon which he forever leaned. "I think we will do well," he said, appearing quite pleased. "People seem prepared to spend."

"How can you tell?" she asked coolly.

He chuckled. "I have been told the size of their most recent electronic transfers from offshore banks."

"Just a coincidence, no doubt," she muttered, thoroughly disgusted that he always seemed to be able to get away with things, no matter how underhanded, how close to illegal.

"Sarcasm doesn't suit you, my sweet," he told her in amusement. Seeing her frustration and outrage, he added, "I've told you often enough, my dear . . . you need to be more practical. Pick the winning side. It is rarely the publicly acceptable one."

Elizabeth chose to ignore him, turning instead to search the room one more time. Where, oh where, was Jacques' dear substantial bulk? She'd been hoping for hours to see him lumbering to her rescue. He'd been on the list of attendees, but that was no guarantee that he would be there. As the final minutes ticked slowly by, her hope was fading. It was nearly time to open the bidding, and she hadn't heard a word from Jacques or anyone claiming to represent him today. She had been so sure.... She bit her lip and tried to keep calm. One more scan of the room....

She saw a man looking at the photograph of the gold and sapphire necklace that had been handed out as an addendum to the sale catalogue, noticing that he seemed particularly taken with it. Her heart sank lower. If Jacques wasn't coming, there was nothing she could do to prevent anyone in the room from buying the necklace. And Dorian was prepared to deliver almost immediately.

She closed her eyes, feeling faintly ill. Fifteen years of her life were about to slide down the drain with one flat strike of an auctioneer's mallet. Fifteen years of anguish and loneliness and sacrifice and suffering. She had been so close. So very, very close.

"Are you all right, my dear?" Dorian asked solicitously.

She forced her eyes open and lifted her chin defiantly. She'd go out of this with her head up if it killed her! She turned an icy smile on Dorian and replied, "My feelings are none of your business, Dorian."

"Tsk, tsk," he chided, lifting his brows in censure. "It isn't over quite yet."

Her gaze returned to the doors, and she watched the people still trickling into the room, hoping a miracle would somehow materialize in spite of the deteriorating odds. Most of the dealers and their representatives had already arrived; individuals seeking expensive baubles for their personal collections were now filling up the chamber.

She had seen the list of names of people planning to attend, and one of them had caused her to stare long and painfully at the paper. Katrin Louwens. And her father, a member of Washington's diplomatic corp.

She wondered if they would arrive in one of those long limousines with little flags flapping on either side. Well, maybe not for a non-official function such as this, she thought, wishing she didn't feel such catty antagonism toward the woman.

Elizabeth gave a cursory glance to the attractive blonde just stepping into the room; then she noticed the dark-haired man following immediately behind, and her heart stopped.

Blake lifted his head, transferring his attention from the blonde to Elizabeth. His eyes narrowed, and the look he sent her was hard enough to turn coal to diamonds. Deliberately he looked away, turning his attention back to the blonde. She seemed momentarily mystified and gave Elizabeth a light assessment followed by a puzzled frown.

Dorian murmured, "It looks as if you have competition."

"I don't know what you're talking about," Elizabeth muttered stiffly.

Dorian nodded toward Blake, who was escorting the blonde to a seat on the far side of the room. She kissed his cheek as she sat down. Elizabeth was appalled to see him smile and kiss her lightly back before straightening. Elizabeth glanced at the seating chart she held in her hands. The woman was Katrin Louwens.

Well, what had she expected? Blake hadn't made any promises. There had been no commitments. She had carefully avoided them herself. She had been saying goodbye for days now, and yet... Seeing him with another woman was like pouring acid on her heart.

She saw a commotion at the door and turned to see Jacques Martin hurrying in, his chubby face flushed and sweating, looking as if he'd run all the way from France. Her burning heart soared. He was scouring the room for her, and when he found her he had a look of such profound apology in his face that she knew that all hope must be gone. He was shaking his head and holding up his hands in that quintessentially French way of saying, But what can I do? It is beyond me to influence this.

The guards were closing the doors. Elizabeth choked back a bitter laugh. She was going to have to stand here and watch her own execution. She wished Blake were with her, holding her, telling her it would be all right. Against her better judgment, she let her gaze wander back to Katrin Louwens. Blake was no longer there.

"Looking for me?" he asked softly.

She whirled. He was behind her, and he had seldom looked more grim. Or more determined.

Her gaze flicked back to the blonde. "She's very pretty," she said, scarcely conscious of the aching envy in her voice.

Blake heard it, though, and his expression became somewhat sardonic. "Katrin?" he asked mildly, sliding a warm look her way.

Elizabeth's eyes flashed. He was deliberately dragging this out, taking pleasure in her jealousy. She couldn't believe it. It wasn't like Blake. "Yes, *Katrin*," she hissed as the auctioneer's gavel snapped smartly against the block.

Blake pulled Elizabeth back along the wall, to a corner where they could speak without Dorian being able to simply tilt his head to overhear every word.

"Katrin is an old friend."

"She carries her age well."

"My, my. Is that jealousy I hear in your voice?"

"Don't be silly. We don't have that kind of relationship."

"No. Of course we don't. So you won't be upset to hear that I went out with Katrin when I was in Europe a couple of weeks ago, will you?"

Elizabeth's eyes flashed. "Not at all."

And you wouldn't be annoyed if I told you that she dropped in to see me at my apartment...."

She swiveled her head, her mouth open in surprise. "N-no..." It didn't sound very convincing. "You can have anyone in your apartment that you wish," she said unsteadily, hating every word.

Blake smiled, but his eyes were humorless. He looked frustrated and furious. "I'm glad to hear that," he said, each word well garnished with sarcasm.

The tense silence between them was filled with the voice of the auctioneer steadily climbing the price scale. The first item was going well indeed. Elizabeth folded her arms protectively across her chest and tired to keep her chin up in the face of disaster on all sides.

Blake propped his shoulder against the wall, leaning close enough to Elizabeth's rigidly erect body that he could inhale the fragrant memories that he'd grown to love. The fury in his eyes began to soften into a complex combination of anger and desire. Damn her, anyway. She wasn't going to give an inch. She'd beg Martin for help, but not him. He wanted to wring her neck for that. And he wanted to know why. Why wouldn't she come to him, damn it?

"I saw someone else while I was in Europe...." he said neutrally.

"Oh? Was she as pretty as Katrin?" Elizabeth closed her eyes. Why did she have to sound like a jealous woman? Well, the answer to that was disgustingly obvious. She tried to get a grip on her raging desire to scratch the woman's eyes out.

Blake grinned slightly. "It wasn't a she," he said softly.

Elizabeth caught the undercurrent of warmth in his voice, and she looked at him guiltily. "I jumped to a conclusion," she said weakly. "I guess maybe I am a little...jealous." She sucked in her breath. "Of course, it isn't permanent. Just...the result of...so much togetherness."

"Really?" he asked dubiously. Under his breath he muttered, "I hope not." Then, a little louder, "Getting back to what I was trying to say...I saw someone else while I was in Europe."

"Sold! For 122,500 dollars, to the Jarl du Lac Companies, Limited, represented by..."

Elizabeth gave Blake a pleading look. "I'm sorry.... You're trying to talk to me, and I'm not paying attention. But this next item is...of special interest to me." Her voice tapered off to a whisper.

He nodded grimly. "Yes. I know."

There was a note of complete comprehension in his rich baritone voice, and it feathered through her like an alarm. She looked up at him as the auctioneer called out, "The next item is a special addition. Number one B. An 18k gold necklace with beautiful clear white sapphires, 'Depression Diamonds' obtained from the estate of actress Violetta Rossi, known for her work in silent films. The necklace was designed and created by the actress's son, well-known designer Karl Rossi..."

Blake murmured in surprise, "Karl inherited the sapphires from his mother?"

"It was all he had to work with," she whispered. "She had sold her diamonds and replaced them with white sapphires to keep Father fed and clothed in the early thirties. She was having no luck making the transition to talkies. She went to work at a department store to make ends meet. When she died, the sapphires were all she had left to bequeath him. Then, later, they were all he had to make that first necklace...."

Blake slid his hand behind her head and forced her to look at him. "Why didn't you tell me all this before?" he demanded, the words dangerously even.

"Tell you about the sapphires?" she asked in confusion.

"About everything?"

She paled. He couldn't know. And yet she could see in his eyes that he did. His fingers were hard, but he wasn't hurting her. If anything, *he* seemed to be the one who was hurting, and the pain was flowing through him, pouring into her like a high-voltage electrical charge.

"I spoke to Karl this morning," he told her.

"You couldn't!"

"I could and I did. I should have done it weeks ago." He made a sound of disgust. "Let me amend that. I should have talked to him *years* ago. Fifteen, to be exact."

In the background, Elizabeth could hear the bids, and she was desperate to know who was competing for the sapphires-and-gold, but she found she couldn't turn away from Blake's anger.

"I told you I saw someone else while I was in Europe," he repeated. "It was your old friend, Jacques Martin." He smiled tightly, watching the play of expressions across her face as she realized the implications. "No. He wouldn't tell me what was in your letter. But don't relax yet. I heard enough. And, more importantly, I worked out a special deal with him. It involves you."

The auctioneer shouted, "Sold! To Jacques Martin...."

Elizabeth looked across the room and then back at Blake. "What deal?" she asked frantically. "What have you done?"

She saw Jacques go to finalize the purchase arrangements. One of the officials began an exchange of documents. A big, strongly built man in a fashionable brown tweed jacket and dark slacks joined him, appearing to participate in some way. She didn't recognize him, and she frowned, wondering who he might be.

"Did Jacques tell you I would be working with him from now on?" she asked faintly. "That...I'll be moving to Paris...as soon as he wants?"

"No." He chewed on his lip, considering. "Is that what you'd like to do, if you were completely free to do as you wished, Elizabeth?"

She laughed bitterly. "If I were free..." She said it with such longing that tears nearly came to her eyes.

"Let's get out of here," he said abruptly, taking her firmly by the arm and guiding her straight to the nearest exit. "I have a few things to say to you, and I'll be damned if I'm going to say them here."

"I can't leave.... The auction..."

Blake uttered an explicit, Anglo-Saxon phrase regarding what could be done to the auction.

Elizabeth took one look at his face and decided it might be wiser not to argue the point. He looked as if his patience had just hit rock bottom. One more push and his civilized exterior would be shed like a suit gone out of style.

She twisted to see what had happened to Jacques and the man in the brown tweed jacket, but they were nowhere to be found. At least she had a temporary reprieve...she hoped. Jacques had bought the necklace. But why had he looked so apologetic? And what did Blake mean by that "special deal" that involved her?

"Where are we going?" she asked anxiously.

Blake ignored her and jabbed the elevator button for the lower level of the garage. Before the doors opened, the big man in the brown tweed jacket came down the hallway at a brisk walk. He handed Blake a soft velvet bag, which Blake dropped into his coat pocket.

"So you're Elizabeth," the man said, grinning and looking her over with interest.

She stared at him, wondering who he was.

"This is Grant Macklin," Blake said. "One of my two partners."

Grant held out his hand, shaking hers when she reciprocated. It was like having a bear swallow your hand, she thought. There was a catlike grace and power about him, too, she noticed. He wasn't someone you could sneak up on unawares in the night.

"If you want his autograph, why don't you ask for it?" Blake growled.

Amazed by his irritated outburst, Elizabeth tilted her head to better see his face. He sounded jealous!

Grant laughed. "You've got it bad, man. Take it easy on her. She looks as if you've scared her witless. The color's drained from her cheeks." Grant put his hand up when he saw the expression in Blake's face. "Okay. Forget I said anything. About the other item on tonight's agenda . . . Alex recognized a couple of familiar faces in the crowd . . . and a few in the immediate neighborhood. We've called his old buddy, Jones, and faxed him the pictures we got. He's interested in Dorian's Colombian emerald salesman. Apparently when he's not selling emeralds, the guy's selling munitions to both sides of the local civil war, smuggling dope, laundering money. Anything that pays well and isn't taxed."

"Charming," Blake muttered. "Do you think we can use any of that to our advantage?"

Grant laughed. "Oh, yeah. I think so." He noticed that the elevator doors were opening and motioned them inside. "I'll walk you to the car." He smiled at Elizabeth. "Shelby's going to give me the third degree about you when I get home tonight."

Elizabeth wasn't following him at all. "Shelby?" She looked at Blake. "The one in your picture?"

"Yes," Blake growled irritably. He gave Grant a deadly stare. "Too bad you won't have anything to tell her."

Grant looked quite amused. "Oh, I think I'll be able to come up with a few things." He saw Elizabeth's perplexed expression and explained, "I'm Shelby's husband."

Her expression cleared, and the smile that lightened it was one of relief. It was nice to know the woman was married. Before she could think of anything to say, the elevator doors were sliding open at their level and Blake was hustling her to the car. Once they were locked in and ready to leave, Grant went to his own car.

"He's still following us!" Elizabeth exclaimed as they pulled into Blake's apartment garage, a half hour later.

"He'll take off now," Blake predicted as they got out of the car.

With a honk of his horn, Grant obliged and, as Blake had predicted, drove away. Which left the two of them conspicuously alone.

"Well, I can see where I'm going," she said, trying to be lighthearted about it as they rode the elevator up and got off at Blake's floor.

He ushered her into his apartment and locked the door after them with a sharp and final-sounding click. Loosening his tie and flipping open his shirt collar, Blake went over to the liquor cabinet and proceeded to pour himself a drink. Bourbon. He glanced across the darkened room at Elizabeth. "Can I get you something?"

The thought of alcohol made her stomach queasy, and she turned away, feeling sick. "No thanks," she said weakly.

His expression hardened. "Suit yourself," he muttered, knocking back a good healthy swallow as Elizabeth sank down on the edge of his couch. He walked into the middle of the room, barely leashed fierceness emanating from every stride he took.

"Tell me, Elizabeth," he said. "Were you going to say goodbye, or were you just going to leave town without a word this time?"

The fury just beneath his words singed her, and she flinched. She wanted desperately to know what was happening to the sapphire necklace, where Jacques had gone and what Blake was talking about. She opened her mouth to ask a dozen questions at once, but he had already begun to speak again himself.

"Let me guess," he said sarcastically. "You were going to call me from the airport and mention in passing that you were leaving because of an older, wealthier man. 'It's been a wonderful time. We've really been great in bed together. But I'm off to take care of the parts of my life that you know nothing about.' Was that what you were going to do?" he demanded, standing with rigid fury in the middle of the dark and shadowed room.

Elizabeth fought off another wave of sickness and the urge to lie down and curl up in a miserable ball. She had to deal with this, whether she wanted to or not. Licking her lips nervously, she tried to find a good point to begin.

"What exactly did my father and Jacques tell you?" she asked faintly.

Blake laughed and looked at the ceiling. "It isn't fun being kept in the dark, is it?" he asked angrily, thinking of all the years that he had been kept in the dark about her, about why she'd left him. He exhaled roughly and came to stand over her, staring down at her with very mixed emotions. "What did they tell me? Damned little, but enough. Enough for me to finally have a rough idea of what's been going on." He rubbed the back of his neck, looking very tired. "Jacques respected your confidences up until he arrived in Washington. When he got here, I told him if he didn't let me step in and help you, I'd hound him for the rest of his life."

Elizabeth stared at him. "You did?" she murmured. "That doesn't sound like you," she said weakly.

"That's more or less what Jacques said. But when he realized I was willing to be ruthless instead of my usual easy-going self, he finally outlined what you wanted. I think he'd already come to the conclusion that I could be of greater help to you in the long run than he could when I talked with him in Paris. But he's as stubborn as you are, and he dragged his feet, trying to avoid telling me any more than he had to."

"Oh," she said miserably.

Grimly, he went on. "I also know that Karl labeled the necklaces he made during a certain period of his life with a higher gold content than they had. And that the necklace Dorian auctioned off today was one of them."

She stared at him miserably, not knowing what to say. "I'm sorry..."

"No thanks to you, however," he added pointedly. "Karl helped fill in that crucial detail. He literally walked me through the facts."

"My father?" she whispered. "How on earth . . . ?"

"I'll explain that later," he said grimly. "From what Jacques told me in Paris, I assume Karl did it to scrape together the money he needed to take care of you and your mother. I've wondered for a long time why you've kept working for Dorian, but obviously it must have been because he discovered Karl's fraud and was blackmailing you."

Elizabeth nodded slightly.

Blake became angrier. "I suppose the miserable bastard then threatened Karl with exposure if he didn't agree to work for him?"

"Yes," she whispered, wondering in despair what would become of her father now.

"I assume he made the same threat to you?"

Horrified that Blake now knew virtually everything, Elizabeth could only stare at him helplessly and nod. "Yes. I think at first Dorian simply wanted to make sure my father would do as he demanded. If I were with them, it would be a constant reminder that I could be hurt if Father didn't cooperate. He didn't know that Dorian had made his blackmail threat against me, as well, though. Dorian preferred it that way. It let him control both of us. He warned me not to tell my father that I was being threatened, too. Eventually, of course, he did find out, and you see what it did to him. But in the beginning, I did what Dorian demanded because I was afraid to tell Father. I thought he might do something rash, admit his guilt or go to the authorities, or . . ."

"Or kill Dorian?" Blake guessed. When she nodded, he muttered, "Believe me, the thought holds definite appeal." When she looked aghast at his vehemence, he shook his head. "Don't worry. I won't do it, either. But don't deny me the fantasy of thinking what a pleasure it would be."

"Dorian threatened me the afternoon before we were going to elope," she explained softly.

Blake gave a short, bitter laugh. "And you fell right into his hands."

She felt tears fill her eyes. "I just wanted to protect..."

He waved a hand dismissively and said with anger in every word, "Yes, I know. You wanted to protect the man you loved... the older and richer man... your father!"

"Yes. But I also..."

He was pacing back and forth. "Why didn't you just come to me and tell *me,* damn it?"

She jumped to her feet, furious and frantic. She disregarded the wash of illness sweeping through her and shouted, "What could you have done? Become an accomplice after the fact? Should I have ruined your life as well as my father's and mine? Should I have dragged you down with us? I *loved* you, Blake. I loved you with my heart and soul. I loved you with every breath I ever took. As much as I loved my father, I loved you more! Don't you understand? I wanted you to be free of us. I was also trying to protect *you.*"

He grabbed her shoulders, and his hard fingers bruised her soft flesh. "Did it ever occur to you to ask *me* what *I* wanted? Did it ever cross your beautiful mind that I might not have wanted to be free of you? That I would gladly have stood by you and tried to find a way out of the mess?"

She swallowed hard and closed her eyes, trying to forestall the awful roiling in her stomach. "Yes," she said in a whispery voice. "I told you, you're the noblest, kindest man I've ever known. I knew you'd stand by us." Hot tears began to roll down her cheeks, and she crossed her arms in front of her stomach, trying to hold on. "I loved you too much to accept such a sacrifice," she said, beginning to sob. "All those years, you were with me, Blake. While I drew designs in that basement in Zurich. I'd open my trunk and..." She bit her lip.

"... see the roses," he finished for her, his own voice a thin, jagged saw of pain. He closed his eyes. "While I was going insane thinking you were with some other man...."

"There never was another man," she whispered, feeling the perspiration begin to bead on her cold face and breasts.

"Elizabeth..." he began, his hands gentling on her, sliding down over her shoulders.

She pulled away from him frantically. "I'm sorry. I'm going to be sick...."

She made it to the bathroom in time, but felt thoroughly humiliated, realizing that he'd come with her, held her while she retched, cooled her with a glass of fresh water.

She was shaking like a leaf, staring at him in misery. The fierce anger in his face had been supplanted by concern. His hand was warm and smooth as he felt her forehead.

"You don't feel like you have a fever," he murmured, frowning at her. He lifted her in his arms and carried her back to the living room, sitting with her cradled in his lap.

"I don't think that's it," she said weakly. She rested her face against his neck, unable to stop the tears. "I'm sorry," she whispered. "I've never been prone to weeping like this."

He held her close and released a frustrated sigh on a kiss against her cheek. "Maybe you should go lie down." He trailed his knuckles across her jaw. "Grant was right. You do look pale. Why don't I put you in my bed? We can finish this conversation later, when you're feeling better," he said huskily.

She leaned back against his arm, searching the worry and remorse in his eyes. "I want to know what happened to the necklace, Blake. Please . . . ?"

He reached in his pocket and removed the velvet bag. "Hold out your hand." When she did, he dropped it into her palm.

It was heavy, and she could feel the rocky coil quite easily through the soft folds. She stared into his enigmatic eyes.

"It's yours, Elizabeth," he said quietly. "You're free."

She blinked rapidly, determined not to burst into tears again. "I don't understand. I saw Jacques bidding. . . ."

Blake's gaze roamed over her face. He looked like a man forced to stand at the gates of heaven, never allowed to come inside to stay.

"Jacques and I thought we'd be more likely to get it without a fight from Dorian if Jacques was the one to do the actual bidding. Grant wrote him a check and purchased it from him as soon as Jacques took possession from the auction house staff."

Elizabeth slid her arm around his neck and frowned. "But I told Jacques I would work for him, pay off whatever it cost him. . . ."

A slight smile lightened his hard mouth. "So that was what was in the letter." He paused.

"Yes. Along with my plea to him to purchase it."

His face tightened as if he'd been stung. "It's yours now, free and clear. You don't owe me anything in return," he said tightly. "But . . . you could have asked me," he pointed out. "You could have offered me the deal, instead of Jacques." He cleared his throat. The pain was unmistakable now in his face. "Why didn't you ask me, Elizabeth? Are you so eager to get away?"

She felt another wave of sickness. "I think I'd feel better if I lay down," she murmured.

He stretched her out and leaned over her worriedly. "Elizabeth? What do you think it is? Food poisoning? Flu? Too much worry?"

She rocked her head slowly back and forth. "I thought I had it all planned out," she said weakly. His hands were warm and comforting on her now, and she smiled through the warm tears that had renewed their assault.

"There's something else, isn't there?" he said tightly. "Something to do with me . . . with us."

"Yes. You had intended to get over wanting me, and I agreed," she said, her voice becoming higher pitched as she tried to be lighthearted about it and failed completely. "I had sworn to myself that I'd be honest with you, and then I told you that I would take care of the birth control, but when it came time, all I could think of was how I wanted to feel your child growing inside of me, and then, when you told me you wanted children with a woman you could trust . . ." She drew in a sharp breath at the painful memory. "Well, it was too late then."

"You didn't use anything?" he said in amazement.

"No. I'm sorry. I just . . ." She put her hands over her face. "I'd been so lonely for so long, Blake. And I loved making love with you, being with you. I ached to hold our baby in my arms. I kept telling myself it was selfish and crazy, but . . ."

He ran his eyes over her body, and traced the curve of her breast and the smooth plane of her stomach with his hand. He rested his palm over her belly and asked huskily, "I take it your period is late?"

"A little. It could be all the stress...."

His gaze connected with hers. "Or you could be pregnant."

She nodded. "That was another reason I thought perhaps I should work for Jacques. In France, I could get good medical care. If I was pregnant, you could see the baby and not be burdened with us, if you didn't want us...."

His sudden stillness forced her to find the nerve to look at him. He looked thunderstruck. "If I didn't want you?"

"Well, sooner or later you would have gotten me out of your system," she explained, embarrassed and guilty at what she had done, and loving him with every breath in her body. She caressed his hard cheek tenderly, the love for him shining through her silvery tears. "I knew you'd go on with your life. And I would have to go on with mine... trying to get the sapphire necklace back. But—" her voice ached and her eyes filled with longing, "—but you see, I thought if I couldn't have you, at least I could have a part of you...."

Emotions worked his features, and his eyes became strangely glittery. "Get you out of my system?" He laughed, but it came out as a harsh, choked sound. "I'll never get you out of my system. You're as embedded in me as the blood that heats in my veins every time I look at you. You've been saying that you *loved* me, Elizabeth." He searched her face intently. "Is it in the past tense for you? Or do you think..." He closed his eyes and lowered his cheek to caress hers. "If you want me to beg you to stay with me, I will.... Just don't leave me again."

She felt his surrender in the way he touched her, as if she were the most precious gem in his possession and he would hold her with the greatest delicacy possible. His need for her made him completely vulnerable, and he laid bare his soul and let her see it in his face, in his eyes, in his touch, in everything.

"Love you? Of course I still love you," she murmured against his jaw, feeling the muscle working against her lips, as if he were struggling against feelings too strong to expose. She held him close as he stretched out fully alongside her to wrap her tightly in his arms. "You are my one and only love. The only man who makes my heart glow. The only man whose arms I want to feel around me. You're the love that has kept me alive through all this. If anyone should do any begging, let me be the one to do it. Let me beg your forgiveness for the way I've deceived you.''

''I'll forgive you the deceptions if you'll forgive me for not being able to save you fifteen years ago,'' he said raggedly.

''There was nothing you could have done,'' she murmured. ''Please, darling...''

''All right, all right,'' he said with a deep sigh. ''The past is gone. The sooner we forget it and concentrate on the present, the better.'' He lifted his head and stared into her eyes, molding her face with tender hands. ''If you're pregnant, I'd like you to consider marrying me,'' he said huskily.

''You don't have to...''

He silenced her with a finger laid gently across her lips. ''Yes, I do. And if you're not pregnant, I'd also like you to consider marrying me....''

''But...''

''I've loved you for fifteen years,'' he said, as if each lonely year was excruciatingly painful to recall. ''I'll love you for the rest of my life. If you don't marry me, or at least let me keep seeing you, I'm going to be facing one hell of a miserable future.'' He swallowed and rested his forehead against her hair. ''I close my eyes at night and remember the feel of you in my arms...how the scent of your skin makes me feel dizzy with pleasure...how your laughter makes me want to smile...how hot your skin is against mine when you cry out when we're making love....'' He feathered several gentle kisses across her cheekbone, curving her into his body as if he would shield her from all of life's blows. ''I love you, Elizabeth. I've gone through hell thinking I'd lost you. I don't want to walk across those hot coals again, damn it.''

He caressed her slowly, cherishing each curve, each beloved dip and swell of her shape. ''I hope you *are* pregnant,'' he whispered fiercely. ''Because that will make it very hard for you to escape me. I can hound you forever, if need be. You'd *have* to see me once in a while, because I'd insist on exercising my paternal rights.'' He slid his hand over her stomach and murmured against her cheek, ''I'm glad you didn't use anything, Elizabeth. If you want to go back into my bedroom, I'll demonstrate just how glad. And if you're not pregnant yet, I'll be more than happy to keep working on it.''

She slid her fingers into his hair and gently pulled his face around so she could see it. ''Do you really mean that?'' she breathed, surprise and hope blossoming strongly within her and flowering in her sea-green eyes. ''You want me? You'd like a baby someday... with me?''

''Want you?'' he echoed, mystified that she could not know how much, and he swore softly to underscore the fact. ''Yes. I want you. As I want to take my next breath, as I want to see the next sunrise, as I want to grow old and see children at your feet.'' He lowered his mouth to hers and kissed her, sliding his tongue in deep, intimate strokes past her lips, caressing her with a delicacy that spoke of tenderness and patience and a deep and abiding love. ''I love you and will forever, Elizabeth,'' he whispered against her lips. ''Please don't leave me. I don't think I could survive with my sanity intact if you walked away again.''

''My love, my love,'' she sobbed, tightening her arms around him protectively, nuzzling close in an effort to ease his torture. Joy was bursting in her like fireworks on the Fourth of July. ''I don't want to leave you. I never did. I never will again,'' she swore, sealing the promise with a kiss that slanted and became warm and wet and very quickly urgent.

He tilted her head back, his eyes glittering in the darkness. ''Will you marry me?'' They were both breathing a little harder, and the nerve endings were coming alive all over their bodies. He wasn't about to leave anything dangling this time. ''Marry me, Elizabeth,'' he repeated urgently, kissing her over and over again, lighting fires that swept across her skin and ignited the passions deep within.

She laughed giddily, and the happiness flowing within her made her radiant with newfound hope. ''Yes.'' She arched in pleasure as he caressed her. ''Yes,'' she sighed. ''Yes and yes and yes.''

He caught her tightly in his arms, groaning against her neck, ''I'm going to hold you to it, so don't pretend you didn't know what you were doing.''

She laughed tremulously. "I won't if you won't. You're sure of this, aren't you?"

"I have never been more sure of anything. This has been a long time coming for us." He found her lips with his and moved persuasively over them with another sweetly tingling kiss. "I love you. I'll always love you. My partners have seen it for weeks. If you have any doubts, ask them. They'll be happy to confirm it."

She hugged him, relishing the feel of his solid, muscular body close to hers. A sigh of contentment slid effortlessly out of her.

"When will you know if you're pregnant?" he asked huskily, tracing delicate whorls over her clothing with his fingertips. He smiled as he saw her eyes half-close in pleasure at his gently erotic touch. He tugged at the edges of her dress, drawing it up a little at a time.

"The test results might be reliable within the next couple of weeks, I think."

He stretched out more comfortably, gently pulled her over him like a human coverlet and began working her clothing around until he could caress bare skin.

She moaned softly.

"I'm sorry," he said hoarsely. "You don't feel well. I shouldn't be doing this."

She murmured against his ear, "Actually, lying prone seems to make me feel a lot better. All the nausea's gone."

He laughed. "In that case..." He kissed her tenderly and slid her hands to his belt buckle. "Why don't you let me spend the rest of my life showing you just how much I love you...starting right now?"

She murmured her acquiescence against his eager mouth, and the joy they had found in each other before, they found again. And when the hot tide of satisfaction crashed through them at the end, their muffled cries entangled as one. The sound was loving and joyous and triumphant.

*   *   *   *   *

SILHOUETTE·INTIMATE·MOMENTS®

IT'S TIME TO MEET
THE MARSHALLS!

In 1986, bestselling author Kristin James wrote A VERY SPECIAL FAVOR for the Silhouette Intimate Moments line. Hero Adam Marshall quickly became a reader favorite, and ever since then, readers have been asking for the stories of his two brothers, Tag and James. At last your prayers have been answered!

In June, look for Tag's story, SALT OF THE EARTH (IM #385). Then skip a month and look for THE LETTER OF THE LAW (IM #393— August), starring James Marshall. And, as our very special favor to you, we'll be reprinting A VERY SPECIAL FAVOR this September. Look for it in special displays wherever you buy books.

MARSH-1

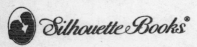

Bestselling author NORA ROBERTS captures all the
romance, adventure, passion and excitement of Silhouette in
a special miniseries.

THE CALHOUN WOMEN

Four charming, beautiful and fiercely independent
sisters set out on a search for a missing family
heirloom—an emerald necklace—and each finds
something even more precious . . . passionate romance.

Look for THE CALHOUN WOMEN miniseries
starting in June.

COURTING CATHERINE
Silhouette Romance #801

July
A MAN FOR AMANDA
Silhouette Desire #649

August
FOR THE LOVE OF LILAH
Silhouette Special Edition #685

September
SUZANNA'S SURRENDER
Silhouette Intimate Moments #397

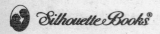

Silhouette Books®

SILHOUETTE BOOKS ARE NOW AVAILABLE IN STORES AT THESE CONVENIENT TIMES EACH MONTH*

Silhouette Desire and Silhouette Romance

> May titles: April 10
> June titles: May 8
> July titles: June 5
> August titles: July 10

Silhouette Intimate Moments and Silhouette Special Edition

> May titles: April 24
> June titles: May 22
> July titles: June 19
> August titles: July 24

We hope this new schedule is convenient for you. With only two trips each month to your local bookseller, you will always be sure not to miss any of your favorite authors!

Happy reading!

Please note: There may be slight variations in on-sale dates in your area due to differences in shipping and handling.

*Applicable to U.S. only.